Robin Langley was born in Chester in 1969 but was brought up on a hill farm in Wales. He was fascinated by hairdressing from the age of six when his mother used to go to the hairdressers. After working in Greece as a hairdresser and back-packing around the Middle East and China, he started to work for an ex-colleague who brought out his wilder side.

To Julian Whitley, for bringing the party-person out of me, and to Emma Lousie Jones-Mason, for allowing me to write *The Stretch* in between clients while I worked in her hair salon 'Springs'. But most importantly, my wife, Becky, for allowing the wild parties. To my children, Jade, Ethan and Alfie. My grandson for bringing new fun into my life.

Robin Langley

THE STRETCH

AUSTIN MACAULEY PUBLISHERS™

LONDON • CAMBRIDGE • NEW YORK • SHARJAH

A CIP catalogue record for this title is available from the British Library.

ISBN 9781528997263 (Paperback)
ISBN 9781528997270 (ePub e-book)

www.austinmacauley.com

First Published 2022
Austin Macauley Publishers Ltd®
1 Canada Square
Canary Wharf
London
E14 5AA

I would like to thank Julian Whitley, Carlton Fox, John Brockshaw, David McKinley and Mike for an amazing trip to London.

Chapter 1

Two officers entered the house, stun guns at the ready, and jabbed Baz in the back sending ten thousand volts through his great bulky body and into Carey's tiny innocent body, instantaneously sending her muscles into spasm. Her muscles jerked furiously before her body relaxed. Then the jolting started again. Her pure, blue eyes bulged out of their sockets and her mouth opened, but no noises came out.

Baz held her blonde head in his hands. "Carey, Carey!" There was no reaction. Then the officer behind Baz kicked the back of his legs sending him into a free fall and followed up his kick with a punch in the back. At this point, Baz lost hold of Carey altogether. The policeman raised his cosh for another blow but then he caught sight of Carey's limp, lifeless body impacting on the laminate flooring – her head bouncing like a cricket ball – and thought better of it.

Pulling her body towards him, Baz lay Carey flat on her back, leant forward and breathed into her mouth, filling her lungs with his breath. He checked her chest was rising and then started compressions – one, two, three, four, five. Watching her tiny chest rise and fall, he started compressions again and by now, Rockin had moved to her side. "Carey, come on, Carey, can you hear me, Carey?" He lifted her eyelid but he wasn't sure what he was looking for.

Three weeks earlier.

December 11th was a dark Friday morning with a slight frost. The black 911 Porsche Carrera swung into a long, freshly tarmacked drive, back end sliding out as it did so, and snaked its way up the drive under the sheer power of the engine alone. The headlights swept towards a grand 19th century red-brick farmhouse and into a courtyard, with more Edwardian farm buildings to the right and a curve of mature trees to the left. Ahead a black, freshly polished stretch limo gleamed in the moonlight, with almost invisible leaves brushing against its tyres in the morning breeze.

To the far end of the yard in the dim morning light sat a lowered, dark blue BMW with three-spoke alloy wheels. Inside the car was a heavily-built skinhead at the wheel and next to him a dark, tanned man. Their eyes followed the Porsche as it turned into the parking slot and came to a halt, and the skinhead made a speed dial call, spoke for about 20 seconds and hung up. Then the lads noticed two men walking towards the limo, the tallest of the two carrying a package in his right hand. The other man, who was of athletic build, scanned the vehicles but didn't spot the lads in the BMW, and his gaze soon turned to the Porsche as both doors opened.

A Hispanic-looking man emerged from the Porsche, glanced up at the two men walking towards him and shouted. "Are you ready?" They smirked, and the second guy in the Porsche climbed out checking for something in his inside jacket pocket as he straightened himself up.

No one paid any attention to the Beamer as they walked towards each other, hardly breaking eye contact. Instead, they stopped beside the limo and quickly getting past the pleasantries, they started talking about the deal.

Back inside the BMW, the passenger (known as Phil) spoke to the driver, revealing a missing front tooth as he did so. The skinhead looked at his watch and nodded turning off the car's interior light. The doors clicked open and the two men slowly climbed out, quietly pushing the doors half shut to avoid making any noise.

Crouching down, the two men waited and listened to see if they had been seen or heard, and then quickly moved in a large arc, unnoticed, towards the others. In one swift movement, the skinhead launched his full bodyweight on top of the Hispanic man, who immediately fell towards the ground, his head hitting the limo's door with a dull thud. Finally, his face contacted the tarmac, filling his mouth full of gravel.

The second man from the Porsche noticed a figure moving to his right, so he quickly swung round and pulled his hand out of his jacket pocket just in time to come face to face with his attacker. Rockin lost grip of the metal object in his hand and it fell to the floor making a loud clunking noise as the metal hit the tarmac. Phil still running, lowered his upper body and drove it straight into Rockin's stomach lifting him clean into the air. Then, straightening his body to an upright position, he started spinning Rockin around on his shoulder just like a ballerina.

The Hispanic's adrenalin rushed through his veins as he turned his grazed face to try and make out who had brought him down. He noticed a distinctive red, white and blue Tommy Hilfiger top and then he saw the skinhead's face. "You bastard, Baz. What did you do that for?" Baz released his grip and allowed Marco to stand up and brush the dust and gravel off his clothes, laughing as he did so. "You bastard, I'll get you back," Marco added.

Phil lowered Rockin to the ground, allowing him to regain his posture, and asked, "So what do you reckon to the limo?"

Chapter 2

The limo driver introduced himself as Tony, and the lads looked at the beautiful car with glee and expectation of the day to come. Rockin and Marco had made most of the planning arrangements, but even such a simple thing as trying to book a limo for six lads had its problems – and that was just the beginning of the day's deceptions. The first step of the plan had started and everyone was feeling buzzy with excitement. Poor Tony thought he knew what was in store for the day, but how wrong he was. He was totally oblivious to what might happen as the lads loaded their bags and a few classy Tesco carrier bags into the limo.

Rockin checked that he still had his silver credit card case he'd been fiddling with before Phil had jumped on him, and he finally discovered it next to a pile of leaves before climbing aboard the limo. Phil was already sitting inside stretching his legs and tilting his head back on the plush, brown leather seats. As he took a deep breath, he couldn't quite believe his luck. This was the first time he'd worn his black Top Man suit since his son's baptism, and now to be sitting in a stretch limousine was a dream come true, especially after what he had been through in the past few years. Despite the fact the car was a stretch limo, it was still a tight squeeze with six lads – two of them bodybuilders, who ate far too much powdered protein!

Baz and Phil were introduced to Will and Giles, and because none of the guys had ever been in a limo before, they were certainly planning to make the most of it. Dreaming about what it would be like to be a celebrity with no money worries, girls throwing themselves at their feet. If only. But they all had a cheesy grin on their faces nevertheless.

Tony lowered the window, which separated him and the lads, to ask them if they were ready and as he glanced in the rear-view mirror, he thought to himself, *What a strange bunch.* Something wasn't right but he couldn't quite put his finger on it yet. Perhaps he was still a little sleepy from having to get up so early to take this weird lot on a four-hour trek to London. The lads all looked at each other and Rockin said, "Let's roll."

Experimenting with a few different buttons on the walnut console above his head, Baz soon found the one to make the partition go back up. He said slightly louder than a whisper, "We don't want that bugger listening to what we're saying." Everyone understood and Marco checked that the phone to the driver on the rear parcel shelf was not off the hook. The limo's six-litre engine roared into action and elegantly pulled away, following the twisting drive to the main road. It turned right onto the A483 – soon they'd be on the dual carriageway heading towards Shrewsbury. The adventure had started and there was no turning back now.

Will opened one of the Tesco bags and pulled out a couple of bottles of Asti, at which point everybody's face lit up, except Giles who was kicking himself for not bringing some decent plonk. *Still, it was better than nothing,* he decided. Pouring Asti as the limo snaked up the road was a messy business indeed, but no one cared – they were already having the time of their lives. They made a toast to the day ahead and everyone downed their glass of champagne, except Giles who sipped his gracefully. Giles' family owned the farm which they had just left – the grandest in its day and, in fact, it still is today. From the best oak wood panelling in the house down to the glazed tiles in the dairy, no money had been spared on building this lavish farmhouse.

It wasn't long before the conversation got around to how Phil had lost one of his front teeth. Phil was reluctant to tell the story but he didn't want to lie, so he decided to tell the truth – well part of the truth anyway. He explained how he was in town shopping and had collapsed, knocking his front teeth on the window sill of the local travel agents. There was silence for a couple of seconds while the lads mulled this over, and then Baz put his hand over his mouth and started to chuckle. Baz was a bouncer, and like squaddies, bouncers constantly take the piss out of each other – the harder things got, the more they thrived on it.

"This fucker," Baz said, pointing to Phil, "got himself arrested and dragged off to the police station for an interrogation. He's lucky he's here at all."

"Why did they arrest you?" asked Giles. At which point Baz answered on Phil's behalf.

"Because he was wearing a bloody balaclava and had a tool in his coat pocket!" The lads all looked at each other. To be honest, Giles would have preferred it if everyone on this trip had no police record whatsoever, especially for armed robbery! Giles had never actually met someone who had been to prison, and the comprehension of what it meant to serve time hit home. In the back of his mind he started thinking about what might happen if something unexpected happened today. He'd never hung around with people like this and he was starting to wonder whether this whole trip was a good idea. Glancing over at Baz, he decided that he looked like a cross between a gorilla and one of the EastEnders' Mitchell brothers. His neck was twice, if not three times, as thick as his own and his shoulders were wide and imposing.

Baz could feel Phil's embarrassment and decided to change the subject. He explained how he ran his own gym, which Giles and Will automatically assumed was filled with even more gorilla-type men. Baz had a nice side line of selling steroids to the budding Arnold Schwarzeneggers of this world, but he thought it best to keep this information to himself. The gym was far from the nicest in the world, and in the winter your breath would freeze as you exhaled – you'd almost get frost bite as you tried to lift any weights. The material was ripped on the benches and the padding, which was falling on the floor, had worked its way into the carpet. Yet he did keep the place as clean as he could, whipping the duster and vacuum out when no one was looking.

Baz explained how he had started his businesses, progressing from a mere gym owner to running the biggest security firms in North Wales. He'd already been a bouncer in town, mainly for the girls rather than the fifty quid a night he was paid, and starting up his own security firm was a natural progression from this. Now he employed more than one hundred men who covered three separate towns. Baz had set up 'Door Angels' at a very rough time in Wrexham when people were more scared of the bouncers than the other punters. For example, two drinkers had died in fights in the same number of weeks, all by the hands of a firm of bouncers from Manchester. They did do an excellent job of clearing out the drug pushers big and small, but only to sell their own gear instead.

Wrexham Council and the police took drastic measures to clean up the town, and all the bar owners were given an ultimatum – either get rid of these bouncers from Manchester or lose their licenses, so obviously, the bouncers were given the boot. The council spent two million on state-of-art CCTV systems and every pub and night club doorway was monitored – even the fire exits in case some poor soul was taken around the back for a beating. This had all left a void for door security staff, which is where Baz stepped in.

Chapter 3

After two and a half hours of driving the limo pulled off the motorway into a service station just off the M1, and drove through the car park trying to find a suitable parking space. Eventually, though, Tony had to admit defeat and headed towards the bus section, as there was nowhere adequate to park such a long vehicle. Rockin clicked the door open and was the first to emerge, closely followed by Marco who swished his long, dark, wavy hair and looked around to see if anyone was watching him. A few people turned around to see who was in the limo, but most people carried on about their business without anything more than a second glance.

The rest of the lads gathered around the trunk and started lifting their black bags out, checking them one by one. Making their way to Costa Coffee, Will ordered three Lattes, two Cappuccinos and an Americana for Phil, who wasn't into fancy coffee. Rockin also grabbed an apple Danish pastry to calm his hunger pangs. After the quick refreshments and a stop in the newsagents to buy The Sun and the Daily Sport, they made their way to the toilets to change, only to discover that the toilets stank! "The drains must be blocked," said Will. "Rockin you go and complain – you're good at that. You're always whingeing to me about something," he added, taking the piss as usual. The lads looked around for somewhere else to change, but it seemed that it was the stinking cubicles with brown excrement lining the bowls and piss on the seats or nothing.

Dropping his jeans to reveal abnormally bulging leg muscles, Baz had decided to change right in the middle of the washrooms. The rest of the lads timidly followed suit, until five lads were standing in all their glory, covered only by their boxer shorts.

First to open his suit carrier was Giles. The suit, which had been supplied only the day before by a wedding hire shop, was a black morning suit with a gold waistcoat and gold cravat, crisscrossed with a diamond shaped pattern. Feeling very self-conscious indeed, Giles hurriedly whipped his pin-striped trousers on, followed promptly by his crisp white dress shirt. Then, turning to the mirror, he started to tie his cravat, "Who's the swanky bastard?" Marco shouted.

Giles turned and said in a posh accent, "I've always been swanky, I'll have you know."

"And don't we know it," added Rockin. All the lads were laughing and smiling, and the rest of them soon donned their suits, except Phil who was going to stay in the black suit he was already wearing. They all helped each other tie their cravats, making jokes, laughing and smiling, while the other customers who had come in for a slash could only stare in total amazement.

When they were all dressed, they stood in front of the mirrors in a long line, all standing proud. Rockin said, "Anyone would think we were going to a wedding!" And all the lads laughed.

Phil had a sudden thought and said, "Which one of you is going to be the groom for the day then?" They all looked at each other and then to Rockin and Marco who then looked at each other.

"It should be either one of you two because you both set up today," Baz said, looking at Rockin and Marco. This was one thing that hadn't been planned, and there were certainly no volunteers. Consequently, neither Marco nor Rockin answered. Marco loved being the centre of attention, but he really wasn't keen on being a fake groom.

The stench in the loos was all becoming too much, so Rockin got the ball rolling, "We'd better get moving if we want to make it to London." All the lads gathered their clothes and threw them into the empty suit carriers and then made their way back to the limo.

Watching them approach, Tony got out of the limo and said, "Ah I see, you lot look like you're going to a wedding. I was starting to wonder. So, which one of you is the groom then?"

"Shit," said Marco under his breath, and there was a deadly silence until Baz shouted,

"It's Rockin!" Rockin was standing at the back of the group but Tony had no idea who Rockin was anyway! He soon guessed, however, because Rockin's face flushed bright scarlet gave the game away.

They all climbed silently into the limo thinking about what had just been said. Would Tony start asking questions and pull the plug on what they had planned? The silence continued until they reached the slip road onto the motorway, at which point Baz pressed his favourite button and wound up the

16

privacy glass again. Marco turned the stereo on. First to break the silence was Will, "I knew we should have decided who was going to be the groom before we got into the limo."

Everyone seemed to agree without saying much, although Marco commented, "Well we have our groom now," nodding at Rockin as he spoke.

"Yeah just what I wanted," Rockin replied. "Cheers guys!" He had a worried look that he would be getting all the crap if anything went wrong.

Giles added, "Well that's one thing we've sorted out!"

Rockin was engaged to be married, but not today. His wife-to-be, Lara, was a strict Catholic girl and she taught at a Catholic primary school. She went to church once a week and would never have more than two drinks, as she said it would give her a hangover. Rockin, on the other hand, had always liked women and had spent six months in the party capital of Greece indulging his passion for wild, crazy girls. It had come as a bit of a shock to many of his friends that he was settling down, especially with a Catholic girl. After all, Rockin hated religion. The other lads were all still single and loved partying, except Marco who was married with one child and another on the way.

Marco had strategically implanted the idea of getting engaged into Rockin's head, and he had also found him the ideal platinum ring – an antique bow ring with 48 diamonds. "It would be perfect for Lara, and you won't find another ring like that around here – or maybe not even in the whole country!" Marco had informed him. In fact, Marco would have popped the question for Rockin, but that was maybe one step too far, he'd decided. Later, Rockin found out that Marco's wife had wanted the ring, so he had saved himself a couple of thousand pounds after all.

Suddenly Marco piped up, "Hey Will, have you found the telephone number yet?" Will was staring at page 3 of The Sun.

"Hey, that girl has lovely breasts," he said pointing to the centre of the paper.

"You're not supposed to be looking at her breasts, you old pervert. Give me the paper," Marco snapped, practically ripping it out of Will's hands and breaking off a small chunk as he did so. Then he started leafing through the pages, going back and forward several times until he came to the page he wanted. Smirking to himself, Marco said, "I've got it, pass the phone." Baz passed his phone to Marco because Rockin was playing battle ships on Marco's phone, to distract himself from the whole situation.

Marco started dialling the number in the advert. It rang four times before someone answered. "Good morning, you've reached The Sun's news desk. If you have a story press 1, if you…" Marco removed the phone from his ear before the message had finished and pressed the 1 key. The phone began ringing once again.

A rather abrupt-sounding voice answered, "News desk?" A little burst of adrenalin rushed through Marco's veins and his voice went slightly higher pitched as he said, "Hi, I've got a story."

Sounding rather bored, the journalist said, "And what is it?" Marco started to explain what was supposed to have happened this morning.

"Well basically, I'm a best man for a wedding that was supposed to be happening today. However, the groom found out on the way to the church that the bride has been sleeping around." Marco's voice was becoming higher and higher pitched with every word. So much so that he had to pause and take a deep breath.

"Carry on," said the journalist. Marco felt like he had gone back 10 years and was in the headmaster's office being told off, as he tried to make his excuses. He rushed through the next part.

"Yeah so he phoned his bride-to-be and confronted her about having sex with one of his friends and she admitted it. So now we're on our way to London to have a blow-out." The reporter asked for Marco's number.

"Leave it with me. I'll talk to my manager and then call you back," he said.

By now, the atmosphere in the limo was electric. The lads, full of nervous and excitable energy, were firing questions at Marco, wanting to know what the reporter had said. "Did he believe you? Is he going to phone back?" Then, much to Marco's annoyance, Baz began to criticise him telling him that he should have made it sound more exciting. Marco's heart was still pounding after the conversation and he certainly didn't need a confrontation at this moment. Plus, he wasn't really used to anyone moaning at him – the worst he usually got was from some blonde he'd picked up whingeing about her hair.

But Baz was different matter – he was a bit of a nutter who got easily upset, not helped by all the steroids he took. Marco handed the phone over to Baz and said, "Well, if you think you can do better, you can make the next call."

"OK sorry," replied Baz. "You're much better at the talking than me."

Holding Baz's eye contact for a second longer, Marco said, "Yeah you could say that." Baz gave a disgruntled grunt and pushed the phone back to Marco.

Then Will piped up, "Hey mate, you'd better use a different phone just in case that another reporter tries to phone back!"

Giles held up a copy of the Daily Sport revealing several topless beauties spread-eagled over a flashy car. With a huge grin on his face, he spoke in his usual posh accent, "There's a telephone number here to call if you have a story to share?"

Marco grabbed the paper from Giles, who responded with, "I would have passed it to you if you had asked." Ignoring this comment, Marco scanned the page skimming through several ridiculous stories – one about a double-decker bus being found on the moon and another which showed pictures of the lady with the biggest boobs in Britain. Then his eyes found the advert he needed, so he carefully dialled the number on Rockin's phone, clearing his throat as he did so.

A cockney girl answered the phone "The Daily Sport, how I may help you?" Marco replied in as cool a manner as he could.

"I've got a story you'll be interested in."

"I'll just put you through to one of our reporters," the cockney lass told him, before putting him on hold. This time Marco told the same story but he made it a lot more exaggerated.

The reporter asked Marco who the bride had slept with. "It was me!" Marco told her.

"And who might you be?" asked the reporter.

"I am – well was – the best man."

There was a silence for a second or two and then the reporter asked, "What about the groom, is he still talking to you?"

"Yeah just about. We've been through a lot together over the years," Marco added.

By now the reporter wanted more details. Where was the wedding supposed to take place? How can they get in contact with the bride? Did we have any topless or nude photos of the bride? The last question stumped Marco for a moment. "Leave it with me, I'll try to get hold of one," he told the reporter.

"OK, I'll go and talk to my boss," the reporter answered. Once again, the lads wanted to know what had been said, and by this time they were even more excited – even Baz was in a better mood and congratulated Marco on a job well done.

The next moment Baz's phone rang and Marco grabbed it – it was the reporter from The Sun wanting to know the bride's name, where she lived, what she did for a living and how they could contact her (unfortunately the lads hadn't thought of that!). He also wanted to know the groom's name, Marco's name and the ushers' names. Marco gave him all the information he wanted, making up a name for the bride – well actually he gave his wife's Christian name and made up a surname. Then he hung up. Moments later, Baz's phone rang again, and everyone looked confused as Marco lifted the phone and said, "Hello darling!" It was Baz's girlfriend Wendy. Marco had styled her hair for several years and Baz was jealous of their over-friendly relationship – well Baz thought it was over-friendly, but no one else did.

Marco had always been a natural flirt, and in his younger days he'd modelled himself on Tom Cruise after watching Top Gun. Baz suddenly twigged and realised that it was his phone Marco was talking on and the 'hello darling' was aimed at his very own girlfriend.

Baz held out his shovel sized hand and Marco looked down at it. He was certainly not going to rush to hand the phone back. In fact, he relished the thought of Baz getting jealous and irritated. Marco chatted some more until he could see Baz's face starting to twitch with frustration, so he slowly but reluctantly handed the phone over.

As Baz chatted to Wendy, Marco snatched his phone off Rockin, dialled his hair salon and asked to speak to his wife, Alex, who was also his business partner. Once they had got over the pleasantries, he started explaining how the morning had gone so far.

He dropped the bombshell that the newspapers were interested in their story; and Alex couldn't believe her ears. She knew they had struggled to get a limo to take six lads to London, and that's why Rockin had come up with the idea that they should pretend they were a wedding party.

The idea had worked, they had the limo so all they had to do was hire the outfits and get some button holes, which she was fine about. But she didn't have an inkling about the newspapers and what the lads had planned for the rest of the day. She couldn't believe what Marco was saying. He was supposed to have slept with the bride, paid the limo driver to go to London and on top of that he was going to tell the nation the whole fabricated story – pictures and all! Through the eyes and words of the Daily Sport and The Sun.

Marco wanted Alex to phone or take phone calls from the newspapers saying she was the bride, but she refused point blank. She could imagine the story being totally blown out of proportion. Then, with a sudden thought, she said, "Did you give your own names or did you make some up?" There was silence for a couple of seconds while it dawned on him that he'd made one big mistake. People would think it was true!

He replied nervously, "Yeah."

"What do you mean yeah? Did you give false names or not?" Alex replied.

"Err, I gave our real names," Marco admitted. His wife couldn't believe it, but just as she started having a go at him, Baz's phone rang. Saved by the bell, Marco quickly said, "I've got to go." He hung up before he got more of an ear bashing.

This time Rockin answered the phone. It was the reporter from The Sun. He handed the phone eagerly to Marco, and the reporter told him that the editor might be interested in their story and that they were trying to arrange for a reporter to come and meet them.

Then phones started ringing left, right and centre and the excitement in the limo was soaring with every ring. Marco coolly picked his phone up, looked to see who was calling and turned it off. Baz was somehow holding Rockin's phone and had already answered it. It was the Daily Sport, and the reporter thought he was speaking to Marco until he heard Baz speak in his Welsh accent. At this point he asked to speak to Marco instead. Baz told the reporter that Marco was speaking on another phone, which seemed to annoy him.

The reporter told Baz that someone was ready to meet them, and he wanted to know what time they would be in London. Baz pressed the button to wind down the partition window and asked Tony how long they would be. "You haven't told me which part of London yet!" Tony replied.

Baz thought fast and said, "Covent Garden."

"About forty minutes if the traffic is OK," Tony replied in a cheerful manner. Baz put the window back up and repeated this information to the reporter, who then told Baz that he'd meet them in the bar of the Savoy.

"We've done it, we're going to the Savoy!" Baz shouted to the others as he put down the phone.

The whole group cheered and shouted, "Yes!" except Marco who was still talking to the other reporter. He just grinned like a Cheshire cat and carried on with his conversation.

In fact, all their faces were gleaming with anticipation, as they all started to chat excitedly together. Phil tilted his head back, took a drag on his cigarette and smiled to himself for the second time today. He was in a limo and he was going to be in the Daily Sport. All his mates and fellow bouncers would read this story. As Phil was daydreaming, his mind slowly crept back to his children. Was this an omen for the future? Were things going to get better? Would he get visiting rights to see Charlie and Carey?

The negotiations with The Sun were more complicated and Marco was aiming to sell them a story that he'd only come up with five minutes ago. He was not doing too well, but he was standing firm. He wanted £20,000 for this story, but all they wanted to pay for was today's drinks.

To celebrate their achievement, Will grabbed the last bottle of bubbly and hastily popped the cork, sending a cascade of champagne all over the limo's interior. Will ended up with most of it on him, but he wasn't bothered because he was enjoying the moment as much as everyone else.

Phil's Past

Five years previously, the second heat wave had arrived. The hospitals were struggling to cope with people suffering from heat exhaustion and dehydration and a hose pipe ban had already been in force for a month. The ground was parched and all the vegetation had changed to a burnt yellow colour.

Charlotte sat next Phil in his red Mark 1 Golf GTI, which he had just picked up from a local dealer. He was especially pleased because this car had appeared on Top Gear and had been hammered around the track by the man himself, Jeremy Clarkson. The car had come complete with a signed photo of Jeremy sitting in his car, which Phil had had framed and put on top of his TV.

He floored the accelerator and the car came out of the sharp left-hand bend, headlights searching for the road ahead and the tyres kicking up dust which obscured the tail lights. The country lane was narrow and steep with hedges on both sides, only inches from the sides of the vehicle, while it accelerated into the unknown. Charlotte was a cautious driver but the thrill of sitting in the passenger seat of a speeding car sent the adrenaline surging through her veins, turning her on with each increase of velocity.

After a couple, more bends and screeching tyres, Phil came to the top of the mountain and the road straightened out with only a couple of minor bends. Phil slowed the car down as he explored the road for an appropriate lay by. He spotted one on the right and braking softly, he glided the GTI to a halt.

Charlotte leaned over, placing her hand onto Phil's lap, and they kissed passionately. Phil slipped his hand under her tight T-shirt, moving upwards until he touched her soft lace bra. His fingers began caressing her firm breasts.

In the dark, a figure moved silently behind an old dry-stone wall, gradually raising his head to peer over the top with his cold evil eyes. His eyes fixed on the GTI, which gleamed in the moonlight, and his bitter and twisted mind watched the couple become entwined in their moment of passion. Soon, however, the windows starting to steam up which obscured his view.

He noted that the male was of large, muscular build and was tanned with dark hair. *All the better,* he thought as his breathing became heavier. The woman was slim with blonde, flowing hair. She was small but had firm breasts – just the way he liked them.

On arriving in Britain, he had looked with disgust at all the overweight women. They didn't even try to cover their obese bodies as they wore cropped tops with their bellies hanging over the top and skimpy skirts or tight jeans which revealed their cellulite.

He had decided after his escape, and his long journey, that the women he was going to take were going to be stunning with only exquisite figures, and he selected his pray by following them, learning their habits, where they worked, trained and socialised.

Sabir took the greatest pleasure in watching them shop, choosing their clothes, imagining them in the changing rooms, what their breasts looked like and what they would feel like. No one noticed a beggar or certainly they preferred not to!

Sabir watched as Charlotte placed her hands-on Phil's shoulders and mounted him, and the car started to rock softly as she rode him, arching her back in pleasure. After a few minutes, they both reached climax and at the same time, the car stopped moving. Sabir could barely see through the windows as he just managed to make out Charlotte bending forwards to kiss Phil and lifting herself off.

The Arab couldn't wait any longer – he had to get closer. Sliding over the wall, imagining he was in the special forces, Sabir carried deep scarring. Sabir, which means patient, had been tortured by Saddam's henchmen and all his finger nails been pulled off one by one. Electrodes had been attached to his testicles and he'd been kept in a solitary underground cell, measuring just 2 ft. by 4 ft.

Sabir was whipped on a daily basis – for good measure and only God knows what else.

The Iraqi's mind had been mentally twisted before that, but he was much worse now.

He had been found guilty of raping and brutally murdering two university students and had been sentenced to death by the judge. However, the military had a different idea and decided that he would be used as a guinea pig in the art of torture.

As Sabir crept closer through the long, dry grass, the seeds sticking to his wrecked clothes, a broken bottle cut into his elbow drawing a small trickle of blood. This reminded him of his escape from his hole in the ground at the army base, which was bombed by the allies in the first Gulf war.

The explosions had killed most of the soldiers and the ones who survived had run away like cowards. Sabir had run in the opposite direction, hitching lifts and stowing away in the back of trucks, which was much more comfortable than the hell he had been living in. He entered the UK and applied for asylum, and with his scars, they took a sympathetic view.

This little prick of pain hardly registered with Sabir. In fact, it gave him pleasure knowing that it wouldn't be the last blood spilt tonight. As he approached the tail light of the car, he could smell the fresh car wax, so he breathed deeper smelling the dry earth. Then he got a hint of aroma – the aroma of sex – and he felt a surge of passion take control.

Phil kissed Charlotte on the lips telling her, "I love you." Charlotte just winked back oblivious to the fact that just a few feet away lay an uncontrolled mad man. Phil carefully slipped the condom off, tied a knot in the end and winding down the window, he threw it into the outside world.

Sabir could not resist, so he crept forward on all fours and placed his hand near the rear tyre. The sexual aroma had grown stronger as it filtered through the open window. Then he heard a click as the driver's door opened and the Iraqi moved back quickly and silently. He'd learnt to move without being noticed back in Iraq.

Phil emerged from the car and took a deep breath, inhaling the dry arid air. His chest expanded as he breathed in, but then he smelt something strange – like a tramp. He looked around sensing that something felt wrong. Standing motionless for 30 seconds he listened intensely to silence until Charlotte's voice cut through the air. He swung around on his heels and glanced down at her. Her cleavage was still showing as she told him to hurry up. He turned to the rear of the car, undid his zip and started to piss, but the ground was too parched to absorb the liquid. Some of it bounced up and hit the Iraqi in the face and the rest snaked along the dry earth finding a path to his leg – the warm urine being absorbed by his jeans. This brought back horrible nightmares, but he lay still all the same.

Phil turned the ignition and the engine roared into life, the wheels thrusting dust and gravel into the Iraqi's face, which was the second insult. Sabir stood up watching the red lights disappear into the distance and without bothering to brush the dust off himself, walked over to the condom.

The next day the temperature was still raging, so Phil left going to the gym until the evening, hoping it would be a bit cooler. Baz heard the GTI pull up outside the gym and one final rev as Phil killed the engine. Baz stopped making a strawberry protein shake for one of his wannabe bodybuilders and headed for the open door, instantly admiring the car. Baz mocked him a bit, "That's too good for you, you'll wreck it."

"Piss off," Phil replied. "She's my new baby." He skimmed his hands gently over the bonnet full of admiration for his new wheels.

As Phil walked into the gym, he glanced down at the Wrexham Evening Leader, which lay on the work top. In bold black type the headline glared up at him, 'Local Girl Raped and Butchered'.

Two years later…

Christmas was fast approaching and the conversation between Phil and his wife turned to buying presents, so he agreed to put in some extra shifts at the weekend. Because of his shift pattern, he would have to do double shifts and that would mean working a sixteen-hour stretch. But Phil didn't mind. He just thought of his kids' faces lighting up on Christmas day.

As the shifts went on, Phil was becoming more and more tired, until one night he was virtually falling asleep at the machines so the manager sent him home. Phil arrived home to find his wife in bed with some bastard and he didn't know how he kept his cool. Instead, he just turned around in shock and walked out, and after that he only went back to see the kids. Then the trouble started when Phil decided that he wanted the kids to come and live with him because Charlotte was too occupied in being a tart around town.

After several arguments, Charlotte started restricting his access and so the matter went to court. Charlotte made up a pack of lies until Phil's access became even more restricted. Even the law was against him as it always favours the woman's side. He contested the judgements as soon as he had saved enough money, and borrowed some along the way, but each time there were more lies from his wife and the judge always sided with her. Eventually all his access was taken away, which was killing him.

Charlotte's mother brought the kids around secretly to see him because she knew he had a good heart, but then his wife found out and it all went back to court. It resulted in the judge informing him that he would be going to jail if he answered the door to his own children again. The judge might as well have ripped his heart out and thrown it into a skip.

This went on for over a year and then out of the blue, Charlotte met a new man who booked a romantic holiday for them both. There was one problem, though, she had no one to have the kids, as her mother's health had taken a down turn caused by all the stress.

Phil was totally gob smacked when he received a call from Charlotte asking him whether he would have the kids while they were away. In fact, it was a dream come true. He had a couple of meetings with the kids beforehand and they were all ecstatic as they talked about what they were going to do. He had managed to save up some money, so he decided to take them to Euro Disney. On his next day off, he excitedly went to the local travel agency and booked the flight, hotel, car, insurance and tickets to the theme parks. The high he was feeling was amazing and for the first time in ages, he felt confident again. So, confident that he was even flirting with the assistant and they had made eye contact several times.

The day before the final payment for the holiday was due, Phil lost his wallet and all his cards. He cancelled them as soon as he realised and after several phone calls to the bank, they agreed to let him have cash. Dashing into town, before the travel agents closed, Phil thought he had made it with five minutes to spare, but to his disbelief they had closed. *God, this is too stressful. I need a drink,* he thought to himself, so he headed off to Weatherspoon's and ordered a pint, almost downing it in one. Feeling a little more refreshed, he ordered another pint and drank this one more slowly. Just as he'd almost finished his second pint, a couple of his friends came in and were surprised to see him. "What are you doing here, I thought you didn't drink when you were weight training?"

"Yeah but after the day I've had, I needed one," Phil replied.

The pub began to fill with customers who were coming in for a drink after work, and the atmosphere grew with the hum of conversation and clinking of glasses. Phil and his friends chatted away and before he realised, it was closing time and the alcohol had really gone to his head. He said his goodbyes and staggered out of the doors.

When he got home, his head started pounding and his throat felt like he had swallowed sand paper. He staggered to the shower, and as the hot water hit his face and hair, the waft of stale smoke filled the shower. His mind slowly started to emerge from the drunken haze and a shock of fear shot through his body – the money. Flinging the shower door open so hard that it swung back and nearly hit him in face, Phil dashed along the landing and into the bedroom, grabbing his jacket and quickly rummaging through the pockets checking them again and again. His heart was pounding through his chest and he could feel himself starting to sweat. Next, he tried his trousers, but there was nothing except for a few coins. The money was gone. Lifting himself from the floor, Phil sat on the edge of the bed, placed his head in his hands and started crying.

The next thing he knew, he was walking out of Millets carrying a balaclava and he turned into Bank Street, which is a small alley down the side of the Halifax Bank. Placing his hand in the Millets bag and pulling out a balaclava, he pulled the black balaclava over his head as beads of sweet pierced his forehead. He walked back onto the high street, past W H Smiths and headed towards the travel agents. He started to go light headed but managed to make it to the door and placed his hand on the handle. He swung the door open under his weight and collapsed onto the travel agent's floor.

When he came around, his hands were cuffed behind his back with blood streaming out of his nose and mouth. He was curled up into the foetal position like a little baby with tears rolling down his face as he sobbed hysterically at the feet of a policeman. The realisation of what he had done hit him like a bolt out of the blue, and his body was shaking as he cried hysterically for the second time that day. He had blown it, and all he could see in his mind was his children being dragged away by two policemen as they tried to cling to his legs.

Chapter 4

The Savoy

The limo wove its way through the traffic heavy streets of London and finally turned slowly into the small private road to the Savoy, coming to a graceful halt outside the revolving doors.

Tony got out of the driver's compartment and walked leisurely around the limo to open the passenger door and let the lads out. One by one they climbed out, straightening their jackets as they turned to watch the next lad clamber out. And clamber is what they did – after all, they weren't the most graceful bunch.

Rockin went to pacify Tony, who wasn't happy because he hadn't taken them right to the church. "It's most unusual," he told Rockin.

"We fancy a beer and then some fresh air before I get shackled," Rockin replied. "So, don't worry about it."

Tony wondered if the 'shackled' meant he didn't want any pressure, before adding, "Well here's my card and I've given the tall guy with dark hair my number as well, just in case."

Rockin followed the rest of the lads into the Savoy, his eyes scanning the reception area. He was suitably impressed by the vast and elegant chandelier hanging in the reception area. Giles knew where the bar was, "I've been here a couple of times before," he informed the lads. Phil rolled his eyes as they all followed him up the sweeping staircase.

It was quiet in the bar – just a few men having an early business lunch on one table and an American middle-aged couple sitting at a table near the window. Once in the bar, Giles seemed to hold back a bit. Marco, on the other hand, wanted to get some alcohol into his system. "What does everyone want to drink?" he asked. They agreed they wanted a beer, so Marco ordered six bottles of Stella, plonked himself down on a high bar stool and sparked up a cigarette.

Just as Marco was savouring his cigarette and thinking back to the day's events so far, the barman said, "That will be £28.50 please." Marco started choking on the smoke and then fell backwards, crashing to the floor with shock! He lay their eyes wide open, with smoke drifting from his mouth and his arms spread out to the sides, like he was nailed to a crucifix.

Panicking, the barman came running to the other side of the bar. "I'm having a heart attack!" exclaimed Marco with a huge grin on his face. The barman dropped to his knees and started going through his first aid routine when Rockin, who was used to Marco's antics, reassured the anxious first aider.

"Don't worry he's fine. You watch, he'll be break dancing next!"

Will held out his hand and Marco grabbed it heaving himself up. As soon as he was back on his feet Marco said, "I think we should have a kitty."

"You scrooge," said Baz, as he handed the barman £30, much to Marco's annoyance.

Checking his watch, Rockin suddenly realised it was ten past twelve – time to phone Lara at the school where she worked. He took his phone out of his pocket and flipped it open, looking at it nervously. What would Lara's reaction be, and what should he say to her? Rockin felt like the first time he had phoned her to ask her out on a date – he had butterflies in his stomach. He started to search through his phone to find the school's number, but he was in no particular hurry. Then Marco's phone rang, which distracted Rockin from what he was doing. It was the reporter from The Sun, and all in a split second, Marco's face changed from happy and smiling to miserable. All he said was, "OK thanks," before ending the call.

With a huge look of disappointment on his face, Marco told the lads the bad news. The reporter from The Sun wasn't coming after all. Everyone's faces changed to a look of disappointment, except Rockin, who was a bit relieved, until he saw how gutted everyone was and then he felt disappointed, too – only not quite as much. One down, one to go, and with a bit of luck he wouldn't have to make that phone call to Lara after all.

All the lads wanted to know what the reporter had said, so Marco repeated the short conversation. "Basically, the editor didn't want to pay, and he didn't believe the story as he thought it was a bit farfetched," he explained.

Giles stood up and walked up to the bar to order six more beers. As he carried the bottles of Stella back to the table, he noticed two young guys in casual dress walking into the bar. His heart lifted as he wondered whether they were the reporters from the Daily Sport. They stopped at the entrance and looked around. "They must be the reporters," Giles shouted to Marco excitedly. "They're here!" But then one of the men pointed to a table on the opposite side of the bar, they walked over to it and took a seat. It wasn't the reporters after all.

Marco dialled the number for the Daily Sport and asked to speak to the reporter he'd spoken to earlier. The receptionist then placed him on hold for what felt like an eternity.

"Hello sir, he's away from the desk right now and I can't locate him," she told Marco.

"Oh."

"Could you try calling again later?"

He finished the call and everyone seemed to have got the gist of the conversation. Baz said, "They're all backing out, and I think that receptionist was covering up for them." Everybody seemed to think the same, and they all went quiet for a minute or so.

Rockin felt a huge sense of relief coming over him. It was like having a bad toothache but feeling the pain ebbing away as the dentist gives you an injection. He wouldn't have to make the call to Lara after all! Rockin stared at the rest of the lads who all seemed disillusioned. With blank faces, they all carried on sitting in silence, and once again, he began to feel guilty for feeling relieved.

Half way through the second bottle of beer, Marco stood up announcing that he was going to the toilet. "I'll come with you," Rockin replied, and they both headed out of the bar and down the corridor to the toilet.

When they were inside the loos, Marco confided in Rockin, "Baz is starting to get on my nerves!"

"Yeah, I'd noticed," said Rockin.

"I keep thinking he knows about that time Wendy and I had a snog in Scotts."

"I reckon he knows something has gone on, but doesn't know what."

"He would have beaten the shit out of me if he thought that!" replied Marco.

"Just watch your back today, Marco, that's all," added Rockin.

As they walked back through the lobby, Rockin's heart took a sudden jerk as he noticed a scruffy bloke with a camera slung over his shoulder walking into the hotel, with a slightly better dressed man behind him. Rockin automatically nudged Marco, who was in a world of his own and didn't appear to notice at first, but then he felt the same jerk as Rockin had.

A massive wave of relief and excitement welled through him. He felt like an excited school kid on Christmas morning. The two men walked straight towards Rockin and Marco which confused Marco for a second. How did they know who they were in a hotel this size? Then he realised that it was obvious because they were dressed up in morning suits.

The reporter spoke first, "I need to speak to Marco," he said. "And which one of you is the unlucky groom?"

"It's me," Rockin said, with a hint of nervousness. The reporter looked him up and down and then asked him if he was feeling alright. "I'll be alright after a few more beers," he told the reporter, who had introduced himself as John.

"Are you still talking to the best man?" John replied.

Marco had reached the doorway to the bar, walked straight over to the lads and said, "Look who I've found!" Turning back towards the door, the lads watched Rockin and his two new friends walk in. They all grinned like Cheshire cats feeling that their day was coming together at last.

Gathered around the table, everyone stood up as the introductions were done, except the photographer who hung a few feet away and was not introduced to the lads. He didn't seem particularly interested anyway. The photographer was the shortest of the group. With his short dark hair coming forward over his face and a Nikon D2 digital camera slung over his shoulder, he looked a little unkempt and totally out of place in this posh hotel.

"Well," said John. "I'll take a few details and then get some photos of you all with the limo. Then later, we're going to try and get some girls organised."

"That'll do me," said Baz. "Will they be topless?" John smirked at Baz's comment, but didn't answer.

"So where do you come from?" John asked Marco.

"Wrexham," he replied, before Giles added,

"I live in Bangor on Dee," in his usual posh accent. Baz shook his head in disbelief.

Looking at Marco, John replied, "I thought you were from Wrexham. I used to work for the Wrexham Evening Leader."

"Bloody hell, it's a small world," said Will butting in. "Come to the big smoke and you get interviewed by someone from back home."

At the mention of home, Rockin started to think of Lara. It was now or never he thought, as he reached into his pocket and pulled out his phone and flipped it open once more. Looking at it for the sixth time that day, he had the same feeling come over him as he did earlier, but he wasn't going to get out of this now! After finding the number, Rockin glanced at his watch. It was 12.51, so there wasn't much time left. Lara would have to go back into class at one! He pressed the green button on his phone, placed it to his ear, and after a couple of seconds it started to ring. He was about to give up after about a minute or so, when he heard someone's voice and just caught the end of a female voice saying, "St Mark's School?" Rockin told the girl who he was and asked to speak to Lara. The girl went off to find her, which seemed to last forever and made Rockin feel worse and worse every second. After nervously tapping his foot for about a minute, the phone was picked up. "This is it," he told himself. "This is it."

However, the voice wasn't Lara's, it was the same girl as last time. "Hi, Lara's taking the children into the hall for their Christmas lunch so she can't come to the phone right now," the girl told Rockin. Rockin's heart sank to the floor. What was he going to do now? Then the girl asked him if she could take a message.

"How long is she going to be?" he asked her.

"She won't be available until the children have finished their Christmas lunch," the girl replied.

Rockin felt like shouting at this dozy girl, but instead he just said, "It's really important."

"She's going to be sitting with the governors!" said the girl.

"I really need to speak to her!"

"Is it life and death?"

He thought to himself that it could be life and death when she finds out what was about to happen, but he realised there was no way he was going to get to speak to her right now.

"This sounds very strange," Rockin started, "but please can you tell her." He paused and then added, "Tell or ask her." Another pause. "That we are going to be in the Daily Sport?" Another pause. "And we are going to be photographed with some topless girls."

The phone went quiet for a few seconds and then the girl said, "I'll go and get her."

By the time the girl had reached the hall, everyone was sitting down to their lunch. The other staff, governors and the priest all sat on the top table – just like a wedding. The girl, who was Lara's student teacher and named Kate, walked over to the front of the table until she was opposite Lara. "I think you should talk to him," she said. Lara looked confused.

"Talk to who?"

"Your fiancée!"

"Why, what does he want?" Lara was looking annoyed and embarrassed.

To make things worse, and before Kate could think, she accidentally blurted out, "He wants to know whether he can appear in the Daily Sport."

Lara's expression turned to stone. At that moment, she wanted to crawl under the table and never come back up. She could feel the priest and the governors on the table looking at her, their eyes burning inquisitively into the side of her face. She could feel her body temperature rising, her hands becoming clammy as she made her excuses and left the table with her head down in shame. As she walked out of the hall, down the corridor and into the staff room, she looked around to check no one else was in the room and then closed the door behind her. "Hi darling," she said. Rockin repeated the pleasantries.

"How's your day going?"

"Alright. We've made it to London and we're having a drink in the Savoy."

"What do the Daily Sport want?" she asked him in a cool and calm voice.

He started to explain as quickly as possible because the credit on his phone was slipping away, and most of all because he wanted to know what Marco was telling the reporter. He was trying to eaves-drop, but it was extremely hard to talk and listen at the same time. He explained how he had become the groom back at the service station, and then one of the lads had called the papers for a laugh, but one paper had actually turned up, much to his disgust. He never mentioned the topless models because Lara seemed to be taking it all really well, so he wasn't going to risk it.

He also added that he had tried to talk someone else into being the groom, but the reporter already knew his name and what he looked like. Lara was not fazed at all. She just told him to behave himself and have a good time. He couldn't believe his ears, but then he remembered that was one of the reasons why he loved her. She had always been easy going and she trusted him.

Rockin felt like a huge weight had been lifted off his shoulders and he could now relax and enjoy the day! He said his goodbyes to Lara, and as he came off the phone he winked at Marco. Walking across to join the rest of the group, Rockin was surprised when John considerately asked how he was. He had thought that all reporters were hard faced and arrogant, but this guy seemed to be different.

John started to ask him some questions about his bride to be. He already knew her name, and Marco had filled him in on some of the basic details. Rockin would have loved to know what these details were! John asked how long they had been together, where they had planned to live in the future and where they were going on honeymoon. "Have you got any topless photos of her?" John asked Rockin.

"Not on me, no!" Rockin replied. "It's not the kind of thing you take to your wedding. She was my bride-to-be, my future wife."

John thought he'd hit a raw nerve, and he could feel someone's eyes burning into him. He turned around to see Baz and Phil staring at him. John did not feel like upsetting these two 'gorillas', especially after seeing the size of Baz's bucket hands, and Phil reminded him of Vinnie Jones, who would pound you into mush without even trying. Little did he know that this was the last thing on the two lads' minds. They were just curious and didn't want to miss out on any of the action!

John was determined to get them on to a more positive mood, so he informed them what the paper was willing to pay for. The paper won't give you any cash, but it will pay for the drinks all day and to get you into several strip clubs and pay for a few dances. Himself and the photographer would follow them around, take the odd photo here and there, and get the best story they could. The lads thought this was magnificent, especially having their drinks paid for at these extortionate prices. And gorgeous half-dressed girls dancing for them for zilch. What more could they possibly ask for?

Marco caught the bar tender's eye and gestured for more beers. It was time to start celebrating. John then turned to Marco, who was feeling very jovial, and asked him if he could organise for the limo to come back to the hotel so that they could get some snaps with it. The next round of beers arrived along with two extra for the paparazzi. John stopped asking questions and relaxed with the lads while they waited for the limo to reappear, which was taking some time.

Then Marco's phone rang. It was Tony. He was stuck in traffic and needed to fuel up. Then John's phone started to ring. It was his boss. While John was talking, Marco and Rockin filled the rest of the lads in. "It sounds too good to be true," said Phil, while Rockin started to slip into a daydream filled with scantily clad girls dancing around him and giving him more attention than the other lads. In his dream, he was the envy of them all.

Chapter 5

John gave the lads the low-down on what his boss had said. The offer was to supply them with booze all day, take them to a couple of lap dancing bars and later to Peter Stringfellow's, which was to be the highlight of the day. In return, the editor wanted all the dirty secrets of their relationship and photos if possible. "Check his phone to see if he's got any pictures on there," John's boss had told him. "And if he can't provide any, we'll mock some up."

"There are some models on their way down now to have their pics taken with you guys and the limo," John told the lads. "What time is the limo coming?" he added, turning his head towards Marco.

"It's on its way," Marco replied, "but the traffic is heavy."

"Well we might as well relax then because we have a long day ahead of us," John decided. He was quite looking forward to the day as well. After all, any hot-blooded male likes to look at half-dressed woman.

John would have to watch how much he drank today because he needed to keep his writing skills honed. Not because so many people read the stories in the Sport – it is more of an adult comic book than anything else – but you never know when one of the editors from another tabloid might notice one of his stories and pass some work along. A slim chance, but you just never know.

As the lads were happily chatting amongst themselves, he looked at them all, noticing the huge grins across their faces. Even Rockin looked happy, which was strange he thought. John couldn't decide whether to keep his distance or try to befriend Baz and Phil, as both looked like they could start a fight at the drop of a hat. In fact, it would add another dimension to this story if they did start a punch up, if neither himself nor the photographer was involved. Or maybe he wouldn't mind the photographer being involved. He wasn't overly keen on him to be honest.

Half an hour had passed and there was still no sign of the limo. However, three top-heavy women had walked into the bar – two blondes and a brunette.

36

Will was the first to notice them as they strolled in, and they looked around to see who they were supposed to be meeting, trying to catch someone's eye.

"Fuckin hell, it's Jordan," Will blurted out, with a mouthful of beer spraying across the table. Everybody turned around.

"She looks smaller in real life," Phil commented.

"Well her chest does anyway," added Baz. Everyone in the bar – businessmen, tourists and waiting staff – watched these three lovely ladies walk over to the lads. The brunette gently placed her hand on Rockin's shoulder, and he could feel her warm, tender touch through his shirt and waistcoat. It felt completely natural somehow. Immediately, he could feel the stress ebbing away. He turned his head to the left and looked up, staring up at her deep, velvet brown eyes. Her face looked perfect with its olive toned skin, beautifully shimmered cheek bones and moist lips. Rockin had died and gone to heaven.

Everyone apart from Rockin, whose mind was elsewhere, was thinking the same thing. Was it Jordan? Having been sure from a distance, now that she had come closer, they were having doubts. Baz, who thought he was a bit of an expert, had already decided it was not her, but that she would do. After all, they had been supplied for the lads' enjoyment and they were free. *All the better,* he thought, as he licked his lips and just about managed to restrain himself from putting his hand on her arse.

John took the lead seeing as his bosses were paying all the bills. He introduced himself and Rockin first and then the rest of the lads. The girl who they'd thought was Jordan introduced herself as Julia. She had long, straight, blonde hair, which had been professionally coloured. Her make-up was slightly overdone, with pink lipstick, and she wore a Tiffany necklace hanging just above the start of her cleavage, which naturally drew your eyes down to her more-than-ample bosom.

Fiona was the next to introduce herself. She looked more like a traditional tart with her dramatically fake blonde hair, heavily applied make-up and bright red lipstick. Her chest was far too heavy for her frame, and her flimsy top could scarcely keep her breasts under control. She didn't look like the brightest in the bunch, but she was pleasant enough and grinned like a Cheshire cat.

Then Abigail introduced herself as she continued to tenderly caress Rockin's shoulder. It was as if she was trying to ease the traumatic pain which he had gone through that morning. Rockin wondered how she knew he was the groom and how much the paper had told her, or even whether she had any idea of what was going on. Her eyes flitted from one person to the next, taking in every gesture they made and making eye contact with everyone who looked at her – which was everyone in the bar. These six lads were quickly falling under her spell.

After the introductions, John filled the girls in on the story so far. Rockin was introduced as the poor groom, so he adopted a glum expression to play the part well. He could feel Abigail's eyes surveying him. Abigail knew she had been right. As soon as she'd seen them all sitting there around the table, she had noticed a different look in Rockin's eyes. *How could someone do that to him?* she thought to herself.

Abigail was convinced that she had a sixth sense and was heavily into supernatural stuff. She lived her life by horoscopes and had a personal reading of the stars done once a month by one of her mystic friends. In fact, her mystic friend had highlighted today, telling her, "There's energy and strange power coming from the alignment of the planets for you Abigail. Someone needs your help to understand what is happening to them, and you'll need to guide them through this important time in their life." As soon as her agent mentioned this job she had been filled with excitement. Maybe her time had come. Maybe today things would change for her.

Rockin had no such time for religion, tarot cards, horoscopes or Feng shui. It was all a load of crap to him to be honest. Life was what you made it – you make all the decisions as life twists and turns not the planets or cards. He believed that luck was a big factor, and some people were luckier than others – he had no doubt about that. Rockin's only religion was positive thinking. Think positively and the mind would work out how to turn a situation to your advantage – hopefully anyway.

How could a card tell the future? How could some old girl with a crystal ball and bad eyesight tell the future, when she could hardly see the damn ball? As far as he was concerned, all these people can see is the reddies in your pocket, and they were all taking advantage.

The biggest con of all, as far as Rockin was concerned, was religion based on a book of fairy tales. He did agree that the bible was most probably a good rule book – treat people with respect, help where you can and so on – but most miracles can be explained, and science produces miracles every day.

When it came to women, Rockin understood them more than most men. He'd heard his mates boast about the amount of horse power their car has, how brilliant or rubbish their football team is or their conquests in life – all things that bore a woman to tears. Rockin was different, though. Because he understood women, he knew that whether you agree with them or not, listen to them, guide them and best of all even twist their beliefs and nudge them gently into the direction you want to go.

Rockin had learnt to be a good listener, which is one thing he was aware that most men never do. He learnt this very early on in life. Listen, repeat a couple of things they said so they know your listening, drop in the odd question, add some advice and Bob's your uncle – they think you're wonderful.

Giles stood up and offered the blonde closest to him, Fiona, his seat, pulling it back slightly to allow her slim, curvaceous legs to slip past. She sat down slowly crossing her legs, and her flimsy knee-length skirt started to ride up to reveal her tanned, silky thigh. Pinching the end of her skirt, she slipped it back down her leg, looking up to catch Giles watching her. Immediately Giles's cheeks started to flush red with embarrassment, Fiona threw him a cheeky smile and he blushed even more.

Marco, noting Giles's gentlemanly gesture, quickly stood up flicking his long, dark coloured, shiny, black hair over his shoulder. Sweeping his hand down in an arc, he invited Julia to sit down. Julia took him up on his offer, but she showed no emotion as she did so – not even a chink of a smile. Sitting down she folded her arms, signalling a defensive attitude.

Marco was not into challenges when it came to women. He worked on the principal the easier, the better. Just as celebrities show off their houses in magazines like 'Hello', 'OK' and the cheaper versions, Marco was a mini celebrity in his home town. Bouncers would let him come to the front of the queue at clubs. He would get served quickest at the bar. Most lasses in the local pubs and clubs knew him, or if they didn't, they wanted to. He had his own business, a Range Rover, a Porsche 911 Carrera and a six-bedroom house worth over half a million. It was no hidden fact that a lot of girls – and blokes – hated him, but most of it was jealousy.

Marco once got into a fight because some slapper told her boyfriend that Marco had chatted her up and had asked to take nude pictures of her. Marco honestly couldn't remember talking to the woman, but her boyfriend decided to have a go. He chose the wrong night, however, because Marco was out drinking with his brother-in-law – an ex-paratrooper called Clive – who didn't suffer fools lightly.

When the boyfriend took his first swing, which hit Marco straight on the nose, Clive elbowed the attacker across the temple with the force of a sledge hammer, dropping him instantly. As he lay on the floor, Clive went for his gonads, crushing them like a banana in his huge hands then twisting and crushing even more. The boyfriend's face contorted in agony and as the twisting continued, he tried to push Clive's hands away, but it was a feeble attempt. He had no strength – it was being ripped out of him. Tilting his head back in suffering and glancing at one of his mates, his eyes pleaded for help – his voice had stopped working by now. His mates just stood there with their eyes wide in shock and horror. They certainly weren't going to get involved.

For the record, it took four bouncers to remove Clive and one to remove Marco.

Chapter 6

John sat back in his chair and listened to all the chatting that was going on. All the lads seemed to be telling the same story to the girls, as they attempted to chat them up, but they were careful not to go into too much detail.

The photographer was well versed in situations like this, so he took a seat, put his camera on the floor and tried to look inconspicuous. The Savoy was well known in the industry for removing paparazzi, even if they were invited by their clients. After all, they wanted to keep their establishment classy and luxurious, with as much privacy as they could provide. They knew only too well how their distinguished guests could get themselves into comprising situations. Unlike some hotels, who loved the free publicity, the Savoy frowned on unwanted attention to the hotel and its guests.

Abigail was sitting next to Rockin listening to his sad story. She was hanging on to every word and analysing each syllable. Her beautiful, chocolate-coloured eyes were barely breaking contact with Rockin's blue gaze, and he could hardly believe his luck. As Abigail began to relax in his presence, she knew the astrology was truthful. She could feel herself being drawn in to Rockin's life and she was feeling the pain more than he was. His pain and anguish would come later, she thought. Maybe tonight, when he tried to close his eyes, all the emotion would start flooding and whirling around in his head. Today was too busy. All his mates were here, they were in a plush hotel with three sexy girls, there was a journalist present and then, of course, the drink was numbing the pain.

Rockin could feel something touching his leg and as he glimpsed down to see what it was, he discovered it was the bare, sexy, silky skin of Abigail's leg. The warmth and tenderness of her touch sent a feeling through his chest – there was only a hundredth of a millimetre of material separating them.

He wanted to touch and caress those gorgeous legs; he wanted to kiss her there and then. But he couldn't because it would change his world. Rockin could not stop looking at the picture of pure beauty. Her long, flowing auburn hair and those deep chocolate eyes that you could just fall into and never come back up. She was unadulterated glamour – not glamour in a porn type way, but glamorous, or perhaps elegant was a more accurate word.

A new Audrey Hepburn or a modern-day Elizabeth Taylor, perhaps. Abigail was slightly top heavy – and there was nothing wrong with that. She had a small waist and perfectly bronzed legs with a sheer glow, Rockin noted. Abigail asked Rockin if he believed in the stars and destiny and because he'd had other girls ask him this question before, he knew how to play the game. It was like fishing – give the girl the bait and they would soon be hooked. Although, reading by her body language – legs touching his legs, exposing her wrists, her gaze – he would say she already seemed hooked just by the story he'd delivered to her.

Rockin wanted to say that she didn't look like a hippy chick, but sometimes an off-the-cuff statement could blow the ship out of the water – and all your hard work with it. Instead, he said, "Yeah I do. I read my stars most days. I don't live my life by them, but I do think there is something about them." Abigail's face lit up like a Christmas tree. *Hooked, line and sinker,* he thought.

She asked him what star sign he was. "Guess," he answered, which made her study him even deeper. She was staring into his soul. He could see her mind churning the information he'd given her, the cogs were turning, and he could imagine the warmth building in the frontal lobes as her mind went into overdrive.

After a few seconds, Abigail spoke, "Well," she said. "You seem well-balanced, you think things through, you don't rush into anything." *Not bad,* Rockin thought, giving her a small, kind smile.

"Come on then, which star sign am I?" he added, teasing her.

"If you ask me, you're a Libran," she said with total confidence.

"Fuckin' hell, you're good!" Rockin was taken aback. Not one girl in the past had managed to get it right. He paused for a few moments before asking her, "So what does my future hold for me now that everything has gone up in smoke?"

"I'll have to do a reading for you!" She looked deeper into his eyes, and Rockin was amazed by her intensity. She hardly broke eye contact at all.

He glanced around at the rest of the lads. Marco had given up on the girl who had taken his seat. She was so miserable that he thought she looked like she'd had an argument with her fella before she left home. Instead, Baz had moved in for the kill. He was used to a challenge and actually liked it. His philosophy was if you don't have to fight for it, it's not worth having.

Baz always liked everyone to believe he had come from a tough neighbourhood, having to fight his way through the graffiti-covered back streets, dodging muggers and drug pushers. In fact, he was brought up in the country, living in a converted barn. He went to a small village school, gaining good grades at primary school and half way through secondary. It was only at this stage of his life that he started to drift into the wrong crowd. He never actually bullied anyone himself, but he did hang around with bullies. He liked the image of being a hard man and having power over people. He liked the fact that he could make people do what he wanted them to do by threatening them with violence, although deep down, Baz hated violence.

Marco caught Rockin's eye and gave him an ever so slight wink – hardly noticeable to the untrained eye. Will and Giles seemed to be doing well with their 'bit of stuff' – Julia. She was laughing and smiling at whatever posh crap they were throwing at her.

Abigail and Rockin were now deep in conversation and their hands were ever so nearly touching. He was working her good style, thought Marco. Just at that moment, Marco's phone rang. It was Tony. "I'll be with you in a couple of minutes," he told him. Going to fuel up in a limo was easier said than done!

Marco gave John the nod and they all started to make their way down to the front of the hotel. Rockin left Abigail's side and went to talk to Marco to fill him in. "She's a bloody nutter. She's into Zen and the stars."

"Is she?" replied Marco, not having a clue what Zen was.

"Anyway, what's the plan now?" Rockin enquired.

"We'll have some pictures taken and then tell Tony to piss off." Marco paused before adding, "And you should shag that girl in the back of the limo. She's gagging for it."

"Yeah, but Tony thinks I am getting married in an hour!"

"We're paying him, so he'll do what we want."

True, Rockin thought.

"She could be your last fling!"

Tony was pleased, assuming that they now had come to their senses and wanted him to take them to the church. He turned left into the Savoy's private road and straightened the limo, and then he thought to himself, *I've got to turn this thing around again – twice in one day.*

As he approached the hotel, he could see all the lads on the other side of the glass doors, proudly standing in their attire.

Chapter 7

Giles saw the limo slowly approaching and nudged Jo with his elbow startling her. He winked and nodding his head towards the limo, as if he was saying "have you seen one of those before." Of course, she'd seen limos countless times, common as muck in London. She had never actually been in one, but she was not going to give that away.

The sky was still clear with no breeze, the temperature only hitting a maximum of nine degrees not bad for December, the streets and pavements were dry with the sun glinting on the paint work as Tony followed the solid straight white line dividing the road into two lanes.

He swung the limo around ninety degrees in the turning area stopping it parallel to the polished doors of the Savoy, his back was starting to ache after sitting in the same position for so long. He had slipped a disk a couple of years ago, while trying to clamber under one of his buses twisting his body trying to get into awkward positions.

His body wasn't what it used to be, he was now approaching retirement, but often wondered if he ever would hang his keys up for the last time, it was always more difficult when you run the shop and people depend on you for a wage.

His grey hair had thinned leaving a tanned scalp, even in the middle of winter; his waist line had expanded of the years of sitting behind a wheel. His wife was always nagged on at him to get some exercise, go on a diet lose some weight, she worried about his heart and arteries and becoming clogged.

She had watched one to many documentaries about heart attacks and bad diets she was now becoming paranoid. She offered to make him a salad for lunch but he always declined. A paste or a sausage roll would do fine, he wasn't grossly overweight just a bit tubbier than he should be, but it was enough to cause problems to his back.

He pulled the chrome lever to unlocked the door and pushed it open, lifting and swinging his legs out, grabbing the door frame by his puffy yet wrinkled hands and pulling himself up groaning faintly under his breath.

By this time the concierge was standing by the rear door ready to open the door for the lads thus removing them from the hotel swiftly with no fuss. But John put his hand out indicting for him to halt, which he did without question.

John knew they hand to be quick at this hotel, they would move them on like lightening. John arranged the lads in a line along side of the limo Rockin and Marco in the centre, Baz and Phil to the left and Giles and Will to the right.

No girls present, they were instructed to pose as if this was the pre wedding photos, which Tony thought was a strange comment to make. The photographer walked backwards getting the Savoy sign in the view finder and started snapping.

All the lads felt awkward with the exception of Marco, the girls watched them and a few people stopped, including a couple of American tourists in their sixties, she had tan tights with beige comfortable walking shoes bright red jacket and a traditional yank shampoo and set with no bang.

He was about six feet, a good head of hair matching red jacket, covered belly hanging over his tartan trousers, holding hands as they watched the proceedings a smile beamed across their love-struck faces.

While the photographer checks his camera in between shots, he lets go of his wife's hand and marches in a peculiar military style and places his hands on Marco's and Rockin's shoulders and leans in even closer and says, "Who is the lucky man?"

"It's me," Rockin replied with nervousness in his voice.

The yank eye balls Rockin not letting his gaze go, both hands are now on Rockin's shoulders with a serious look on his face, he immediately starts asking personal questions. "This girl you're marrying," a pause, "is she your best friend?"

Rockin thinks of Lara, "Yes."

"Is she your soul mate?"

Rockin stares back into the yank's eyes almost catching a glimpse of his soul which sends a weird sensation through his mind, he could feel the answer being drawn out of him. "Yes," he replied.

The yank gunned him a smile and tenderly patted him on the shoulder, "Best of luck." Abigail had been too far away to hear what had been said but she sensed something spiritual had just happened.

In one of the rooms behind the huge dark oak reception the manager and two security guards sat in front a wall of security screens, relaying images from all over the hotel.

The manager had been alerted as soon as the paparazzi had arrived in the hotel, and had started watching the screens soon after the girls had arrived. He had noted they were keeping a low profile, but something was definitely about to happen.

The two security guards were definitely not the bouncer type; they were more the breed you saw in shopping precincts. Skinny, late twenties and gaunt looking, never getting enough fresh air, couldn't find a better job it was one step up from a factory but just as boring maybe more boring starring at screens all day.

The lads were again posed in front of the camera leaning on the limo grouping around Rockin, changing their expressions to what the photographer wanted glum, happy moody. Then he wanted just the groom and the best man, he asked for the same expressions as before, but then he asked for a strange request.

They did not know quite what to do at first then John guided them, the request was for them to look if they were about to have a fight. They soon figured it out, he managed only took a couple of shots of them looking like they were having some heavy words.

The alcohol was now taking effect they were all feeling a bit tipsy, the attempt of them both trying to be actors, sent them into a fit of giggles.

Next, he wanted all three of the girls in the shot, the lads were thinking this the moment they got their tits out for the boys, and they waited in great expectation. The photographer only required Rockin in the next pic which sent Marco into slight sulk, the girls all gathered around.

The lads looked jovial but there was a slight under current of resentment creeping from their eyes. Not that they disliked Rockin or anything, they would love to have all the girls wrapping their bodies around them instead of him, to tell their mates and hopefully have a full page spread in the sport.

The photographer instructed Rockin to sit on the front wing of the limo the girls did not need prompting Abigail leaned on him lovingly placing her head on his shoulder pulling him closer. Placing a hand on his chest and cast him an upwards glance through the corner of her eye, they made contact and held it for a second which felt like time had stopped and they were the only ones in the universe, well she did. Rockin was thinking more of her tits what he was hopefully about to see, what would they look like.

Wills bird followed suit she also placed her arm around his back making a nice little threesome; this was what dreams were made of. The grumpy one had perked up now and the camera was brought into action, she slowly sauntered over to Rockin swinging her hips seductively as she moved.

She gestured to him to spread his legs wider, which he did revealing the front wheel. She slipped her four-inch black stiletto heeled boots in-between Rockin's legs lifting her foot towards his crouch, gently she placed it on the top of the tyre. The split in her blue knee length skirt fell open on the side of the camera exposing her slim toned thigh, everyone was now in ore, and she had taken on a new sexy persona!

Back in the security office the three of them sat watching the screens, a look of mild envy sat on guard's faces. Nothing like this every happened to them, the girls usually turned away if they tried chatting them up, never mind having girls draping themselves over them. Even the manager felt a tinge of jealousy, these guys were young, good looking the world was their oyster and by the look of it knew how to make the most of it. They all looked so happy vast grins across their faces, oh to be young he thought.

They watched on the black and white monitors as grumpy gradually lowered herself forward oozing sex appeal Placing her elbow on her knee and holding her jaw seductively in her finger tips she turned to face, opening her mouth sexily, eyes directly into the camera. These images instantly being recorded.

Marco was the next up; he strutted over flicking his wavy black hair over the shoulder for the hundredth time today. Abigail stayed by Rockin's side making small chit chat about where she thought they should meet up after. The other two girls beckoned Marco over to them which put an extra swagger in his step; he leaned onto the white paint work. The models brought themselves in close to his sides caressing his chest, flicking one of their legs backwards into a sexy pose. A smile beamed across his face, more than a child in a candy shop much more.

Grumpy was now pressing her large rounded chest into his side, pushing up her cleavage making them look even larger. Her leg was teasingly placed in front of his, and tenderly pressed, moving ever so slightly in minuet circles. Marco was now finding he had to concentrate really hard to stop an embarrassing moment from happening with so many people watching.

But no breast had been bared yet, but one of the security guards had notified the police they might need their help with some paparazzi. Several beat officers came regularly to the Savoy especially in the winter months, when the cold nights numbed their feet while pacing the streets.

Tea, coffee and something to eat usually a cheese toasty, the plod wasn't that adventurous while on the beat, some grub, a hot drink and to put their feet up for fifteen minutes.

They were never charged for their snacks and encouraged to drop by when they liked as long as they stayed back of house as not to unnerve the guests that some dodgy dealing was going on in the hotel.

Officers would tend to do the round to different restaurants and hotels, like any one they always had their favourite places to drop by. The manager thought it would inspire them to arrive promptly to repay their favours.

Marco loved posing so having his picture taken was a real buzz knowing he had got himself under control, he always said he would have been a model if he was taller and better-looking. So, he had been itching to get in front of the camera, he always loved to be the centre of attention.

When Rockin was having his photos taken, Marco was extremely jealous and envious, he had to dig his feet in to stop himself jumping in front of camera or on top of the limo which he had done once before but it was not exactly a limo.

While in a queue with his wife, Rockin and Lara and about another one hundred people waiting to get into a night club, which he never did, usually he would strut to the front, but his wife hated it all those people watching and staring as they walked past, whispering or shouting comments about them.

The queue was not moving. Marco was becoming bored and started break dancing on the street, this would not have been too bad but he was crap, at least he was then, he has perfected it a bit more since then. A few people watched; he wanted more attention.

Parked next to the kerb was a knackered blue Ford Sierra which was at least ten years old if not more. Lara had noticed him eyeing this car up for a while but did not expect him to do what he did next. He jumped onto the front wing then onto the roof and tried unsuccessfully to spin on his back. He did spin, he spun off the roof onto the bonnet and crashing to the floor. Luckily or unluckily the bouncers had rushed over to pick him up from the dirt encrusted road.

He tried to brush himself down but was frog marched down an alley way around the corner to the back of the club, and the bouncers demanded he pay up

£200 by Monday or they would come to the salon and beat the shit out of him. He paid up the same night after a quick walk to the cash machine; the best bit was they then let him into the club without having to go to the back of the queue!

All the lads were called back into their original positions, one girl in between each set of lads. Abigail headed straight for Rockin and Marco, but the photographer wanted a different girl with the main men, she reluctantly swapped with Grumpy. Marco and Rockin exchanged excited expression while Abigail was walking away, not that they didn't want Abi, but this girl oozed sex appeal now.

The Photographer said on my count I want this to be the shot, one two three and the lads for a second stared smiling straight into the camera as they had before, but the girls were moving.

Perplexed they turned their gaze away from the camera to the girl which they were posing with. The models were whipping their tops off revealing bare breasts, nipples hard and erect from the cold. Giles couldn't help but think what happened to their bras, they were wearing them before he had noticed them for sure. A quick fiddle with their hair, one hand behind their back holding their tops.

The manager shouted "go, go, go" as if ordering his troops out of a plane to parachute to earth. Both chairs the security guards had been sitting on shot backwards toppling over on to the floor. The second one nearly falling flat on his face as he caught one of the legs, he rebalanced himself by grabbing a desk to his left. The receptionist was nearly pushed over the top of the reception into a guest's face which happened to be the Yanks. As the manager skidded around the side of the desk, he grabbed the first thing he could to stop himself going flying, but he grasped a grey guest telephone which went hurtling to the floor cracking the side open as it landed.

The groom, best man and ushers took a momentary look at the topless wonders standing next to them, time seemed to slow, adrenaline and testosterone was pumping through their veins, this was what today was all about. Their delicate soft silky skin seemed to irradiate something, maybe it was magic.

This was magic bare flesh was never exposed in the winter months; it was tucked away under layers of clothing or bedding only to be revealed in the endless months to come.

The Photographer shouted "ready" and all the girls in different variations told them to "come in tighter, get closer" this they did not need to be told twice.

They all gleamed into the camera, proud as punch, hands wrapped around their tiny waists. Marco hand was pushed higher than the rest, touching the bottom of the breast feeling the warmth against his cold fingers. The Nikon clicked away taking countless images, no time for change positions, just clicking.

The Photographer shouted "security" turned on his heels and was jogging down the street camera still in hand. Everybody twisted their heads around in time to watch the guards come barging through the polished doors of the hotel.

The girls had turned their whole bodies around to shielding their breasts from the small crowd of people who had gathered. But exposing their chests to the approaching security, who instantly stopped in their tracks. Eyes transfixed onto Grumpy's tits. For a millisecond their expression changed to desire, looking at her perfectly formed chest, plastic or not, it didn't matter the second guard even licked his lips.

As the girls turned Will left his hand on her waist naturally bring it into position on her stomach, he then lifted his arm and cupped his hand around her breast, raising his thumb so it made contact with her firm rigid nipple and brushing it back and to. She just stared at him with an all-knowing look, but did not remove his hand. Will left it there for a second longer relaxed his hand gradually lowered it.

The manager blundered through the door, shouting, "What do you think you are doing? Get out of here now." Being careful not to swear in front of the guests. The guards rounded the limo coming face to face with Baz and Phil; they weren't sure what to do.

If they touched the girls they could be done for assault and they did not fancy their chances with these two guerrillas. The manager started again, "The police are on their way."

Tony was in the limo starting the engine; he had an unblemished record and did not want to start its demise now. Tony started his ten-point turn because of the confined space; the lads jumped in while Tony stopped to change direction, they beckoned the girls into the limo as well but they refused. John had squeezed in just as Tony turned for the last time and straightened up, flooring the limo towards the open road.

Chapter 8

The open road did not last for long, because once Tony had turned into the Strand, the traffic slowed to a near halt, stopping and starting at the traffic lights, buses and lorries belching out nocuous black diesel fumes and white van men beeping their horns.

Tony had felt like a getaway driver, and sweat dripped down from his forehead. By now, however, his pulse had started to slow down and his body was beginning to relax again. It didn't help matters that all the lads in the back were shouting, "Faster, faster." Had something else happened in the hotel that he was oblivious to? And what was going on with those girls? Would there be blue flashing lights in his rear-view mirror at any moment? He wondered. This notion sent his temperature back up, and the sweat trickled down his spine soaking his clean, crisp, white shirt at the base of his back.

In the rear of the limo the atmosphere was electric, and you could feel the energy leaping from one person to the next. Sparks of ecstasy were almost flying! To the lads, it felt like they had just pulled off a huge bank robbery, or won the lotto rollover. Oh, the relief, the excitement. In those few seconds, they had all become one, and any envy, jealousy or personal grudges had evaporated in an instant. It would usually take years to have a bond like this and even then, it probably wouldn't be as strong.

The closest most people got to feeling like this was in adolescent years – between childhood and adulthood – when you and your best mates broke the law, got into trouble and had to run and hide. Then you'd go and get wasted on cheap cider, forming what you thought was an unbreakable bond.

Or on your graduation night when all rules were thrown out of the window. You'd drink copious amounts of alcohol, snog as many people as you could, steal something you didn't need or didn't want. Whether it was getting plastered, having wild, passionate sex with one or more of your fellow students or the waiting staff, you were invincible. The world was your oyster and you could accomplish anything.

The lads relived the moment, raising their voices in exhilaration and already exaggerating the truth. Marco told them how he had slipped his hand onto Abi's tits, how she had loved it and how he could tell that she wanted him. She hadn't stopped looking at him from the instant she walked into the bar, he told them. He seemed unable or unwilling to recall that he could scarcely get a word from her back at the hotel, and that she had spent the whole time with Rockin. But that no longer mattered and no one cared anymore.

Will was next up. "I felt Abi's nipple," he injected into the conversation, and everyone, including John, looked around at him.

"You did what?" asked Rockin.

"Yeah it felt beautiful. Her tit felt plastic and her nipple was hard. And she looked me straight in the eye."

Rockin felt a surge of jealousy, but it soon ebbed away, *I was supposed to have her,* he thought to himself in a serious but joking tone. He pushed it to the furthest, deepest part of the back of his mind, and thought to himself, *What am I thinking? I've got Lara at home.* John seemed rather impressed by Will's statement.

"Bloody hell, you can't touch those girls usually," he commented. This drove the jealousy back through Rockin's body, but he was careful not to show it.

"Well, she's got my number," exclaimed Rockin, trying to fight back, but Will was too quick and witty for Rockin.

"A bird in the hand is better than two in the bush," he said, which sent everyone up in a wall a laughter, Rockin included. Even Tony, sitting on his own in the front, felt himself have a little chuckle.

Oh, to be young, he thought. But they weren't young – well not that young depending on who you asked. Most of them were in their late twenties.

Tony's mind drifted back to the day's work, and a realisation that he now had all the wedding party back with him, so he could finish the part of the job that he was getting paid to do. To deliver the groom to the church was his main aim now, and he felt quite fatherly about the job. After all, he was getting to know these lads. They weren't bad. They were… well he couldn't quite put a name to it. Mischievous maybe. After all, they were enjoying their last moments of freedom and all that.

The lads certainly did understand how to enjoy themselves – that was beyond doubt – and he did suspect that the police had been called, but what could they do? Maybe arrest the girls for exposing themselves, but the girls weren't with him. Or at an extreme long shot, they could have the lads for accessory, but he concluded that this was unlikely. The police down here, he summarised, had far more pressing obligations.

John was watching and listening once again, and glancing over at Rockin, he saw that he was deep in thought. The rest of the lads were still joyfully telling their version of the same story.

By now, Marco and Will had both lit up a couple of Silk Cuts, taking a deep inward breath while appreciating the essence of the nicotine which clung to their lungs. At the same time, Marco was patting his chest slowly and softly. His eyes were shut and he had a chink of a smile. This patting of the chest had nothing to do with smoking or a cough – he was subconsciously patting himself on the back for a job well done.

Phil was being his usually cool self – non-boasting and solid in mind and body. His expressions only went from happy laughter to showing no emotion. Phil just had a stiff upper lip, and he didn't like revealing his feelings to anyone. This had been part of his problem in the courts when he was trying to gain access to his children unsuccessfully – well that's what his mum said afterwards, anyway.

Giles looked pretty smug, no doubt going over the event in his mind, and thinking of the expressions on his friends' faces when he showed them the newspaper clippings at the next pheasant shoot. They would pretend to be disgusted at first at the fact that he'd appeared in such a low-life newspaper with all the common people. He also knew they would secretly be envious, and that he would be the talk of all the young farmers throughout the region, if not nationally. He would become a mini celebrity, with friends and social circles opening many paths to daughters of the wealthy Cheshire Farmers. Giles was a good catch and not short of a few pounds – far from it in fact. He had just taken delivery of a brand-new BMW M3 with dark metallic blue paint and grey leather interior, which his mother thought was a tad too flashy.

At that point, Giles decided that he would be attending the 'ladies' day' meeting at Chester races next May. It was more than a good few months away, but this would allow time for the stories to spread around. By that time, he'd be a legend.

Tony seemed to be oblivious to where he was heading. There seemed to be no rush, and he didn't know where he was going and no one else seemed bothered either. He drifted into a daydream – his subconscious was driving now – and he started to picture the images of the girls standing next to his limo stripping their tops off.

Just as he was enjoying his daydream, a piercing siren went off behind him jolting him back into the real world. The lads behind him looked startled too. Flicking his eyes up to the rear-view mirror, Tony could see where the noise was coming from. A white Volvo police car sat on his tail with its blue and red lights flashing. "Shit," he said under his breath.

Tony looked for somewhere to safely pull over, and he soon noticed a layby up ahead. But as he drove closer, he saw the huge yellow letters BUS STOP with double yellow lines skirting the edge. "Well, it'll have to do," he mumbled to himself. He brought the limo to a halt, switched off the ignition and glanced up to his mirror to watch the police stop behind him on the road.

The cop driver seemed to be waving at Tony so he put his hazard lights on, but then he realised that the driver was shouting at him to pull forward.

Just to annoy the pigs, Baz had turned the music up a notch. Baz worked closely with the police, but he still appeared to hate them, or maybe it was the image he was trying to portray. Even Phil couldn't work this out, and he was one of his best friends.

Baz felt that people were always trying to be something they weren't and never would be. Like all those years ago back in school when they spent hours practicing their signature – different slants, different loops, larger, smaller, smooth, gagged and aggressive or sometimes not much more than a line. He had read somewhere that your signature displayed the type of personality you had or wanted to depict, and a lot of the geeks in school seemed to reinvent themselves, especially if they went on to university, where no one knew their old persona. That way they could take on another cool, hippy or whatever other personality they wanted.

Baz was the complete opposite. He had always loved his family, his brothers and especially his little sister, with her fine blonde hair and blue eyes. Although she wasn't that small any more. She was at university, and he wondered whether she would reinvent herself too. He hoped not because he loved her as she was.

Then there was his daughter, who looked the same as she did all those years ago. He had lost contact with both his children – a son and a daughter – through a bitter divorce, and had to watch them grow up from afar. Charlotte – the ex-wife – had just denied him access in the beginning for no real reason, except revenge because he had filed for divorce. But even that wasn't Baz's fault because Charlotte was the one who'd been having an affair while he was working night shifts.

Maybe it was his fault she'd cheated on him, he often found himself thinking. Perhaps if he'd studied harder at school, got a better job, earned more money and therefore didn't have to work extra nights to pay for the essentials. But Charlotte had known he was a factory worker and bouncer when they had met. He'd always found it hard to show deep down emotion, which probably hadn't helped matters.

The police stayed in the car for what seemed like an eternity, while they checked the vehicle's details. They knew that taking their time tended to make the car's occupants apprehensive, nervous and more likely to slip up.

Eventually they emerged from the car and tension started building in the limo. "Are your tyres legal?" Marco asked Tony. This just seemed to make everyone's anxiety higher.

The officers split and worked both sides of the car, stopping to have a good look at the tread on the tyres, even on the inside. They ran their hands around the back tyres as if they were trying to find a puncture, and then did the same with the front ones. One officer moved to the front of the car, signalling Tony to put his headlights on. A second cop leaned down to check the tax disc, removing some dirt from the motorway which obscured part of the date.

Both officers wore black body armour, which is standard in the capital, with a white shirt and a black pin-on tie. Their equipment belts held various items including truncheons, pepper spray and handcuffs. Both in their late 20s to early 30s, the officers were a similar age to the lads and they both had crew cuts.

Officer Wilkinson, as he introduced himself, beckoned Tony to get out of the vehicle, which he did with a rather pained look on his face, as if he was trying to get the sympathy vote. "Is this your vehicle, sir?"

"No, I've just nicked it, along with the wedding party back there," Tony replied, regretting it as soon as he opened his lips.

"I'll ask you again. Is this your vehicle, sir?"

This time, Tony replied in a deep voice, "Yes, officer."

"Then can I see your documents?" the officer asked Tony. He already knew who owned the vehicle, that it was fully insured and that Tony had no points on his licence. It was more to be a pain in the backside following Tony's cocky answer.

Tony fumbled in his back trouser pocket for his wallet. "I've only got my licence. My wife's got everything filed away back in the office," he explained.

"You'll have to produce them at a police station of your choice within the next seven days, or you'll get a summons," Tony was informed. He just nodded.

The second officer had moved around to stand face to face with Tony. "You're a fair way from home, aren't you?" This made Tony take a step back. He hadn't told them where he was from and his accent wasn't strong enough to give it away, he thought. He realised that they must have done a vehicle search which had showed up where he lived. They must have known he was insured in that case, too. He stopped himself saying anything because by the tone of their voices, they were dying to do him for something!

"Who's in the back, anybody famous?" one of them asked.

"No just a wedding party," Tony replied. The lads had turned off the loud thumping music so that they could eaves drop on the interrogation. The officers looked at each other as if to say, 'we've got them', and the second officer walked over to the back door, knocked on the window and then opened the door. The first person he saw was Marco, who looked dubious at the best of times, with his fake tan and long dark hair. Baz was sitting next to him, staring straight ahead, rather than looking at the pig.

"Would you all mind stepping out of the vehicle?" the officer asked. So, one by one they all clambered out. "All line up and face me," they were told, which they did without question.

Officer Collins – the policeman who had asked them to get out of the car – had a two-inch deep scar on his left cheek, virtually connecting his eye to his lip, and his skin was rough with a five o'clock shadow.

"Who's the unlucky man?" There was silence.

"That's me," Rockin replied.

"Where's the wedding?" Silence again. The lads had told different lies to different people and they were at a loss for words. After all, Tony still thought he was taking them to a wedding, even if he didn't know where the darn thing was being held.

John was still in the back of the limo hiding behind the blackened glass. He was led to believe the wedding was supposed to have taken place in north Wales, but had been called off last minute. This story seemed too far-fetched to tell the police though.

The silence lingered, and Collins was still looking at Rockin, who was the obvious one to answer. But Rockin hardly knew any street names in London, never mind addresses of churches.

The noise of the traffic and the pedestrians gawking seemed to intensify the waiting, and eventually Giles was the one who broke the silence, much to everyone's relief.

His voice had turned up a level on the posh accent scale – he spoke with a true plum in his mouth. It sounded natural, but he spent most of his time trying to water it down after years in private education. "Westminster Abbey, officer," he said with great pride.

This made the officers blink. "You're pulling the yarn," Collins said. Rockin interrupted, his voice suddenly sounding well-spoken, too. "It's in one of the side chapels not the main bit," he clarified. There was silence yet again, and this time an unbelieving one. Rockin remembered his mum saying that if you were a grandchild of a commissioned high-ranking officer from the army you could get married there. He blurted this out nervously, but Rockin had an excuse to be nervous – he was the groom!

Officer Wilkinson scanned this merry group, all standing in a line. In fact, they looked like they were in a line-up back at the station, standing with their backs to the limo and all looking rather guilty of something. He noticed that the skinhead one seemed to have gone pale and hadn't said anything since they had all emerged from the limo. The long-haired, tangoed one looked a bit too cocky, staring him straight in the eye. He definitely fancied himself, thought Wilkinson, what with the way he was flicking his hair around all the time. The posh one seemed level and the groom was understandably nervous, but something wasn't right, that was for sure.

A moment later, a coughing noise erupted from inside the limo. At first it didn't seem to register with the officers. John placed his hand over his mouth, tensing his neck muscles to strangle the cough, but then the coughing exploded.

Walking up to the open limo door Wilkinson peered in. He didn't see anyone at first but when he tilted his head to the left, he spotted a figure squashed into the corner and cowering as he tried to make himself invisible.

"Out," Wilkinson shouted, feeling frustrated that he hadn't noticed this extra man earlier. John gradually eased himself out of the limo, but he didn't look Wilkinson in the eyes, he stared at the floor instead. "And who are you?"

Eventually, looking up at Wilkinson, John replied, "I'm a reporter."

"Shit," Wilkinson said under his breath. "What's a fuckin' reporter doing with a wedding party?"

The passing motorists and pedestrians shot some strange looks – some even stood and watched – and a couple of Japanese tourists started taking pictures. It was a strange sight seeing a bridal party and chauffeur backed up against the limo, all in a row, with two police officers interrogating them.

Soon a red double decker bus indicated to come into the bus stop. The driver, who was a middle-aged man carrying too much weight around his face and most probably the rest of his body, looked annoyed. As he edged the bus forward, he let off the air brakes so that they hissed noisily. It was as if he was trying to make a point. Collins gave a stern look towards the bus, and the driver started waving his hands frantically and shrugging his shoulders, miming to the policeman. "Where am I supposed to stop, you berk?"

The policeman took a large breath expanding his body armour, and feeling the cold polluted air in his lungs. Then the bus driver lifted the handbrake off and released the foot brake, discharging more compressed air and letting them all now that he was still waiting impatiently.

Wilkinson looked towards Rockin. "What time's the wedding?"

"Err, one o'clock," Rockin replied, not sounding very convincing. The officer looked down at his chrome watch.

"It's twenty to one – you should be there now."

Giles replied in his posh voice, "I hate to sound rude, but if you hadn't pulled us over, we would be there now."

"The bride will be arriving before you in this traffic," said Collins, rubbing his forehead. A tense headache was building around his temples and eyes. If his boss found out that he had wrecked someone's wedding, and then seeing the fuckin' reporter. He remembered seeing a flash going off somewhere in the background.

This could blow a simple stop and check out of the water, but it wasn't a simple stop and check. He had only pulled them over as a favour to one of the beat officers and he didn't really have any reason to do so. "I'll tell you after, just wind them up a bit," he'd told him. Collins couldn't help but think he was in the shit again. After all, it was only a week ago that he and Wilkinson were in the Super's office getting a right rollicking, and this bloody reporter could blow everything out of proportion if he wanted to. It could even end up being plastered across the front pages! The news had been dull for a while now, so God only knows what they could print. He felt the throbbing pain of a migraine really starting to kick in.

Looking at Rockin Collins said, "I'll see if I can get clearance to give you an escort to the church – sorry I mean cathedral." This lit up Rockin's face in an instant.

"I've never had a police escort before," he said loud and proud. Collins knew he couldn't risk getting his name splattered across the front pages. Then he looked at Giles and thought, *And you never know who those posh gits know!*

"Just get in the limo, the lot of you," Collins said in a stern commanding voice. Then he stepped into the patrol car, picked the mic up, held it for a second, pressed the button and started to explain the situation to control, telling a couple of small white lies to stop all involved from getting into trouble. After all, that sodden reporter would never know what had been said.

Once Collins received the clearance he wanted, he pulled the patrol car onto the road and stopped opposite Tony's open window, Collins kept looking forward, while Wilkinson barked out orders for Tony to keep a close, constant distance between both vehicles. "And don't let anybody push in between us," added Wilkinson. Tony nodded and even felt quite excited.

The blue lights were already flashing as the Police Volvo edged forward making sure Tony had pulled out after them. Collins switched on the siren, which sent a shrieking noise through the London traffic. Both vehicles carved their way through the traffic, diving to the left and then the right.

The lads were ecstatic, jumping up and down in their seats like excited school children. Will shouted, "This is even better than being with those tarts we were with earlier!" they all enthusiastically agreed.

"Ha ha, we're like the celebrities!" said Will.

"No! Celebs don't have police escorts. Only royalty and the prime minister get that service!" Rockin announced.

They were making good progress, Tony informed them. "A couple of minutes and we'll be there," he said. This statement immediately stopped the excitement in its tracks, and the whispering started. They had all forgotten that they were now on route to Westminster Abbey.

"What are we going to do now?" asked Will.

"We'll just get out and run," said Baz, but Marco interrupted. "No, we can't do that."

Phil spoke up for the first time in a while, and everybody stopped and listened, "We'll get out, say thanks to Tony for all that he's done, and walk into the church. It's as simple as that."

Everyone nodded in agreement and Rockin piped up, "The simplest way is always the best way." They all nodded again.

Giles was sitting on the very back seat and he soon announced that he could see the Cathedral coming up. Thirty seconds later both vehicles started to slow.

"This is it then," said Rockin, feeling slightly nervous and almost as if he was about to get married.

Giles snapped his head up, almost shouting but managing to restrain himself. He said in barely more than a whisper. "Fuck! There's a wedding at Westminster Abbey."

Chapter 9

The Wedding

The patrol car with its blue lights flashing came to a halt ahead of the gates allowing the limo to slip in behind so that it was adjacent to the entrance. Tony eased himself out of the driver's seat for the officers, a lot easier than he had done earlier. Straightening his jacket, he looked around at the few official guests by the cathedral door who were looking down quizzically at the limo with its police escort. With elegance and a little showmanship, Tony opened the passenger door for the last time formally that day, he hoped.

By now a crowd had gathered outside this architectural masterpiece, which dates back to pagan times, with tombs of kings, queens, statesman, warriors, musicians, poets and scientists. Built in between the 13th and the 16th century, Westminster Abbey is one of the best recognised in the world, with its two imposing towers.

Tourists, especially the American and Japanese, loved to see a good, traditional British wedding with the bride in her flowing white dress, the sometimes beautiful, sometimes hideous, bridesmaid dresses, the Groom, best man and the ushers dressed in their morning suits. Their cameras always came out at British weddings making the wedding party feel like celebrities. And the Americans could never help themselves. They always had to go and tell the bride how stunning she looked.

A group of tourists clapped as Marco emerged from the limo, then Rockin and the rest of the gang. They seemed very impressed at the police escort, and soon began gossiping that they must be royalty or from a high-powered family to be receiving a police escort.

Then a couple of beat officers, who happened to be passing the gates as they had pulled over, stopped to relieve the boredom of walking their endless beat. They too wanted to see who was receiving a police escort to Westminster Abbey.

The cameras continued to click away, and Marco was posing in front of them all, trying to act natural, as he flicked his hair and caught Rockin in the face.

By now the people in the crowd were convinced that this must be a celebrity wedding, what with Marco's image and Rockin's spiky hair do. This idea was further confirmed when Baz and Phil emerged from the limo. With the size of them they must be the bodyguards, thought the crowd, even though Baz was in a morning suit. Phil did take on the persona of a bodyguard though as his eyes started darting around the crowd, trying to guide the lads away from the limo.

Collins and Wilkinson didn't wait around for any pleasantries. They had to turn the siren off at the final approach so as not to alarm any guests. John was the last to immerge, and by now he was totally confused at the situation. He wondered what was going on and did think of saying something, but he stopped himself and decided to see how things played out.

The lads had decided what to say to Tony before they had stopped outside Westminster Abbey. Marco calmly walked over to Tony and offered his hand, shaking it with a firm grip. "Thanks for getting us here and sorry for all the hassle we've caused you," Marco said to Tony in a rather concerned voice.

"It's been different, that's all I can say," Tony replied, winking back at Marco.

Releasing his grip, Marco turned to the crowd and flung his hands into the air, which brought a rapture of applause from the people. He then turned to face the lads, who were looking towards the cathedral. "Let's go," Baz said, patting Rockin on the back. They all started walking slowly.

Tony leaned against the limo's side, letting out a huge sigh of relief. He could hardly believe that he'd actually got them here, and he thought to himself, *If I smoked, I'd really need one right now.* Watching them stroll towards the Cathedral, Tony realised he'd love to see the girl that Rockin was marrying. *I wonder what she's like?* he thought. She must be easy-going, was all he could think. Either that or crazy.

As the lads nearly reached the door, Will looked over his shoulder to see Tony still standing by the limo watching them. He told the lads and they weren't best pleased.

A skinny, gaunt man approached them with a camera swung around his neck. Appearing confused, he informed them that they were a bit late, and that they should go straight in. He would take some pictures of them after the ceremony.

In his deep, gruff voice, Baz informed him otherwise. "There's no way we're going in there!" And he meant it, but he wasn't really speaking to the photographer, he was setting the boundaries to the lads.

This confused the photographer even more, especially when the other lads all started to nod and agree. They had all edged a little further back and were standing behind a stone wall, which shielded them from Tony's view. The photographer walked into the cathedral shaking his head as he went.

"What are we going to do?" asked Giles in a sheepish voice. They all looked around at each other, and Tony was still there leaning against the limo. "We could wreck someone's wedding day if we carry on hanging around here," Giles continued.

"Fuck if I know what to do!" exclaimed Marco.

"It's just our luck that some prick put up a 6ft fence," Will said.

"Why don't we just walk out of the gate again?" suggested Marco.

"I thought of that, but Tony will see us," replied Rockin.

"Fuck him, we don't need him," Baz said.

"Um, we do need him to get us home, unless you're going to pay for everyone's train fare," Phil said glaring at Baz.

The atmosphere was starting to turn tense, not only because of Tony standing there, but the very fact that the lads were about to wreck someone's wedding day if they weren't careful.

"What are the chances of a wedding being held here today?" Giles asked, but no one answered.

Will popped his head around the wall so that he was barely visible from the street. He could no longer see Tony, but the limo was still in full view, sitting there motionless.

Tony watched as another usher dressed in what seemed to be an identical morning suit walked over to where his wedding party were. Just as Will was about to tell the lads about Tony, he caught the eye of the usher or maybe he was the best man, even the groom, for all he knew. The man looked intently at the lads in total disbelief. "I hope you lot are at the wrong church! Or you've got the wrong day!" he exclaimed.

The usher was about 5ft 9, well-built and walked with his shoulders back and his chest out. Quite possibly military, thought Phil, but then why wasn't he in uniform? Then again, he was most likely from a military family, with his dark hair cropped at the sides, coming forward on the top. He had the classic square jawline and had definitely been on a sunbed.

Everyone was silent.

"Well which one is it?" said the usher. "The wrong church or the wrong day?"

"We think we are at the wrong church," replied Giles.

"Well this is a cathedral. What church are you supposed to be at?"

"That's the fuckin' problem. We can't remember and we don't even have our mobiles on us to find out. Plus, everyone who knows us is at the church."

"Jesus, you're really in the crap," said the usher. "Doesn't the limo driver know where you are supposed to be?"

Marco spoke up this time. "I only hired him the other day. The bride doesn't have a clue because it was supposed to be a surprise."

"I don't know how to help you, I wish I could," the usher added.

Rockin glanced at his watch. It was five to one and a few more people were wandering out of the Great West door to see the extra wedding party. Phil had been right though. Some of the congregations were, in fact, wearing military uniform – army by the look of it.

The lads felt an overwhelming feeling that this situation was going to go pear-shaped at any minute. The usher turned and politely asked his guests to go back in the church, but some continued to linger for a while staring at the lads. Eventually, though, they went back in, after the usher had held his hands out as if he were rounding up a flock of sheep.

By this time, Tony was back in the limo fiddling with his new CD, mp3 player that he'd had installed the day before. *Too many tiny buttons and too many damn lights,* he thought as he twiddled trying to find the right track on his classic 60s CD, which he'd got free with one of the Sunday papers. He was totally oblivious to the confusion he was causing at this magnificent Cathedral.

"Tony's back in the limo," Will announced. "And hopefully, with any luck, he'll be departing at any moment." This gave a mild sense of relief to the huddled group.

"Well he'd better hurry up, because the bride is due to arrive at any time," replied Rockin.

Time seemed to have stopped, with each second taking forever to tick by. Staring at his watch for the tenth time, Rockin willed it to go faster or somehow magically move Tony on.

Will peeped around the corner once again. "What the fuck is he doing?" he muttered. Will noticed that the engine wasn't even running – well at least there were no exhaust fumes coming out of the fully leaded five-litre V12 engine.

"The engine's not even running!" he informed the lads.

"Shit, what the fuck is he doing?" asked Baz.

"Can't see, the windows are blacked out."

"Fuck shit, state the bloody obvious, why don't you," Baz returned.

Agitation was building once again, and a couple of the lads started to shuffle their feet. Marco fiddled with some crumpled ten-pound notes in his trouser pockets, slightly tearing at the edges. Giles had started biting his nails, which were already ground down to next to nothing from working at the leisure park. Rockin continued to look at his Rolex GMT master, which he had told everyone was real. Admittedly it was a good copy, thanks to a good mate who had brought it back from Malaysia for him.

Rockin had done this mate a couple of favours while he'd been working out in Malaysia for four months, and one of them was buying and delivering a huge bunch of flowers with extra red roses to mate's girlfriend's work place for Valentine's day. Rockin was a bit of a romantic, which was one of the reasons he wanted out of here before the bride arrived.

Rockin piped up, "Once the bridesmaids arrive, we've got to go," and most of the lads nodded but said nothing.

"Have another look for Tony, can you, Will?" Baz asked him.

"He's still there," Will replied.

Two of the wedding party came back out of the Cathedral. The same usher as before with another guy. They both wore fancy blue waistcoats under their jackets and sported matching large knotted ties.

Striding over to the lads, the first usher asked, "Any luck remembering which church?"

"No, we feel like idiots," Marco replied.

"Well I've had a word with the wardens, and they are going to ring around to see if they can find your church."

"Thank you," said Rockin.

As the lads were discussing this, two old ladies dressed as if they had just come from a WI meeting, appeared. Both wore beige skirts and one had what looked like a home-knitted green cardigan and large oval glasses. The other sported a black Puffa jacket, which looked more like her grandson's than hers, because it was a couple of inches short in the arms. Both ladies modelled shampoo and sets and walked with a determination in their stride.

"Who's the poor lad?" asked the one in the green cardigan. Rockin stuck his hand halfway up as if answering a school teacher. "We'll sort this out in a jiffy," she told him.

I hope not, Rockin thought to himself.

The two ladies introduced themselves as Gladys and Audrey, and they gave the lads the impression that they could track down any wedding in any country in a 'jiffy'. Gladys gave Rockin a reassuring look and walked towards him to give him a grandmotherly hug, patting him on his back as she did so.

Audrey took a step back, clasped her hands together in front of her chest in the pray position, holding Rockin's gaze and giving him a reassuring smile. "We're going to need some details," she said. Rockin nodded. "Right, what is your full name and the bride's full name?"

Rockin gave his details and said the first girl's name he could think of, which was Lara. Audrey made a mental note. "Can you give me any details about the church?" she asked him.

Rockin replied, "No, I was so nervous, we had a couple of drinks to calm my nerves and now I have no idea."

"OK, we'll phone around, it shouldn't take long," Audrey reassured him.

Hurrying back into the Cathedral, nattering as they went, the ladies made their way into a small office with stone walls and a small antique wooden desk with drawers down each side. A typewriter with no letters on the keys from years of use sat idle next to a neat pile of post and a copy of The Guardian folded in half.

On the other side of the typewriter was a personal leather bond telephone directory with a gold crucifix embossed in the centre, and at the top right-hand corner of the desk sat a modern telephone with the usual numbers, and some extra buttons displaying unlit LEDs for different extensions.

Audrey picked up the directory and started flicking through the pages. They had both decided to start at the closest churches and work outwards. Gladys bent down and opened the third drawer down. She knew it contained a map of all the churches in the city, so she quickly unfolded it. "There are 47 churches," she told Gladys. "I hope we don't have to phone them all."

Audrey paused for a second and made a humming noise. Everyone who worked with her knew this to be a signal that her old – but far from worn out –

brain cells were now working in overdrive. "They've turned up at this cathedral, so I wonder whether they are supposed to be at St Paul's instead." Eventually she found the number she was looking for under P for Paul's rather than S for St.

The phone rang three times before someone answered. Introducing herself as Audrey Green from Westminster Abbey, she asked to be put through to someone who dealt with weddings.

The gentleman at the other end said, "The person you need to speak to is busy at the moment. He's looking after a wedding." This made Audrey's heart jump with excitement.

"This sounds like a daft question," she began, "but has all the wedding party arrived, in particular the groom?"

"I know there has been a hiccup with this wedding," said the man, "but I'm not sure exactly what it is." Audrey described the situation at her end, so the gentleman said he would go and find out and call her straight back.

Bringing Gladys up to date, the ladies came to the conclusion that this most probably was the wedding that the lads were supposed to be at. "I'll go and inform the poor groom," Gladys announced.

As she marched down the nave of the cathedral, a sudden thought hit Gladys. Nave was Latin for ship and this was where people were carried forward and delivered to God. At this instance, she was delivering God's message, 'Sailing above troubled waters of this material world' to the wedding party outside. *God works in many different ways,* she thought.

Knowing that she was carrying out God's work sent an overwhelming warmth into Glady's heart. She turned down the centre isle with her feet barely touching the parka flooring, passing under the great roof which was suspended high above the nave.

Gladys marched towards the Great West door, quite forgetting that she had a bad hip as she walked with a spring in her step. As she approached the door, she glimpsed to the right at the basin of holy water and she felt as pure as the white driven snow. She walked through the Great doors out into the clean crisp air only to notice three brilliant white snowflakes float down in front of her. *A sign,* she thought, which made her stop in her tracks for a couple of seconds to catch her breath.

Looking around through the hordes of tourists milling around, Gladys soon spotted the lads. If she hadn't known better, she'd have thought they were hiding.

"We think we've found your church or rather Cathedral," Gladys informed them.

Rockin looked mystified, but then with a forced, confused smile he said, "Thank God for that!"

"We think you're supposed to be at St Paul's Cathedral, because there's a wedding on today, and we've found out that there's some kind of hiccup with it."

"Great," replied Rockin.

A black Silver Spirit Rolls Royce with 16-inch low profile tyres came to a halt behind Tony's Limo, who was still unaware of what was going on at Westminster Abbey. The driver in the Rolls stepped out, softly closing the door behind him. His black suit was newer and far more tailored than Tony's, but he was also wearing the traditional chauffeur's black cap.

By now, Will was back at his spying post, peering out from behind the wall and watching as the two ushers came out to see if they were still there. Catching a glimpse of Will, they informed him that he and the rest of the party would have to disappear before the bride arrived.

The lads turned in time to see the first bridesmaid get out of the Rolls. She was dressed in a long, pale, yellowy gold, straight dress, which hugged her elegant figure. She was followed by a blonde-haired girl who was only about seven years old and wearing a mini version of the same dress with an extra-large bow on the back. The third bridesmaid was a little taller than the first – a couple of inches taller in fact – but she was incredibly good-looking.

Going over to the girls, the first usher tickled the little girl under her chin before pecking her on the cheek and telling her how beautiful she looked, which made her blush. The same compliment was dished to the other two, but without the same effect. There was some small talk, and then they turned and pointed to where Will was standing and sticking his head out slightly. At this point, a look of astonishment and disbelief came across the two older girls' faces.

The wedding photographer introduced himself to the bridesmaids and told them where he wanted them positioned. Firing off some shots as quickly as possible of the girls standing in front of the car, he then directed them in front of the doors and took some more shots. "We have to be quick," he told them, "because otherwise the tourists get impatient and start wandering into the pictures – especially the Americans."

While they were being photographed, the bridesmaids kept casting glances over to the lads, who were looking panic-stricken. The bridesmaids felt a bit sorry for them and especially for the unfortunate bride waiting alone at the altar, or driving around in circles.

As soon as the pictures were taken, the bridesmaids rushed over to them and exclaimed their sympathy and concern. They asked the obvious questions, and if they could do anything to help, at which point Marco whispered to Baz, "They can come and sort me out around the corner." Baz chuckled quietly.

The bridesmaids walked towards the gate to wait for the bride to arrive. The older girls both agreed that the other wedding party must be a bit thick not to know which church they were supposed to be attending. "They should have stayed at home with the sheep," said the taller one, which made them both laugh.

Just then a second Silver Spirit pulled up, and this time a white one – her father had bought the car especially for his daughter's wedding. The photographer leaned into the car to ask the bride to stay there while he took some pictures. She wondered which of her guests had come in the stretch limo, so she enthusiastically waved the bridesmaids over to ask them. "You don't want to know," said the shorter bridesmaid. This not only confused the bride, but it worried her a bit, too.

Talking to the lads the usher told them they needed to disappear now, either into the Cathedral or out of the gates, but peering around the wall once again, Will noticed that Tony was still sitting there. Something had made Tony look up, and he was unaware of how much time had slipped by. He was startled to see a white Roller in his rear-view mirror, which usually indicated a bride. He checked his side mirror and saw a photographer sticking his lens through the window. Desperate to see what Rockin's wife-to-be looked like, he waited.

The lads, not knowing what to do, decided to wait one more minute and then they would leg it – simple. They would tell Tony that Rockin had bottled it and ran, and that would also explain why he was coming home with the other lads.

Tony watched the chauffeur open the Roller door, and the bride stepped out. She was absolutely beautiful, thought Tony. No other words could describe her. He'd seen enough, so he turned the key, slipped the massive engine into gear, indicated and drove off.

Feeling a surge of adrenaline rush through his veins, Will turned to the lads. "I'VE JUST REMEMBERED WHICH CHURCH!" he shouted in excitement.

"Let's go." The lads didn't need to be told a second time. They turned on their heels and started running, and all the bride saw was her wedding party running for their lives out of the church. Her heart stopped, the blood drained from her strikingly beautiful face, her grip loosened from the bouquet, nearly letting it slip to the ground. Then she noticed Marco's long, black, wavy hair flowing behind him. She glanced at the rest of the party – they weren't hers. Now in total confusion, the bride's body started to shake and her bladder felt weak. A tear welled up in her left eye.

Racing through the gate the lads turned right towards the bride. Everything seemed to be happening in slow motion, she thought, as if she was watching the Bionic Man 20 odd years ago. They jogged past her and waved and winked as they went, except for Marco. He stopped in front of her, grabbed his breath for a second and then said, "You're at the right church, we're at the wrong one. Good luck and God bless." He lent forward, kissed her on the cheek and sprinted off after the rest of lads. *Surreal,* she thought.

Chapter 10

John emerged from Holborn tube station leaving the clattering of the trains deep underground. About 10 feet behind him were the lads who were all having an informal conference on the move, making sure they were out of ear shot of the reporter. It was a quick conference where basically Marco had decided to get as much money out of the paper as possible. They were going to be drinking champagne and the good stuff – surely Moet at least – and Giles would be there to supervise quality control.

Phil had never tasted the real sparkly stuff – well he always had Asti on Christmas day because Charlotte had always insisted. The champagne would get them noticed, if the suits didn't, but what it would show is that they had money and they were spending it. Waiting by the exit, John felt like a school teacher waiting for the stragglers. By now he was feeling the cold and he had goose bumps all over his body. His nipples had turned rock hard and his body was shaking from the inside out. Stupidly, he had forgotten to bring a coat when he'd left the office, and all he was wearing was a white cotton shirt, nylon tie, brown trousers and loafers. He hadn't expected to be standing outside a cathedral for half an hour in the depths of winter waiting for God knows what.

Admittedly he'd warmed up a bit running from the cathedral, trying to keep up with the lads, but he wasn't as fit as he used to be. In fact, he was still confused as to why they had to leave the Cathedral in such a hurry after waiting around for so long, or why they had even been there in the first place. The most he could gather was that it was something to do with the limo.

John suggested an Irish bar around the corner, but Marco and Giles had a feeling that it wouldn't have champagne. However, they were overruled by Baz, Rockin and Phil, who all fancied some of the black stuff. Paddy's bar was a traditional modern Irish bar designed to look old with its dark stained wood interior and smoke-stained magnolia walls.

A couple of scruffy regulars sat propped against the bar nursing a couple of pints of Guinness and the house whisky as chasers. Smoke drifted up from their yellow stained fingers adding to the ambiance of the scruffy joint. Another younger couple sat by a fake fireplace with small gas-powered flames flicking red and yellow. Then there was a couple in their early thirties drinking a pint of Stella and a white wine. Everyone stopped talking as the lads walked in.

John was the first to the bar, and asked the barmaid if they took credit cards. "Well as long as they're not stolen," she said, flashing him a smile.

Turning to the assembled lads behind him, John asked them, "Right, what do you want to drink?" Marco turned away from John to face the sexy, slim brunette barmaid.

"Champagne," he said, "and make it the best you've got!"

Replying in a sweet, soft Irish accent, the barmaid replied, "We have Moet & Chandon."

"Then that'll do nicely," Marco concluded. Turning away, the barmaid slowly bent down displaying her cute, pert ass which was tightly wrapped in dark blue jeans and left nothing to the imagination. The lads were practically drooling. Gently placing her finger tips on the glass to check the temperature of each bottle, she finally selected the centre one, caressing the bottle as she brought it up to show the lads.

She turned the label to show Marco, and he nodded. Unwrapping the foil, untwisting the wire and releasing the cork, letting some of the bubbles spurt out, she placed seven champagne flutes on top of a towelling beer mat and expertly poured the champagne into the seven glasses. Each of the lads lifted their glass and raised a toast to the 'day ahead and the Sport newspaper'. Glasses chinked together. Phil took a sip and nearly spat it back, while Giles and Will savoured the liquid gold.

"I'm not sure about this stuff," said Phil.

"It's an acquired taste," Will answered.

"Why not try a black silk, which is champagne and Guinness mixed together?" suggested John.

"I'm not ruining a pint of Guinness with this shit," said Phil, scrunching his face up.

Phil ordered a couple of pints of Guinness, and Rockin said he wanted one to. Marco ordered another bottle of Moet and leaned on the bar with a smug smile waiting for the barmaid to bend down again. She poured the three pints of

Guinness leaving them an inch short at the top so they could settle. Then she bent down once again, lingering for a while longer than before to tease Marco.

She opened the Moet and even more seductively stroked its neck as she peeled the foil and eased the cork off, letting the contents spurt towards Marco. Then placing four fresh flutes on the bar, she began to pour, handing the glasses to the lads individually, leaving Marco till last and holding his gaze. Their fingers touched for a second around the glass. Informing Marco that she was going on her break, Marco suggested she came around the bar and have a drink with them, which she did helping herself to a dry white wine. She went into the kitchen to inform her work mate Colin that he would have to take over running the bar.

Colin, who was dark haired with deep brown eyes and about five eight, took his position behind the bar and served the two scruffy regulars with fresh Guinness before he noticed the wedding party. He caught Will's eye and asked him what time the wedding was. "About an hour and a half ago," Will replied. This stopped Colin in his tracks.

His brain seemed to have stalled and he rubbed his goatee with his hands, before adding, "Ye what?" in a deep rough Ulster accent.

"Yeah, the bride had been putting it about a bit," Will informed him.

Will knew what the next question would be.

"Who's the groom?" Will was enjoying this now.

"Rockin, the lad with the spiky hair standing next to the lad with long black hair."

Colin raised his eyes and scanned the room. He clocked Marco first then Rockin standing next to him. Cheryl, the barmaid, was also standing with them which made him feel a tinge of jealousy. Cheryl was staring straight into Marco's eyes, listening intently to whatever he was saying, and Colin took an instant dislike to him.

The questions continued, "Who did she go with?"

Giles butted in at this stage, "A couple of guys from her work, Marco and God knows who else."

"Who's Marco?"

Will was the first to answer this time, "The lad with the long hair."

Both Will and Giles watched his face for the reaction, but his brain had stalled once again. His face was frozen as he struggled to take this information in. "You're takin' the piss," he managed to mutter, brain not yet up to full speed.

"Afraid not," Will returned.

Colin could feel the hatred swelling in his body, and his eyes twitched with anger, as he watched Marco touch Cheryl's arm. John broke his trance by asking for a coffee. "Irish or regular?" Colin asked subconsciously.

"Regular," John replied.

Colin walked into the back kitchen shaking his head. He poured a coffee, placing some small milk containers on the saucer and walked back to the bar eyeing up Marco and sloshing the coffee onto the bar. John picked his coffee up and walked to the back of the bar. Finding an empty table, he pushed some used glasses to one side and sat down. He pulled a notebook out of his trouser pocket and started making some notes about what had happened so far. After he'd finished, he scanned his words and decided that this was looking like a really good story, so he reached for his phone and speed dialled his office.

John dictated his story, speaking clearly and precisely, and when he had finished, he mentioned that something was wrong with the lads' story. He told his colleague the discrepancies. That the wedding was supposed to be up north and that Marco had paid the limo driver extra money to take them to London. Then the limo driver had taken them to Westminster Abbey because he was under the impression that this was where the wedding was to take place.

The guy on the other end of the phone said he would do some checking and get back to them. He told John to start asking questions and to keep close to them.

Rockin started to move away from Marco because it seemed he was becoming a bit of a gooseberry. He went to talk to Baz and Phil instead, who were talking about the latest whey proteins to come on the market and what range of body building products Baz should buy in for the gym.

It was only pocket money serving protein drinks, but selling a complete range should bring the profit base of the gym a little higher, the lads concluded. The gym was more of a place to recruit wannabe door men, than turning a profit nowadays, thanks to the larger, plusher gyms. The main reason Baz kept his gym was for recruiting and being able to train doormen when he wanted to, and, of course, the banter between the lads.

Rockin went to the gym three times a week on the way home from work and he had been doing this on and off for five years. He had an athletic, well-toned body with good muscle definition and low body fat. He'd never used steroids but he did use protein drinks and creatine, so he was quite interested in what they were both saying.

Colin kept staring at his watch counting the seconds until he could call Cheryl off her break, but just then a few more customers walked in and he decided this would be an ideal opportunity. "Cheryl! Give us a hand," he called over. Looking at the customers standing by the bar, Cheryl told Marco she had to go and do some work and gave him the tiniest of kisses on the cheek, which Colin saw. Marco took a sip of the champers smiling to himself at the same time. He stood there all alone savouring the moment. He felt his stomach rumble, wandered over to where Will and Giles were standing and asked if they fancied something to eat. They said they wanted to eat in a proper restaurant, but Marco said he couldn't wait that long, so he'd see if they did food here. He went over to see if Baz and Phil wanted anything to eat. After all, they were big lads so they should have big appetites.

Looking around, Phil said, "This place is filthy, and the food will be processed crap – full of fat and salt."

Bloody body builders, Marco thought. *Obsessed with food, but give them a tin of tuna and they're happy.*

Approaching Cheryl, Marco asked her if they did food. She nodded. "What do you fancy?" she asked in her sexy accent. Marco could feel a tingle down below.

"What's on offer?" he replied. She handed him a vinyl coated menu and walked off, and he chuckled to himself silently.

Marco glanced down the menu not really fancying much at all, except Cheryl, and he kept remembering what Phil had said about the food. He eventually decided on creamy chicken soup served with rustic bread rolls and Irish butter. *What could be so bad about that?* he thought to himself.

"I'll have the creamy chicken soup," he told Cheryl, who handed an order to Colin, the temporary chef. Colin went into the kitchen, which was kept fairly clean, and surveyed the cupboard for a tin of chicken soup. On finding one, he opened and poured the contents into a bowl and put it in the microwave for two minutes on full power. Then he grabbed a rustic roll and placed it on a plate with a brown serviette and a couple of portions of Irish butter in gold wrapping. Picking up a white porcelain soup bowl, Colin walked out the back to where the staff toilet was, opened the grubby door and went inside locking the door behind him. He unzipped his trousers and started to bash the bishop as he thought of Cheryl's naked body going faster and faster he soon ejaculated into the small bowl before placing his manhood back in his trousers and his zip up. He left the bowl around the corner from the toilet and went into the kitchen checking no one was in there before going back to get the bowl.

Removing the Pyrex bowl from the microwave, Colin poured out a small amount of soup into the bowl, picked up a wooden spoon and started to mix the soup into his own spunk. Once the semen had blended nicely, he gradually added more and kept stirring. He nearly sampled the soup but had second thoughts. Colin wiped the edge of the soup bowl with a napkin and took his order into the bar.

Marco saw Colin coming over with his food and sat down at a table near Baz. Placing the bowl and the plate on the table, Colin patted Marco on the back, which Marco thought was a bit friendly. "Enjoy your meal," he said to Marco. Colin was just about to walk away when he remembered to ask Marco if he needed any salt or pepper. Marco tasted the soup and said, "It's delicious as it is, thank you."

Breaking open the rustic roll, Marco tried to spread the butter which was rock solid. He hated hard butter, so he raised his hand and clicked his finger, gaining the attention of Colin. Marco asked him if he could have some soft butter, and Colin nodded walking back into the kitchen.

Taking some butter out of the fridge Colin started mashing it with a fork, then he held one finger over his right nostril and blew his nose, sending snot shouting into the butter. He leaned down and scrutinised the phlegm, picked a dark green chunk out and flicked it onto the floor. Then he carried on mashing. Colin picked up an ice cream scoop, pressed the butter into it and then carefully eased the butter out onto a small white side plate.

Thanking Colin, Marco proceeded to spread the infused butter thickly on the crusty bread roll. He wolfed the soup down, proudly telling the lads how good it tasted. After the last of the soup had been spooned out, he picked up the remainder of the roll smothered with butter and wiped the last creamy chicken soup from the bottom of the bowl licking his lips.

Baz and the rest of the lads now felt hungry after watching Marco eat his soup, and the topic of conversation turned to what type of food they fancied for their wedding breakfast. "I'd be happy with KFC," said Phil. Giles was gradually becoming more confident with Baz and Phil, and decided they weren't going to hurt him.

"We should have a proper lunch in a good restaurant," he said, looking around for support. All the lads seemed to be agreeing with him, so that was agreed then. Baz informed Phil that the Sunday Sport would be paying for lunch so he wouldn't have to watch his money.

"We'll sponge every penny we can out of them," Baz added.

Phil looked at Giles and told him that he didn't want to go to a posh restaurant, which showed Giles that he did have insecurities like everyone else. *He's not invincible after all,* Giles thought to himself. By this time, John had finished on the phone and walked to the front of the bar.

"What do you want to do next?" he asked the lads. Giles informed him that they wanted to go a nice restaurant but not too posh.

"What type of food do you want?" John asked, and Giles spoke before anyone else could. "What about Italian? You could just have pizza then if you wanted," he said looking at Phil who seemed happy about this suggestion. It was agreed then. They were going to have an Italian wedding breakfast.

Rockin told John they wanted a decent restaurant. "Not somewhere grotty like this place," he added. John said he knew the ideal place and it was in Soho, so only a few streets away.

Chapter 11

The restaurant, which was called The Olive Garden, was just off Shaftesbury Avenue. Inside, the walls were painted magnolia with large, tasteful pictures of olive groves, except for the frames, which alternated from red to green. The bar, also painted red and green, had tables placed around with red and white chequered tablecloths draped across them.

In contrast to the Irish bar, there was not a bottle of whisky to be seen. Instead, these had been replaced with rustic clay pipes, layered on top of one another, with bottles of Italian wine placed inside each of them. On the bar, there was only one beer on draught – Nastro Azzruro Peroni. No sign of Stella or even Carlsberg.

Rockin looked at his watch. It was two thirty and he hoped they had not stopped serving lunch yet. The restaurant was about a quarter full now, but it looked like they had been busy earlier. He watched as the waiting staff swept away all evidence of previous diners with fresh cutlery and sparkling glasses.

A waiter asked if he could help them and John was ushered to the front. "We'd like a table for seven please."

The waiter looked the lads up and down, almost disapprovingly, and in strong Italian accent replied, "Please enjoy a drink at the bar while your table is prepared gentlemen."

The barman enquired as to what drinks they would like, to which Baz replied, "Got any Stella?"

Looking like he'd been asked that question far too many times and pointing to the only visible tap, the barman said, "No sir, we only serve Peroni." A visibly dejected Baz turned and briefly checking for nods from John, Phil and Marco, ordered four.

Meanwhile, Giles was busy scanning the wine menu. Only Italian wines were listed – not a French, Australian or Californian choice to be found. He pointed to a group of Chardonnays on the second page, with prices ranging from £11 to £45 per bottle, and tapped his finger on the most expensive bottle. Will found this highly amusing and turned away quietly sniggering to himself. Once the barman had finished pulling the Peroni, Giles ordered the wine, smiling broadly at his attempt of an Italian accent. Unimpressed, the barman eased a bottle from one of the many clay pipes and after opening it, placed it on the bar in front of him.

Shortly afterwards, a lady came over and introduced herself as Luisa. She was their waitress and would be looking after them this afternoon. As she led the lads to their table, Baz lent towards Phil and cheekily mouthed, "She could definitely look after me."

The lads sat around the table, with John placing himself between Giles and Will. They had so far been the quietest of the bunch and John felt it was time to try to gain their trust and see what he could learn. Drawing on his experience as a reporter, he'd often found it was the quiet ones who would give you most information, especially if you befriended them.

As everyone settled, Giles took a mouthful of wine, briefly swilling it around his mouth before swallowing, and quietly complimenting himself on his selection. It was a good choice and even better when it was free.

Luisa gracefully handed out the menus one at a time, making eye contact with everyone and smiling pleasantly. She knew eye contact, a pleasing smile and occasionally brushing her hand against customers, even the females, would bring in much larger tips. They would rarely reciprocate and even if they did, it would usually only be on the arm. It was her domain and she could ease away no problem. She stood back as the lads settled down to read the menu, smiling inside at the visible relief on their faces after finding the menu had been translated from Italian to English.

"Garlic bread lads?" asked Marco, to which Rockin quickly replied,

"Not for me, mate. Think about the ladies." With almost uncanny timing, Rockin's Motorola started to vibrate in his pocket. He took it out of his pocket and after briefly glancing at the screen, answered it.

"Hi, it's Abigail," a sweet voice said on the other end of the phone. He'd been wondering if she would call, especially after Will had groped her at the Savoy.

"I've got an hour free, could we meet up?" she asked him,

"Yeah, no problem. We're having something to eat at The Olive Garden," Rockin replied, smiling from ear to ear. He gave her the address and asked her if she'd join them for lunch.

"Do you want us to order you anything?" Rockin asked.

"No thanks," replied Abigail. She'd already eaten.

When Rockin finished the call, John remarked, "None of those girls ever ate, and if they did it was always junk food."

Smugly, Rockin placed his phone on the table in front of him and grinned at Marco. "Lucky bastard," came the reply. Rockin was already facing the entrance, so he was in the ideal position to see Abigail come in.

Shortly after, their waitress Luisa came back to the table and asked if they were ready to order. Baz and Phil were first ordering two Margarita pizzas with added tuna and sweet corn. This came as no surprise to the rest of the group, who knew their eating habits well.

Giles grinned as he had predicted correctly what culinary delights these two would order. The last-minute decision to add sweet corn had been a good choice, albeit a gamble.

Marco, John and Will ordered spaghetti bolognaise, which Rockin thought was a tad risky, seeing as they were all wearing white shirts. So along with Giles, he ordered the safer option – tagliatelle. Luisa asked them if there was anything else, and Marco quickly ordered another bottle of champers – his third of the day. Close behind came calls for more Peroni and Chardonnay. At this point, John excused himself and made his way towards the toilet. Both a call of nature and a check of the mobile were desperately required.

As John disappeared, Will almost shouted, "Christ! The bill's going to be huge!"

"Bottles of wine at £45 a pop? God knows how much Don Perignon, as well as all the grub!" he continued to blurt. Baz looked up and said,

"Sod 'em. These guys all have deep pockets and company credit cards lads." Marco grinned and raised his right hand. Rudely clicking his fingers, which brought Luisa trotting over, he ordered an extra bottle of Don Perignon and a round of expensive brandies. He told the lads he thought he'd better order them now in case John put a hold on things later on.

As the drinks began to flow, Marco and Rockin began to recount the tale of a recent day at the races. "We'd drunk copious amounts of champagne," laughed Marco proudly. "Loads more than today! And that was before the races had even started.

"Next," he smiled, "came the game plan. On the walk down to Chester racecourse, a horse box passed us. The bold signage stated that it came from Tarporley, and that the trainer was called Bailey. And Rockin, in his drunken state, managed to convince both me and another friend that this was the guy who had trained the famous Red Rum!

"On arrival at the course, we rushed off to buy the Racing Post and went through it expectantly. After finding the race that Bailey had a horse running in, we scanned the odds. It was the second favourite – High Artic – running in the fourth race at 3.35pm. The odds were 5/1 and the favourite, Mountain High, was currently being offered with odds of 4/9. It was a sign for sure and bets were laid," Marco continued.

Rockin, spitting bits of breadstick out of the corner of his mouth, jumped in. "After that it was straight to the champagne tent and off to find some ladies!" After doing in several more bottle of champers, Rockin had decided to start a rumour about some hot 'secret insider info' that he had access to. He told this story to any pretty girl who would listen to him.

"What a scream!" continued Marco, turning as he spoke and reaching for a high-five from his partner-in-crime. "There were all these fit women flirting, laughing and drinking champagne with us, thinking we had the inside track!" Laughed Marco. According to the laddish banter, the guys had certainly enjoyed the game and the ladies were both gullible and appreciative.

As the champagne continued to flow, Marco recounted how he added the Red Rum story to back up his apparent insider knowledge about the forthcoming outcome of the 3.35pm. Dropping this seemed to add some weight with the ladies, and the rumour he started for a laugh continued to spread to anyone who would listen. They were always careful to tell everyone to put it on each way. Women, according to Rockin, always seemed to like to bet each way because it seemed safer.

Will joined the conversation now and with a serious face, he glanced across the table. "I got to the champagne tent about 3.15pm, none the wiser to these two having been at it." Pausing briefly to take a swig of Peroni, he continued, "I recognised a few faces and keeping an ear to the ground, I started hearing rumours about the 3.35, a fix was the buzz, and that High Artic was not going to win but would be definitely placed second." Will rocked back on his chair, looked around to check he had everyone's full attention and went on to explain that he had placed three hundred pounds each way on High Artic.

A couple of lads around the table turned to each other and muttered the words, "Shit!"

"Seeing Rockin, I wandered over and told him that I'd put a huge bet on," Will continued, while Marco and Rockin sat opposite were grinning inanely, barely able to contain themselves.

Marco lent over, grabbing a half empty bottle of Dom Perignon, and pointed at Will. "Your face was a picture, mate, when Rockin told you the score – hilarious!"

Rockin carried on the story, "Marco was too scared to say anything, so he just slinked off and left me to explain to Will that it had all been a way of getting in with the ladies, and the rumours were bullshit!"

The two lads were in full swing now, quite obviously used to telling stories of their various antics. Marco said, "Next thing you know, it's race time, everyone goes quiet and turns to the big screen."

Rockin reckoned that they had been responsible for punters placing a grand or two on a rumour designed to get them lucky with the ladies, at which point Will interjected, "Yeah, and a good chunk of mine!" Adding a quiet "Bastards," before winking at them and finishing his third or maybe fourth glass of expensive Chardonnay.

As the lads refilled their glasses, Luisa and another waitress appeared with plates of wonderful smelling, steaming plates of food. All interest in the 'day at the races' conversation suddenly stopped. Even Marco, who had been thoroughly enjoying watching Will's face change as the story unfolded, was halted by the arrival of lunch. Both waitresses worked their way around the table placing the food in front of the lads, who by now were ravenous. After wishing everyone a pleasant meal, they tactfully retreated. No point in asking if they wanted drinks – the table was overflowing with booze and the group was getting noticeably boisterous.

The lads wolfed down their food, soaking up all the alcohol they had consumed earlier, and even Phil, normally reserved in praising his food, reckoned, "That was the best pizza I've ever had." The table then fell silent as the lads tucked in again until from behind Marco, a deep Italian voice asked if everything was satisfactory. Marco turned and eyed over the middle-aged man standing behind him, with badly dyed black hair and definitely carrying a few extra pounds. He was either the owner or a character from the God Father. Either way he was right in Marco's personal space.

Rockin informed him that the food was delicious. "The best I've had for a long time," he told him, which instantly brought a smile to the man's face.

"Has my daughter Luisa looked after you well?" he asked, beaming with a fatherly smile.

Giles answered with his posh accent and said, "She's delightful, and has looked after our every need." A few smiles ran around the table, and an apparently content owner left them to it.

Somewhat on a roll, Giles switched to Rockin and coolly asked, "What time was the wedding?"

Pausing, Rockin thought, *Here we go again,* but just as he was about to answer, Giles added,

"It's a bit unfortunate it's off!" Silence, a slight delay and Giles went full flow into a detailed story, like the one that he and Will had told Colin about the 'wedding'. Convincingly telling it in such a way that it sounded like the truth.

Overhearing the conversation, the owner of the restaurant had quietly returned. Leonardo – or Leon he told the lads to call him – felt deeply graved for the jilted groom. He looked at Rockin and informed him that he should be looking for a girl like his beautiful Luisa. For one moment they all thought, including John, that Leonardo was about to offer his daughter's hand in marriage and march them up the aisle that very afternoon!

Contemplating, Rockin reckoned he wouldn't say no to an afternoon in bed with Luisa, but marriage! No, no, no he told himself and the notion soon passed. Abigail was due to arrive at any minute and if that failed, Lara was waiting for him at home. Leon offered his sincere commiserations to Rockin and made his way back towards the bar.

Another uncomfortable silence followed. The trouble was the lads were still aware that they could not talk openly, with John still on the case, so they sat silently for the second time during lunch until Phil spoke up, "Would somebody bloody well tell me if you lost your money?" Looking towards Will.

Will pondered for a moment then picked up where the earlier conversation had stopped so abruptly. "Mountain High won by about four lengths," he said in a down beat voice, letting the silence hold for a few seconds.

"So, you lost the lot?" asked Baz. Will kept the silence going much to the irritation of everyone who didn't already know the outcome.

"Artic High romped home in second place!" he added, grinning like a Cheshire cat.

"Shit! How much did you win?" asked John. Will replied, still smiling broadly.

"Just under two grand, and the champagne tent went crazy!" As an added bonus, a fit blonde had taken him into the ladies' toilets and paid him in kind.

Phil stared at Rockin shaking his head, and then he turned to Marco and asked, "Do the girls honestly fall for this?" Marco contemplated this, but he knew the answer.

"Yeah, they do, and more sometimes," he said, before adding, "I do alright as well mind, although I reckon Rockin uses hypnosis, or mesmerises them with those big blue eyes of his."

Baz grunted and pushed his plate to the centre of the table. He was the first to finish and he leant back triumphantly, stretching his upper body and arms towards the wall. Meanwhile, John was trying somewhat unsuccessfully to extract information from Giles. It transpired that he came from farming stock, and they were notorious for being tight with money as well as tight-lipped. John asked him about the lads and failed to come up with much. Things were proving harder than he'd expected, not helped by the fact that he'd only just met Baz and Phil that morning.

Behind them, Leon held his hand out letting Luisa through from behind the bar. She was carefully balancing a round of drinks on a silver tray and made her way over to the table, closely followed by her dad. Looking directly at Rockin, Leon waved his hand across several glasses of Brandy and declared in a sincere voice. "Due to what you have been through today, our finest brandy is on the house."

Rockin felt a momentary pang of guilt. Leon seemed genuine and truly believed that Rockin had been left at the altar earlier that day. This was a feeling not shared by the rest of the lads, who took full advantage of the fine brandy on offer.

Baz wanted to ask for some diet Coke to go with his brandy but after Leon had given them a passionate talk on the region, how they made such a high-quality brandy and some distant family ties he vaguely claimed to share with the producer, he decided against it. It didn't seem fair to dilute Leon's pride and joy with Coke anymore. He sat back wondering if Giles would, regardless of Leon's feelings, knowing it was the sort of thing that Giles would do. Leon pulled up a chair and sat next to Phil again, reminding him what fine quality the brandy was and without taking a breath, continued to share fatherly advice about marriage and women to a clearly uncomfortable Phil.

As they sipped the brandy, appreciating every drop, the door opened and in walked Abigail. She was wearing a pair of dark, tight jeans with a stylish brown wool cardigan. Her hair was tied back into a tight pony tail and she looked stunning. She'd taken the time to get changed since their last encounter and smiling, she made her way over to the table.

Leon eyed this stunner walking over to the table, gently rolling her hips as if she was on a cat walk. Abigail stood opposite Rockin dropping one hip down and placing her hand seductively on the other hip. She then walked around the edge of the table and bent down to Rockin, kissed him lovingly on the cheek, and asked, "How are you coping?"

"I feel down now and again, but the lads are doing their best to look after me," replied a glum-looking Rockin.

Leon's eyes had been fixed on her throughout and he somehow concluded that this must be his baby sister. With a nod, he beckoned Luisa over and asked her to fetch a glass of his favourite Pinot Noir wine, intending to give it to Abigail.

Will pulled a chair over for Abigail to sit down, which she thanked him for. She gazed intently into Rockin's eyes, now holding his hands-on top of the table consoling him.

Marco said to the rest of the lads, "Let's give these two sometime together." Even Leon nodded approvingly, thinking of the pain he must be going through.

He turned to the lads and speaking in a kind but firm voice said, "Come over to the bar, and I'll treat you to whatever drink you want."

On arrival at the bar, Leon began to tell the lads the complete history of his restaurant and how he arrived in the country many years ago. As the conversation went on, Will and Giles caught each other's eye and yawned. Both had switched to orange juice by now, and were feeling a bit worse for wear.

Back at the table, Abigail felt like she was really starting to bond with Rockin, and she was sure that Rockin must feel the same. Rockin was in heaven. Abigail was giving out signals and there was no way he would blow this. Her porcelain skin, almost Eastern European features and amazing figure had him hooked.

Marco was getting bored at the bar. Leon had only just warmed up and was enjoying the chance to tell a few stories to any of the lads who would listen. Staring out of the window, he noticed the weather had taken a turn for the worse, clouds were rolling across the sky bringing with them a fine drizzle of rain.

Marco turned back from the window, now lightly covered in tiny droplets, and looked at Rockin who was sitting by himself, clumsily fiddling with his mobile phone. Marco watched him, trying to figure out what was missing from this scene. *Perhaps I should lay off the booze too,* he thought to himself.

Phil nudged Marco and broke his alcohol-induced trance. "Something's not right mate, where's Abigail?" he murmured. Almost simultaneously, the pair's gaze fell to the black sole and a pointed stiletto heel sticking out from beneath the tablecloth.

"Fuckin Hell," Marco said in barely more than a whisper.

Abigail had dropped her earring purposely on the floor and quickly looking around to make sure no one was watching, carefully slipped under the table. Deftly manoeuvring herself, she undid his zip and eased his cock out of his pants.

"Jesus," Phil said smiling and went to nudge Baz. Marco stopped him.

"Shhh, we don't want a scene."

"How does he do it?" asked Phil.

"I told you before – he fuckin mesmerises them," Marco replied.

Before long, Abigail had finished. She'd taken his juice into her mouth and then spat it out onto the floor. *At least he will think that she swallowed, which would give her extra brownie points,* she mused as she zipped him back up. She quietly whispered to Rockin, asking if it was all clear.

Rockin scanned the room and replied, "Yep, all clear." Abigail crawled out, clasping her earring, and sat next to him.

John settled the bill on the company Amex that he'd been supplied with that morning and added a five percent tip. Marco and Phil thanked Leon for his kindness and hospitality and made their way towards the exit. Both were feeling guilty over abusing Leon's generosity.

Abigail told Rockin she wanted to use the toilet and excused herself. A slightly dishevelled Rockin stood up, thanked Leon and made his way to the door where all the lads were now waiting. By this time word had spread about his liaison with the beautiful Abigail, and the lads commented on what "a lucky bastard" he was.

Back inside, John's phone rang. He answered it while waiting for the Amex transaction to clear. It was the chief editor and he was furious! Those gits had conned his paper, he explained. After checking with the local registry offices, it transpired there was no such wedding and the whole episode had been conjured up by a bunch of freeloaders. He instructed John not to pay for a single drink.

"Not one!" he shouted down the phone. After taking a deep breath, John informed him that he'd just signed an Amex slip for over six hundred pounds. The editor was now shouting down the phone so loudly that an obviously embarrassed John had to hold the phone away from his ear by a couple of inches.

Oblivious to all of this, and happily humming away, Abigail walked through the restaurant and headed towards the exit. As she passed John, he held his hand out and mimed for her to stop. When the ear bashing had finished, he turned to speak to Abigail. He gave her the low-down on what he had just learned, all the time aware that her manner was changing from curious to furious!

Shortly afterwards, Abigail came stomping through the restaurant doors and made a bee-line for an unsuspecting Rockin. Looking up his expression said it all. She marched straight up to him, arched her hand right back and brought it forcefully across his left cheek. The impact sent a shock wave through a bemused Rockin's head and he stumbled back several steps.

"You bastard, the lot of you are fuckin bastards," she screamed, turning and running off down the street. An angry-looking John, who had been standing behind her, turned to the lads, none of whom knew how things would go next.

"My editor's seriously pissed at you lot, especially after shelling out all that money," he informed them. The lads said nothing, so he carried on. "I have to give it to you, it was a good prank and you got one over on the paper, which doesn't happen very often."

John went on to explain what the editor wanted to do in an effort to save face. "He wants to run a different story on you and he's offering to pay for some more drinks and stuff." This lifted the lad's spirits instantly.

"It might not be what you're expecting, mind guys," John went on to say. "You've majorly pissed him off and the chances are he'll concoct a story, commission some compromising pictures and print something that, well shall we say, doesn't exactly show you all in a favourable light. Not too damaging to your reputation unless, that is, the story runs in other papers than the Sport."

"Why are you telling us this?" asked Rockin, still recovering from his earlier assault. John smiled.

"Because I like you guys and I've had a laugh. And anyway, the editor's a dick."

Chapter 12

The lads wandered aimlessly through the drizzling rain, along the dirty streets of central London, namely Soho. Passing the down and outs sitting on pieces of flattened, worn-out cardboard boxes, protecting their rears from the cold, sitting crouched in concrete doorways. All the homeless seemed to carry paper cups, in the hope of collecting a few quid. Their efforts today in vain as none of the lads reached into their pockets to donate any money to these helpless souls.

Their minds where dull and dampened. Not only from the rain, but from the shock announcement from John, and the alcohol numbed their senses. An invisible black cloud hovered above their downbeat heads.

They passed an off licence displaying fine red and white wines stacked up in pyramid shapes with a 'Three for the price of two' offer predominantly displayed. Marco entered the shop and bought a couple of cans of Red Bull, followed by some of the other lads. Downing the first can in one, Marco opened the second and sipped the contents as they began their silent journey once more.

Rockin wondered what dreadful story the Sport would publish. After all, they had plenty to work with, what with all the pictures of the lads standing proudly by the stretch limo in all their wedding gear. Worse still, there was a picture of himself and Abi with their arms wrapped around each other.

This caused a pain in his chest. They could make up endless stories from that, especially now that Abi hated him so much. And who could blame her. Adding to this mixing pot of emotions, guilt was starting to wash over him for having extra-marital sex. Waves of torment overwhelmed him, making him go light headed with dizziness. His stomach churned and his heart felt empty.

Then something hit him like a thunderbolt straight in the middle of his head, stopping him dead in his tracks. It wasn't the paper he had to worry about – he could tell Lara that the paper had made the whole thing up. It was the lads he was worried about. Would any of them tell Lara? He wondered.

He eyed them one by one, and eventually decided that none of them would be able to stay quiet. It would be impossible! It wouldn't be done out of spite, but more in a boastful way. He had no doubt that they would try to keep quiet, but it would be easy for it to just slip out when they were recalling the day's events to their mates down the pub. The alcohol would loosen their tongues, exaggerating the story each time. One thing was for sure, it would come out, he concluded.

Marco was thinking the complete opposite to Rockin. He wished he'd been the groom instead of Rockin, and would most probably have played the part better any way. He would definitely have been on the receiving end of the blow job and imagined Abi's luscious lips caressing and sucking his weapon of mass destruction. He would have felt some guilt, but he would have buried it under the boasting and would have had fun exaggerating the story to everyone who would listen, except his wife of course.

Will dreamt of holding Abi's warm, voluminous breasts in his hand in the privacy of one of the rooms in the Savoy, sharing his gambling moments with her. Oh, the stories he could tell.

Giles just wanted the story to be in the paper, so it would bring extra credibility to the story as he told it around the tables at his exquisite dinner parties.

Baz, on the other hand, wanted to take control of this group. He knew he'd have played it differently. Not knowing quite how, exactly, but the paper would still be with them now, that's for sure. He'd organise these lads the way that he organised his bouncers, and he'd start by putting Marco in his place. He informed Phil of his thoughts, but Phil wasn't interested.

Phil's mind was engrossed with his kids once more. Since his separation, Charlotte would change the rules according to her mood swings. Just when he was about to pick the kids up and they were all excited, some emergency would materialise out of thin air, and the whole thing would come crumbling down around him. He cursed her and cursed the judges for believing the lies she told. She was always dangling carrots in front of him and he could never quite reach them.

Things had got even worse since his arrest, even though he had not been charged with anything. Luckily for him, one of the officers he knew well from working on the doors was the first to arrive on the scene. The officer was nearly at the end of his shift and in his slanted view, there had been no crime. Phil had been wearing a balaclava, but as he pointed out, it was winter and his head was cold. And he wasn't carrying a weapon. He was simply on his way to pay for a holiday he'd booked.

The officer checked that Phil did have a booking with this holiday company, which he did. However, the only question the officer did not ask, which Phil was eternally grateful for, was, "How was he going to pay for it?"

The lads eventually entered the seedier side of Soho, passing various dodgy looking establishments all decorated with different shades of red flaking paint, promising peep shows and lap dancing.

Scruffy looking touts in unwashed, faded outfits smoked cigarettes and stamped their feet as they tried to keep warm. They promised the best-looking girls in town, enticing people inside.

The lads slowed down, but they didn't stop. They didn't dare to in case they caught the touts' eye and were coached into entering the establishments.

Baz glared up at a billboard advertising 'Raymond Revue Bar' which brought back memories of his teenage years when he used to sit in the park with his school mates totally engrossed in a porn mag that someone had stolen from their dad. On the back page, there was always a full-page ad for the Raymond Revue Bar, with scantily clad girls in fancy dancing costumes, huge feathers springing from their heads.

He looked ahead at the Revue bar, which didn't live up to his childhood dream. He'd imagined glitz and glamour, like a west end theatre with glowing lights sweeping through the sky, grand steps sweeping up to the entrance. Instead, there was one high vertical white sign with red letters, which looked like it had been there since the day it opened in the swinging sixties or seventies. Proclaiming to be 'the centre of world's erotic entertainment', the letter 'e' was falling off the word 'centre'. A large arrow pointed to a shabby entrance up a dark, narrow alleyway. Baz shook his head. His dreams had been shattered.

They walked down a side street coming across a couple of brightly lit sex shops. Peeking inside, the lads noticed the shops simply sold the usual magazines and sex toys, which seemed dull compared to what they had done this morning.

Outside Giles said, "What's this?" He pointed to a small white sign above a doorway, which read, 'MODELS' in big black writing. "I've seen several of these as we've been walking," he exclaimed!

The lads looked at each other puzzled. Marco was the first to assault the grotty vinyl covered stair case. He leapt the first three steps and took the rest a couple at a time, being careful not to touch the banister and the walls, which were smeared with dirty finger marks built up over the years, never witnessing the sight of a duster.

When Marco reached the top of the staircase, there were two doors. He looked behind him to see who was with him. Baz was there, immediately followed by Will and Giles.

The non-descript doors, painted in an off-white gloss, reminded Marco of the deco in the Irish bar they'd visited earlier. Baz pushed past Marco and proceeded to knock on the closest door, which happened to be the cleanest. The door opened after about twenty seconds, to reveal a highlighted blonde girl wearing only a Basque, black French knickers and pink fluffy slippers.

The only obvious question Baz could think of was, "How much?" he said it in a gruff but highly embarrassed voice. The lads behind jockeyed for position, trying to gain the best eyeful. Replying in an eastern European or perhaps Russian accent, the girl said, "It's £25 and a tip for the Madame." None of the lads had realised it would be so cheap. It was only the cost of a couple of lap dances and a bit more.

"What do you get for that?" Baz asked fascinated by the whole set up.

She sighed as if she was fed up with answering this question. "A massage with extras included. You get twenty minutes."

Baz had never been with a prostitute and he didn't even know deep down if he wanted to. But the thought did tickle his fancy. He stood there in silence, his mind drifting off. The silence hung momentarily in the air as they all waited for Baz's next move.

Marco broke the silence and brought Baz back to reality. "How many girls are working?" he asked.

"Just me at the moment. The rest of the girls come in later." Marco nodded, turned and knocked on the next door, leaving the prostitute standing there. This time a brunette answered the door but her face was far from picture perfect. He asked politely how many girls are working and the answer was, "Three," said in a sharp cockney accent.

Asking to see the rest of the girls, the brunette gently swung the door back leaving it open, and walked sexily, swinging her hips in a rolling motion like a catwalk model.

Marco watched her cute, rounded, peachy arse moves seductively, as he entered a smoke-filled sitting room. There was a plump woman in her early forties watching 'Richard and Judy'. She had a fag in her hand and was slouched in an armchair in a non-seductive fashion. Marco noticed the cracked window pane revealed views of a brick wall.

Another two girls stopped chatting about how drunk they had been the night before and stubbed their Silk Cuts out in the ashtrays in front of them. They lifted themselves off the worn beige settee and brushed some biscuit crumbs off, which landed on the dirty carpet.

Pushing their chests out the girls tried their best to show off their assets. Their cleavages drew the lads' eyes down to their slim waists and further down to the smallest, laciest knickers most of the lads had ever seen. The girls had perfectly rounded hips and their endless legs finished with a pair of tasteful high heels.

The Madame, who was still holding her fag in her left hand, signalled for the lads to take a seat on the two small sofas opposite the girls, which they did. The three girls lined up and paraded in front of them, at which point Giles couldn't help thinking that they reminded him of prize sheep being paraded around the ring in the Royal Welsh show.

Exchanging glances, the lads didn't know if they wanted to stay or go. Most of them thought it would be rather tempting, especially with the two fit ones, and Marco knew the lure that these girls could have over men. He had nearly been enticed once before but bottled it at the last minute. He thought of the guilt he'd carry after enjoying himself, not to mention the worry that he might catch a dodgy disease.

He turned to the Madame, who was still slouched as she inhaled a drag on her fag. She was looking proudly at her girls strutting their stuff as Marco stunned her with a question. "Got any ginger ones?" he asked.

The Madame had heard some requests in her time, but never had anybody asked for a ginger. Her girls were good-looking and two of them were beautiful. She had to admit to Marco that indeed she did not have any ginger ones, but then gesturing towards her girls, she added, "You won't find any better girls around here, darling!" And she could personally guarantee that he would enjoy himself like he never had before. Baz felt a certain temptation and a twinge down below. He could certainly imagine enjoying himself with one of the girls.

Back outside, Phil and Rockin wondered what was taking the lads so long. By now they'd figured out that 'Model' must be a prostitute, in fact, one of the street beggars had told them. They had been inside for more than ten minutes, so Rockin, wondering what he was missing, headed up the stairs followed by Phil and Giles. Coming face to face with the two doors, he chooses the one which was slightly a jar and pushed it open and peeked inside and saw the girls lined up and Marco's distinctive hair.

The Madame told the girl who had answered the door to go and make the lads some coffee, leaving the two others seducing the lads, which she was not happy about. They were having a quiet day and these lads were the first punters they'd had all afternoon. The girls squeezed in between the two sets of lads, bare flesh touching their sides. The smell of seductive perfumes mixed in with pheromones floated upwards, driving up the sexually tension.

Each of the girls quickly began on their sales pitch, placing their hands on the lads' thighs, opening their legs just enough to tease them and revealing the softest, smoothest skin. They were trying to drive the lads wild as they imagined what sex with these girls would be like.

Both girls asked them if they found them attractive, and they all nodded and agreed. Then, because none of them were coming forward with any offers, they asked, "Are you lot gay?"

This hit three of the lads like a thunderbolt. Marco was used to this question, being a hairdresser, but the others seemed shell shocked by this accusation. Baz was the first to answer in his deep, gruff Welsh accent. A firm "no". It took Will and Giles slightly longer to regain their confidence. They came back with slightly squeaky, embarrassed "nos."

The girls knew this question would insult them and maybe push them away, but often it would make them want to prove themselves. They both came straight out with the next question at the same time. "Don't you want sex with us?"

"Shit," they all thought the same simultaneously. There was silence.

"Perhaps you would like a gang bang? Maybe one of you is man enough to take both of us!" Still silence as the lads looked around at each other, waiting for someone to save them.

Phil who had just arrived, questioned them how much it was, the reply came back, "£25 or you can try two for £60," with a noticeable bulge in his trouser, turned to both the girls and said, "I want you both!" The two girls looked at each other and then smiling sexily, they stood up. Sabina, the Polish prostitute, turned to face the other lads and pronounced in her Polish accent.

"We have a real man here!" They both led him into the bedroom.

The rest of the lads were left stunned, hugely envious that they did not have the guts to take on the two goddesses at the same time in front of the lads, and yet relieved at the same time. Marco knew the Madame would be pressing for one of the lads to take Tracey, so he knew he had to get in first. "So, you haven't got any ginger ones?"

"No," came the reply.

"Do you know where I can get one?" The Madame shook her head, so Marco stood up and walked out, quickly followed by the rest.

Phil entered the room with a double bed in the centre with clean-looking sheets and a white towel with tones of grey which looked like someone had forgot to separate their whites. Sabina spoke first, "Take your clothes off and have a shower and make sure you wash your bits with plenty of soap." Phil did not know whether to be insulted by this but then thought and hoped it was procedure.

He started to strip off nervously while the girls watched and talked in some foreign language, he figured they weren't talking about him, as they most probably had seen naked men hundreds of times. He rolled up his trousers tight making it harder for the girls to pinch some cash from his wallet when things got steamy. Then he thought he would have to ask Baz for some extra cash later, as he glanced at the clock which read five past.

He quickly showered not washing his hair but cleaning his bits as instructed, he glanced over to the girls. They both sat crossed legged on the bed, chatting away with their gossip while their eyes lingered on his torso. He turned off the shower and opened the door. Sabina slowly stood up, went over to a pine shelf and passed him a large cream towel.

Once dry, the second girl, Mia told him to lie face down on the bed, which he did without question. Mia with her long wavy hair knelt beside him and started to run her fingers lightly over his back massaging his huge muscles…while Sabina also sat on the opposite side, and glided her fingers from the inside of his knees to his crotch.

Phil started to relax and his swelling started to make him realise that there was no going back. After a couple of minutes Mia said, "You'd better turn over, we only have ten minutes left!" Which sent a sense of fear and excitement through his veins.

Phil rolled over uncomfortably strangely trying to hide his manhood, the girls glanced down at his penis and slowly lifted their gaze over his six pack and up to, chest. Mia started to run her finger over his ripped chest, on the downward stroke she gently scratched him with her long pink finger nails, while Sabina.

94

Sabina tenderly caressed his shaft quickly bringing him to full attention and wrapped her fingers around his cock. *This is paradise,* he thought to himself as he caught sight of the clock which said twenty past, a thought flashed through his head, *I hope they don't sting me for more money,* his heart pounded faster and faster.

Phil felt a warm sensation on the tip of his huge pulsating penis, he lifted his head and saw Sabina with her mouth around it taking half of it as he felt a tightening all the way down his shaft. She blew him for a couple of minutes then felt her warm breath pass over his face then she lowered one of her nipples into his mouth.

Phil felt someone manoeuvring them shelves over his crotch area, he tried to look but was unable to, then he felt Mia lower herself, taking all of him inside her as she let out a groan of pleasure. She rolled herself back and forth then she placed her fingers on his bulging abs and then up to his perfectly formed chest. Phil grabbed her buttocks into his workman hands gently scratching her with his rough fingers, she let out a moan of pleasure.

Chapter 13

The lads stood outside in the dark gloomy London air, Will looked at his watch and told the lads that he had been 45 minutes, Giles pipped up, "I thought you only got twenty minutes," as Phil pounded down the stairs. He was grinning from ear to ear with not a hint of embarrassment on his face. Phil looked at the lads, all of whom smiled back with a trace of envy written over their faces – after all it was virtually every man's fantasy.

Rockin added, "Did they keep you talking?"

To which Phil quickly replied, "Oh my God! It was amazing, I pounded both of them and to an inch of their life and they won't be doing much work today after that session" he said with a massive smile. He told the lads it was the best fifty quid he'd ever spent.

They were all horny after hearing his account and they wanted to see some boobs. Phil said he needed a beer, and all the lads agreed that sounded like a good idea. Baz decided that this was his chance to take control of the lads. "There's a lap dancing bar down there where you pay £20 and get free dances and unlimited beer."

"It's got to be a rip off!" Marco replied.

Baz acknowledged, "It probably won't be Stella, but as long as it's cold, it'll be alright."

Everyone agreed and Baz led the way. They reached a dark red door with faded pictures of the interior, taken about ten years earlier by the look of the curly perms the dancers in the entrance were wearing. Baz pointed to a small black and white sign, which read, "Unlimited free beer and free dances – £20 entrance fee."

They walked down the tatty red carpet until they reached a black-topped pay desk. A bored, tattooed skinhead looked up. He was about 45 years old with a faded blue tattoo imprinted just below his knuckles. It read 'Love and Hate'. Baz went through the details advertised outside and the skinhead nodded, "As much house beer as they could drink and a few lap dances each for twenty quid," he confirmed. The lads gathered together £120 and paid the tattooed receptionist, who casually pointed to a door on their left and went back to flicking through a magazine.

As their eyes adjusted to the light, it became obvious that they were the only customers, and it soon became clear why. This establishment had not seen a decorator's brush for years and there wasn't a girl in sight.

The small black stage was about a foot high, with metal edging, and stood empty at the far end of the room loosely cordoned off by faded red rope. The walls were covered in aged burgundy wallpaper, which was peeling on the edges, and its borders were ripped and torn.

Round brass covered pub tables were scattered around the place accompanied by faded red velvet chairs. The bar was more of a cubby hole or a converted broom cupboard, with one beer pump advertising a brand which none of the lads recognised.

A middle-aged woman, hair scraped back into a tight pony tail, emerged from a side door wearing a black negligee and suspenders revealing pale skin, with unsightly cellulite bulging over the top of her stockings.

She strutted over to the lads in her six-inch high heels, with her big breasts swaying from side to side. Instructing the lads to take a seat by the stage, she said she would bring some drinks over for them.

Phil was grateful for having a break from his wallet. He had expected that they would end up in a place like this and it would be a considerable drain on his finances. A few free pints of beer and dances with a good-looking girl would do him for now.

The beers arrived and Baz took first sip. He hoped the beer would taste alright. *Well it's definitely not Stella Artois, but more like the French beer you buy in small bottles at the supermarket,* he thought to himself.

No lap dancers arrived, so Will opened the Express newspaper, which had been left on one of the tables opposite. The first pint was going down well, and Marco told everyone that the bar maid was getting changed into her dancing gear. "She'll be gyrating her cellulite on Baz's crotch in a minute," he announced. Baz curled his face up and whispered 'bastard' under his breath.

When most of the lads had nearly finished their beer, the first dancer finally appeared. She didn't look too bad and her figure was good, with curves in the right places, reasonably long legs with no apparent cellulite. She had dressed in a bright red and green Hawaiian-style bikini, which made her pasty white skin look even paler. Baz leaned into the lads and spoke in a low voice, "Marco, you should give her some of your fake tan!" Everyone laughed including Marco!

The lap dancer had long brunette hair, which Rockin and Marco noted was greasy at the roots and no doubt had split ends. Marco knew just the right product she needed, while Rockin thought it just needed a good old-fashioned wash.

To start with, the scantily clad dancer came nowhere near the lads, choosing to begin the show from the stage. She began a little half-heartedly, moving to the slow beat of the music, twisting and turning while caressing her body. Her skinny white hands glided up to her breasts then down to her hips and across to her crotch where she badly acted a climax.

It took a painful two minutes to remove her bikini top, hands covering her nipples as she enthusiastically massaged them. Several gyrations later she slipped her hands down to her waist, revealing her breasts for the first time. Just as the lads were beginning to enjoy the performance, the music suddenly stopped, the lap dancer bent down and picked up her bikini top, covered her breasts and walked back out of the door. This did not go down well with the lads who voiced their disapproval.

Baz smiled and announced, "There'll be another one any minute lads and she'll be much better than that I promise." Unimpressed, Will started to study the paper, taking sips of his beer as he scanned the pages. He flipped the pages over until he came to the racing section, checking the results to see if any of the horses he had bet on earlier had won. Fancying a last-minute bet, he went to reach for his mobile. The horse Silent Whisper won at 3/1, which pissed him off. He began cursing under his breath until Phil asked him what the matter was. Will explained why he was annoyed.

"It's always the way," Phil remarked.

He scanned the day's races at Epsom first, then down to Chepstow. Not seeing anything of interest it reminded him of the current venue.

He moved his eyes over to Wolverhampton and checked the race cards. Nothing jumped out at him and taking another sip of his beer, his eyes moved up to the tipster section. There, bold as day, a name beamed back at him. His voice screamed loudly, "I don't believe it!"

Giles laughed, and Baz who was desperate for something good to happen asked him, "What's up, mate?"

"High Artic," he proclaimed in a high-pitched voice.

"Yeah what about him?" asked Baz.

"He's running today at Wolverhampton!" Rockin and Marco both snatched the paper out of his hands, ripping it down the centre.

"It's meant to be!" Will exclaimed with great excitement.

"What time is it running?" asked Phil, who was known for having a small flutter, albeit occasionally, because he hated losing his hard-earned money. Everyone was suddenly highly excited. Will announced that the race would start in about forty minutes.

"We'll have a couple more beers," said Baz, putting a plan into action. "I'll make sure we all have some proper dances, then we'll go and put some money on!" he added, giving Will a wink.

"But how much?" Enquired Phil.

Despite a few blank faces, Will had already decided he was going to put a large bet on, even if it meant a trip to the cash machine. Rockin suggested a tenner each. "It's not worth the effort," said Giles without even knowing the odds.

Giles suggested £25 and Marco immediately upped to £50 wanting to outdo his landlord. Excitement was growing and Baz decided to outdo Marco. "Double it! A hundred quid," he laughed.

Phil had to put a stop to it. Betting this much money could break him for the day. "I can't bet that much, and anyway the horse will probably lose!" He immediately felt like a killjoy, ruining their fun.

Will spoke next, "We'll sort it out when we get to the bookies, and anyway we've got beer to drink and tits to look at!" The rest of the lads seemed to agree and the subject happily moved on.

Marco went to order some more beers from the cubby hole. When the drinks came, he enquired as to when the next dancer would be on stage. The somewhat husky sounding barmaid replied, "She's busy, mate." This startled Marco a little. Something didn't quite add up here, he thought.

They were the only ones in the place, so how could she be busy? He sat back down at the table and pondered over this remark. "What she say?" Baz asked him.

"She's busy apparently, mate," Marco replied. All the lads looked at each other.

"There's only one girl and she's busy! What the fuck is she doing?"

As the lads became more animated and the beer flowed, Phil could see they were going to get kicked out. He decided to go and relieve himself before they did, so he stood up and headed towards the toilet.

Baz's blood pressure began to rise, his face reddening by the second. He hesitated before shouting, "I'm going to sort that bitch out." Giles beat him to it and boldly took the lead. Giles had always considered himself to be a good diplomat. He walked over to the cubby hole and noticed the barmaid half sitting on a stool with a fag in her hand and making no attempt to pour the pints.

He sensed that she was ignoring him. Coughing, holding his hand to his mouth, he politely tried to get her attention. Eventually she shot him a glance.

"Excuse me, darling," he started in a very posh accent. She looked at him like a piece of shit.

"What do you want?" she answered in a dog ruff accent.

"It says on the sign that you get unlimited dances and unlimited beer," replied a now flustered Giles.

"Yeah what about it?" came the reply.

"Well we'd like some more beers and some more dances please," said Giles.

"I told you. mate, I'm busy!"

"You don't look very busy," Giles answered, realising at that moment he had blown it!

"You posh twats – you're all the same! What gives you the fuckin' right to tell me what to do?" she shouted in a smoking-induced husky voice.

Moving forwards towards the bar she leant menacingly over it revealing her aged wrinkly cleavage, and poked Giles sharply in the chest with her badly manicured index finger.

She pushed his chest back slightly but he held his footing.

"Excuse me, there's no need for that. I only want what we've paid for. I'm sure you would like the same," said Giles.

"Don't you tell me what I would like! You little shit," the barmaid shouted. Giles looked down at the beer pump, trying to avert her gaze, and scanned the small writing underneath the brand name. There, as clear as anything, he saw 0% a.b.v. Before Giles had time for this to sink in, the barmaid's ear bashing had started again.

"Alcohol free! It's fuckin non-alcoholic!" his voice was becoming louder with each word, so the lads could hear him. Giles could see the skinhead from reception bearing down on him and before he knew it, he was in a headlock and being dragged towards the side exit of the stage. Probably not his best choice of dealing with the situation because Baz was already on his feet and leaping over tables and chairs. Landing heavily, directly in the path of the skinhead, Baz squared up to him. A huge fist came up and impacted right in the centre of his face, immediately splitting his nose with an explosion of blood splattering 360 degrees. The stunned skinhead toppled clumsily onto the dirt-ridden carpet.

As the grip around Giles' neck fell loose, he took a huge gulp of air allowing oxygen to stream back into his aching lungs. The barmaid quickly pressed the emergency button on a nearby wall and three seconds later the side door flung loudly open.

The bouncer, bounding in, caught sight of his partner cradling his nose and lying on the floor surrounded in a pool of crimson blood.

Baz pushed Giles towards the rest of the lads with an almighty force sending a chair crashing to the floor. By now, Phil could hear the commotion from the toilet and knew that it could only mean one thing, Baz was in destruction mode. He finished going to the loo as quickly as possible, before zipping himself up.

The overweight bouncer ran over to Baz as fast as he could, his belly rolling up and down in sync with his double chin. He was not going to be a match for Baz because his movements were cumbersome and slow. Baz could tell what moves this gross lump of lard would use straight away. *These guys are so predictable,* Baz thought to himself, as he waited for his prey to arrive.

Stepping over his colleague who was still cradling his nose, the bouncer reached Baz and raised his hands as if he was going into a boxing match. He started with a powerful jab with his right fist, but swiftly Baz moved to block the punch with his left arm trying to push it away. Suddenly a left hook travelled towards Baz's exposed face impacting under his chin and sending a shock wave rippling through his skull. Yet Baz hardly felt a thing.

Phil appeared from the toilet just in time to see the punch and he began heading towards the two men, noticing the casualty on the floor on his way. Baz recovered in less than a millisecond, more stunned by the tactic of his opponent than the power of the punch. His training went into overdrive. The bouncer moved in closer for his second punch, so Baz lifted his right leg and forced his foot into the bouncer's stomach winding him and sending him face forward onto Baz's knee. Baz grabbed the back of the bouncer's head increasing the downward force, until knee and head would move no more.

Relishing the hold on his head, Baz then swung his right arm around in a large circle, gaining velocity and bringing it up into an upper cut sending the bouncer's head and body flipping backward in a wide arc.

Phil began to slow when he saw Baz had full control of the situation, until the upper cut! By now, the bouncer's body and head were swaying in a circular movement, and Phil knew instinctively where his head was going to land – on the metal-edged stage.

Phil was accelerating at a good speed now and then Baz spotted another bouncer whirling towards him. *Not another one,* he thought. He'd reached a dilemma. The bouncer's head would be impacting on the side of the stage within moments, so should he save this guy, maybe even his life, and take a beating from the third bouncer or save himself from a beating?

Phil leapt into the air and started diving towards the bouncer. *Fuck it,* Baz thought to himself. He'd always told his lads to save themselves first and foremost, and then look after anyone else. "Health and safety," he would tell them.

Phil flew through the air and not noticing Baz's movements above him, wondered why he crashed abruptly on the floor. He'd hoped to edge himself under the bouncer, thus stopping his head from hitting the side of the stage but he felt nothing. Maybe he had misjudged it. *Shit,* he thought as he tried to turn his head.

Baz lunged down sweeping his arms under the fat bouncer as best he could. The bouncer's weight and momentum were hard to stop, and even Baz's strength wasn't going to be enough. They both continued towards the edge of the stage in almost slow motion.

At the last moment, Baz twisted on his left foot and pushing with the other heaved the great lump to his left side. Baz took most of the impact, winding himself badly in the process, but he had prevented the bouncer from serious injury may be even death.

Marco and Rockin rushed over to help Baz up. The bouncer lay groaning next to him. He had two front teeth missing and blood was oozing from his cracked nose. What stunned the lads was how gently Baz moved the bouncer off Phil and carefully laid him on the carpet in the recovery position.

Phil helped himself up with the aid of Marco and brushed himself down.

Chapter 14

The exterior window of the bookies displayed a huge picture of a footballer about to power a soccer ball into the back of the goal, and next to that was a picture of a jockey wearing blue and green silks, galloping his chestnut racehorse to the finish line. The window frame was painted bright red to match the red and white Ladbrokes sign.

The interior colour co-ordination followed through from outside with the exception of the dark grey carpet and Will commented on the fact that every establishment they had entered so far was red, with the exception of the Savoy.

Baz quickly looked around scanning the shop for evidence of a toilet where he could go and wipe the blood off his hands. These shops usually did have loos, especially the new ones. They had learnt from the American casinos that you had to do everything you could to try and keep punters in your establishment as long as possible. That's why they also provided vending machines selling Coca Cola and bars of chocolate.

In the far corner Baz spotted a door with traditional male and female toilet signs. He negotiated a route through scattered chairs and tables left by untidy customers, managing not to temporarily block the view of the TV monitors beaming live images of sporting events from all over the world.

He had to pass in front of a Middle Eastern looking customer whose eyes were fixed on the lads, not the televisions. Entering the toilet Baz quickly washed his hand using the liquid soap dispenser. The white sink swirled with red water as Baz cleansed his hands. Checking his face for any splats of blood, Baz smoothed his suit, correctly positioned his cravat, glanced in the mirror one more time and then walked back out.

The lads were discussing the stake as Baz re-joined the group, and this was his chance to save his standing with the gang. He quietly asked Phil how much he was willing to gamble. Phil had been considering this ever since Will had announced Artic High was running. "Fifty quid," Phil replied.

"Just go with me. I'll pay anything over that!" Baz whispered. Phil knew there was no point arguing with Baz – he'd been there before!

The stake had already settled on a hundred quid, double of what Phil was willing to risk. "Come on, two hundred quid each," Baz announced to the rest of the group, and to his surprise no one seemed to blink at his suggestion. *All this excitement must be getting to them,* he thought to himself.

"That's nearly all my money gone," Rockin said.

"And mine," Giles announced. However, one by one they all nodded at Baz and started routing through their wallets, eagerly chucking notes at Baz.

Marco said, "Will should go and put the money on since he noticed the horse." All the lads nodded so Baz handed the money to Will. Immediately, Will, who didn't want any fuck-ups, counted it before walking over to the counter. One thing that occurred to him as he stood in line was that not one of them had enquired what the odds were. Maybe they didn't want to be unnerved by the chance of them being long odds, which indeed they were at 10–1.

A pleasing looking girl, hair tied neatly back in a ponytail, sat behind the counter processing the punters' betting slips. She looked like she actually enjoyed her job and gave Will a welcoming, homely look. This was something she hadn't done for the previous customers, which made Will feel warm inside. His face went slightly pink, too.

The girl held her hand out to take the betting slip, but with all the excitement Will had forgotten to fill it out. He blushed even more. Pushing a betting slip and a half-sized biro slowly over the counter, she left her fingers resting on the edge of the slip as Will filled it out.

Will read her name tag before letting her take the slip back over the counter. Her name was Mary. *Nice,* he thought to himself. Mary glanced down at the slip and entered it into the computer. Even though she worked in London, she'd never seen a bet this large.

She looked back up at Will, locking onto his eyes. "Do you know something I don't?" she enquired softly.

"I hope so," he replied handing her the wad of cash, which she duly began to count. A regular, who was leaning on the counter talking to the manager, noticed the sizable bundle of cash being counted and looked on in amazement.

Once Mary had confirmed the amount, Will asked what the odds were. "They've been drifting from 10–1 to 15–1," she told him.

Not a good sign, he thought to himself. Mary gave him a hopeful wink, and handed him a miniature photocopy of the betting slip.

As Will went to return to the lads, the regular stopped him in his tracks. "What horse are you betting on?" he asked Will.

"High Artic," replied Will, who didn't mind passing on a tip.

Will held the betting slip tightly in his right hand and said, "I don't know if it's good or bad news but the odds are drifting!"

"What to?" enquired Phil. Will held the silence for a moment before telling them.

"He's drifting from 10–1 to 15–1," he said. Rockin started calculating what the winning would be.

"About three grand each," he informed the lads.

"A grand total of £19,200 exactly," Giles interrupted, phone in hand set to calculator mode.

"Fuckin' hell, we're going to be rich," exclaimed Phil.

"For the day anyway," added Marco. Phil immediately thought of the extra special Christmas he could give his kids, with all those presents!

This news immediately fuelled their moods and lifted them to the highest place they had been all day. Baz loved it! No way was he going to blow this money on wild women and booze, but then again!

Sabir watched the lads intently. He'd recognised Phil's face as soon as he entered the bookies, and the Wrexham accent had confirmed it. Seeing Phil made his skin crawl, especially when he thought of the night on the mountain, when Phil got out of the car and began to urinate – piss snaking its way along the dry earth, soaking into his jeans and wetting his skin.

On the brighter side, he remembered the beauty of Charlotte – how her skin glimmered in the moonlight silhouetting the shape of her pert breasts, the faint smell of sex mixed with her perfume, which had drifted from the car.

His mind wandered back to the countless days he had spent sitting in doorways waiting for her to pass by, so he could follow her home and take her like he had taken the other one on that very night she had slipped through his net.

He wondered which of them was getting married, and then a thought hit him. Maybe Phil was marrying Charlotte. *Maybe Charlotte was going to be delivered to him, and this was all meant to be!* All he had to do was follow them to the wedding, which had to be soon, and sit and watch from a distance. After all, he had all the time in the world. He could even join them for a drink!

Sabir's image had gone up a few notches. He'd dumped the tramp look for a slightly up market appearance. Out with the dirty, stinking clothes and in with the single-breasted pinstriped suits and Windsor knotted ties. Clean-shaven, his hair was carefully combed into a perfect side parting with some help from Bryl cream. He now played the part of an investment banker, who liked a flutter on his imaginary Saudi family racing stock.

The horses lined up for the race of the lads' lives. The regulars thought this bunch must be a good omen and were all lining up to place bets on High Artic. The lads stretched out in a line watching the bank of monitors, which were all now showing the Wolverhampton racing fixture.

Nearly all the thirty or so punters had put varying amounts of money on High Artic, and all eyes were fixed. The horses waited in the stalls, and each second seemed like an eternity. High Artic moved his head up and down waiting for the off, his jockey in red and green silks trying to steady him.

The horses leapt forward, springing out of the stalls with the power of a supercharged Porsche 911 Carrera. High Artic sailed around the first corner in the middle of the pack, with a real outsider at 100–1 leading at this point. Marco leaned over to Baz, "How far do they have to run?"

"About two miles," Baz replied. Marco imagined himself running two miles, and the thought made him shudder.

The positions stayed the same as they entered the second bend, by which point the 100–1 shot was starting to wane. The hunting pack edged closer until they engulfed him. High Artic and the favourite, Whispering Whirlwind, still held their positions in the centre of the pack, while two more horses battled for the leading positions.

On the approach to the final bend, Whispering Whirlwind made the break as he took a wide corner and easily pushed to the front of the race, leaving Artic High hemmed in. Everyone in the bookies shouted orders to High Artic willing him to push forward, but every angle was blocked. He had to wait and hope for an opening. As they rounded the last and final bend, the pace picked up a couple of notches but not to High Arctic's advantage. The pack grew closer and closer together.

Whispering Whirlwind held first place and his jockey was easing off the whip. High Arctic's jockey in the red and green silks had noticed a gap opening next to the rail – it was now or never. High Artic had noticed the space before the jockey and started to accelerate, slipping into the opening and powering forward. Phil noticed the move first and started to shout louder, punching his fist into the air. A second later the rest of the lads noticed and followed him.

The jockey didn't feel the need to use the whip yet and thought he might not even need to use it at all. This horse knew what the score was and what he had to do. The gap opened even wider, as if it was meant to be, like the parting of the sea. High Artic surged forward taking all the horses on the inside, except one, but Whispering Whirlwind was in his sights.

The whip came down very gently on High Arctic's rump, letting him know that this was the time for true acceleration. He dropped down a gear and hammered the accelerator sending a rush of adrenaline through his veins with dramatic effect. The favourite stood no chance with such a dramatic increase in speed. Hooves dug deep into the ground sending divots cascading into the air twenty yards from the finish line. High Artic battled nose to nose with Whispering Whirlwind and then rocketed forward taking the lead by half a length.

The lads jumped for joy, screaming at defending decibels. Flinging their arms around each other they began dancing with joy. But out of the corner of their eyes something terrible and unbelievable was happening. So, sickening Giles could hardly watch. Phil felt like someone had hit him in the chest with a sledgehammer as he struggled to breathe and the colour drained from his face.

As Baz danced up and down, he caught sight of Phil in his peripheral vision looking as white as a sheet. Baz stopped dancing immediately. "What's happening?" he asked Phil. Phil stood dead still, and all the blood seemed to have drained from his face – he looked like he had seen a ghost. Staring at the floor opposite, Baz followed his gaze down to the carpeted floor. The celebration came to a sudden halt because Will was kneeling on the floor. His body seemed crippled and all bent over, his knees digging into the carpet, his hands covering his face. His fingernails seemed to be gouging into his skin.

Baz's mind whirled, straining to comprehend what had happened. Everything was now happening in slow motion. In the corner of his eye, he just caught the back of an Arab man, who had been sitting by the toilet, as he slipped out of the door. He looked around, his head seeming to take an age to turn. His mind worked over time trying to process all the information.

"We've lost," screamed Will, which just confused Baz even more. He'd seen High Artic pass the favourite and then a terrible realisation hit Baz. Will must have put the money on another horse. He lunged down at Will ready to rip him to shreds. Rage was pulsating through his body, but then something caught his eye on the monitors in front of him.

He watched the replay of the final straight and everything happened just as he'd seen. High Artic burst from the pack on the inside, powering past the favourite. That's when he'd started celebrating, but this time he carried on watching. Whispering Whirlwind held on then surged forward at an outstanding rate beating High Artic to the post. Baz collapsed.

Mary watched the lads' heads hang low and they quickly carried Will across the road to the Golden Lion pub. Back at the bookies, the monitors displayed images of the winner carrying his saddle across the winning enclosure.

Marco ordered six double vodkas and the lads found a table and sat around it in silence. Phil figured that Baz had lost the most – £350, which made him feel guilty. He leant across and whispered in Baz's ear. "I'll pay you back, mate."

"No way, mate, it's my fault," Baz replied, slapping Phil on the shoulder. Baz was more bothered about his standing with the group than the money!

Meanwhile at Wolverhampton Racecourse, more things were happening. All the jockeys had weighed in but there was a problem. Whispering Whirlwind's jockey had dropped weight. All bets were frozen until the official result was announced, but the lads were oblivious. Back at the bookies, excitement was growing. The punters who had placed bets on High Artic were praying. Even the manager willed the result to change. Time ticked by as big discussions took place in an office at Wolverhampton Racecourse. After a long and heated discussion, the result was eventually declared.

Mary hoped that the lads were still in the Golden Lion. After getting the nod from her manager, she rushed from around the back of the counter with a huge grin across her face and ran through the shop, straight across the road almost getting knocked down by a black taxi in the process.

She pulled open the solid oak door of the Golden Lion and slowed her pace to a walk. It didn't take her long to spot the wedding party, who were all sat with their heads down. Mary seemed to float to the end of the table.

"Aren't you going to buy me a drink?" she announced without saying hello. The lads looked up.

"Yeah, sure, what would you like?" asked Giles in a solemn voice.

"Champagne!" she replied in an ecstatic tone, barely able to control herself.

"You what?" Baz asked her.

"You've won!" she screamed excitedly.

It took a couple of seconds for this information to register. Instead of excitement the lads simply looked confused. "How could that be?" asked Will. Mary eagerly started to tell them – in a high-pitched voice – how Whispering Whirlwind had mysteriously lost three pounds in weight and had been stripped of his win, making High Artic the official winner of the 4.30 at Wolverhampton.

The table erupted, launching the empty shot glasses spinning into the air until they crashed down onto the solid oak floorboards. The screams and shouts were amplified even more by the frustrating disappointment of the previous result.

Mary's drink seemed to have been forgotten for the time being, as the lads sprinted across the road dodging the rush hour traffic with the betting slip firmly in Will's hand.

They passed the cheering punters and crashed head long into the counter. The manager looked up at them, "Any damages must be paid for!" he said winking at them with a big smile.

"I've got some good and bad news for you, so what do you want first?" asked the manager. The lads looked confused.

"I can't take much more of this!" Will exclaimed.

"OK I'll tell you straight. You have won, as you know, but…" he paused. "We don't have that amount of cash in the establishment."

"How much have you got?" enquired Baz.

"We can give you six grand in cash and the rest in a cheque," the manager told them, pulling a slightly nervous face. The lads glanced at each other and gave eager nods.

Phil piped up, "Yeah that'll be better, we'll have less to lose!"

Giles added, "Please can we have separate cheques?" Giles had been taught well by his family, who had told him that when it comes to money, don't trust anyone – especially when you're talking large amounts.

"Nothing in this world can split friends faster," he heard his father's voice in his head.

"There's usually a charge of ten pounds per cheque," said the manager. Baz gave the manager one of his looks and stared straight into his eyes. "But I suppose I could wave that charge today," he quickly added.

Will leaned over to Mary, who was back behind the counter, and handed her the betting slips. He whispered something in her ear, "Two-hundred-pound stake each wasn't it, lads?" she asked. They all nodded, with Will giving a cheesy smile.

The manager asked them to write their names and addresses on a slip of paper for the cheques, and then he and Mary started to organise the money. The lads congratulated themselves and started deciding what they were going to spend their winnings on.

After about five minutes, Mary called them over to the counter and handed them a wad of cash, each containing a grand in used £20 notes, which they all had to sign for. Next came the cheques. The manager called each of their names out and handed them a cheque for £2,200. Will was the last to receive his cheque. The manager held onto it for a second, looked at it, then gave Will a knowing look. He handed Will his cheque for £5,400 which he quickly slid into his wallet, not wanting to explain that he'd wagered an extra two hundred pounds!

Chapter 15

The lads proudly showed each other their cheques, except Will who carefully slipped his into a small compartment in his wallet while no one was looking. "A good day's work!" Baz said proudly.

"What's on the agenda now?" Giles asked.

There was silence for a second then Marco announced that he wanted to go to Peter Stringfellow's. Will asked what time it opened, and everybody shrugged. Getting his phone out, Rockin got through to directory enquirers.

"What name please?" came back a female Indian sounding voice.

"Peter Stringfellow's, it's a night club."

"What town please?"

Her voice sounded like a machine, Rockin thought to himself after replying, "London."

She must have been bored brainless sitting at a keyboard, repeating the same questions. She told him she would text him the number, but Rockin asked if he could be put straight through, which she arranged.

Two seconds later, his phone was ringing once again, and this time a machine answered. The recorded voice started to give the opening times, which was all he wanted, so once he had the info, he hung up.

"Seven o'clock," he said to the lads then turned his attention to his watch. "It's nearly five thirty." Phil suggested it was time to get something to eat.

"There's a Kentucky Fried Chicken around the corner!"

"I'd like to get out of the area because we're prime targets for pick pockets," Rockin suggested.

"I'll kill the fuckers if they try and get mine!" Baz announced, and no one in the group doubted this.

"I'd like to go to Jamie Oliver's restaurant," said Giles.

The lads looked at each other. "Come on, we've got the cash!" Giles pleaded with the lads.

"He's right, we should celebrate properly!" said Rockin.

They left the warmth of the betting shop and went out into the cold, damp, dark air of London's streets, the smell of diesel fumes from passing buses and lorries filling their nostrils.

"We'll have to get a couple of cabs," Rockin informed them as he flagged a traditional black taxi down. The cab pulled over, Baz opened the door and asked the driver if he could take all of them.

"How many?" the driver asked.

"Six," he replied.

"It's more than my badge is worth, sorry!" he said shaking his head.

Rockin, Marco and Will boarded the first cab, after telling the cabby where they wanted to go, and they pulled off while Baz attempted to flag down another taxi. Giles didn't feel uneasy being left with these two gorillas on a street corner somewhere in London. One thing he knew was that no one was going to mug them, unless they had a gun. And, he'd grown to like them during the course of the day.

After a couple of minutes, Baz managed to get a cab to pull over for them. He hastily opened the door and climbed in. Giles gave the driver the destination and they sat back in silence reflecting on what had happened so far, and the enormous amount of cash that was lining their pockets.

The taxi wound its way through the London rush hour traffic, the driver dodging down back alleys, virtually scraping parked cars as he squeezed through in an attempt to take short cuts.

After about twenty minutes, the cab pulled up outside Jamie's restaurant with the word 'FIFTEEN' emblazoned on the front of the establishment. Baz slipped the driver a twenty-pound note and told him to keep the change.

Giles couldn't see any sign of the other three through the window, so they walked through the door and scanned the room. There was still no sign. A young waitress wearing a long black skirt with a freshly pressed white shirt came towards them. Her blonde hair was neatly tied back in a ponytail.

She smiled at them and asked in a Scandinavian accent whether they had a reservation. The restaurant looked full to bursting point, packed with businessmen and women after their hard day's graft in the office. Giles and Baz caught some strange glances from customers, but they were used to it by now.

"No," replied Giles. The waitress knew the book was full and was about to speak when Giles cut in. "We've had an awful day," he paused for effect making sure he had her full attention before carrying on. "The groom has been dumped at the altar." He didn't want to go into the full original story. "So, we're trying to make him feel a bit better. He's always talked about coming here, so we thought we'd bring him to try and cheer him up!"

Looking up at Giles and Baz dressed head to tail in their morning suits with golden waistcoats, the waitress could feel his pain without even setting her eyes on the groom. She'd been dumped a couple of times by love rats, but nothing compared to this.

"How many of you are there?" she enquired.

"Six," came the reply from Baz. She ran her finger down the page of the reservations book. She already knew exactly who had arrived, who was due to arrive and most of all who was late. She was making time, while she made up her mind on what to do.

"How long till the others arrive?" she asked Giles.

Baz immediately flicked his phone open and looked through his directory for Rockin's number.

"Alright Rockin, it's Baz. Where are you now?"

"Fuck knows," answered Rockin.

"How long are you going to be?" asked Baz.

Baz could hear Rockin speaking to the cabby.

"Five minutes," came the reply.

Rockin suddenly had a thought. "Are you already there?" he asked Baz.

"Yeah, a couple of minutes ago," came Baz's reply.

"Bastard cabby is ripping us off! I thought we were going around in circles!" exclaimed Rockin.

Just before Baz disconnected, he could hear Rockin having a go at the cabby.

"Five minutes," Baz told the waitress.

"A party was due to arrive at five thirty, but they're late, so if the rest of your party arrives before them, you can have their table," she smiled, but her eyes said more. She really wanted to help.

Baz flipped his phone once again and speed dialled Rockin once more. Without even saying hello, Baz told Rockin to tell the driver to get his arse in gear.

The waitress seemed to take a shine to Giles and introduced herself as Jane. She asked if they'd like a drink while they waited. Phil told her she was an angel and how he could kill for a cold beer. "In fact, make that three-beers, no make it six, as the rest of the lads will be here soon," said Giles.

As Jane turned around, the door opened and Marco burst through the door laughing his head off, Will and Rockin in tow. They'd given the taxi driver a right old ear bashing for trying to rip them off. Jane quickly ushered them to the table before anybody else came in to claim it.

Their drinks were brought over to them, and Phil lifted his glass instantly slugging half a pint down his gullet. Placing the glass back down on the table, he leant back on his white leather chair and let out a huge sigh of relief.

Next minute, Giles watched the entrance door swing open and a gigantic man entered with bulging muscles. He was dressed in full American military uniform, which made Baz and Phil look tiny. They were followed in by another two men in uniform and what appeared to be their partners. Jane greeted them with the same smile she had greeted Giles with, and they told her they had a reservation at five thirty and that they were sorry they were a bit late.

One of the soldiers, who looked like he was in his late fifties, looked over towards the lads and stared for a few seconds, his brain cells whirling, then he turned back to face Jane.

Giles could tell that there seemed to be a problem. He nudged Baz to look across to the reception desk and soon enough the lads both realised who these people were.

Jane handled them like a true professional, apologising for having to let their table go, but without a telephone call, or no way of contacting them, it was the restaurant policy to let the table go after twenty minutes.

She then informed them that all was not lost because she'd had a cancellation just before they had walked in. This statement brought a smile back to their faces, so they agreed to take a seat and have a drink, while waiting for their table to be ready. It wasn't usually the protocol for an American General to have to sit and wait, but his ex-boss President Clinton had recommended he eat here.

The menus came and the lads studied them with glee as they slugged back mouthfuls of beer. Word spread about the disastrous events that had unfolded for the poor groom, and the waitresses skirted around the table glancing over at them. Even the chefs peered out from behind the kitchen counter.

The lads chatted about what brilliant gamblers they were. Will said, "I'd love to go to a casino in London, you know one of the really posh ones!" Baz seemed to like the idea, but then came to the obvious conclusion that they would probably lose all their money. He told the lads so and Marco agreed with him.

Will tried to talk them into his idea, telling them they could set the limit on how much they would be able to gamble. The whole table still looked doubtful. Will decided he would work on them and get them round to his way of thinking before too long.

Another waitress came over and introduced herself in a French accent as Lorraine. She took their orders, and everyone ordered both starters and main course being so hungry. "We've got some celebrating to do, so can we have two bottles of Bollinger?" Will asked Lorraine.

Phil ordered two more beers for him and Baz, indicating that he didn't like the sparkly stuff. As Lorraine walked away, Rockin commented, "There are no bloody Brits left in London! I'm not racist, but it's true." The rest of the lads agreed.

Soon the customers on the table next to the lads got up to leave, all looking very content with the food and alcohol that they had consumed. One of them, a middle-aged gentleman, even patted his stomach as he walked away from the table towards the exit.

The waiting staff efficiently cleared and reset the table, adding two extra chairs to each end, and the military men and their partners were shown to their table.

Chapter 16

The conversation then took a turn and Phil asked Baz what had happened to Wayne, the guy who had been sleeping with Charlotte, Phil's ex.

Baz leant back on the chair and stretched his shoulders, making his muscles bulge, nearly ripping his jacket at the seams and popping the buttons off his shirt like the Incredible Hulk. He was enjoying the anticipation of being the story teller!

"I was picking my nephew up from school one day and Wayne was there collecting Phil's kids," Baz began. "The kids looked terrified when they saw him, and he had to virtually force them into the car. Little Carrie was in tears as she was pushed into his silver Vauxhall Vectra and not even bothering to fasten their seat belts, he slammed the doors shut and sped away.

"I felt awful for the rest of the afternoon wondering about those poor kids, and that evening I went to the local pub and by chance bumped into Charlotte's next-door neighbour. I only knew him by sight, having never spoken to him before, but a glance and a nod later, he came over to speak asking if I was Phil's mate," Baz continued.

Glancing over, Baz and Phil made eye contact for a moment. Baz knew he should have told Phil, although deep down he knew he had done the right thing.

"What he told me shook me up and I didn't sleep a wink all night," Baz went on. Phil was as white as a sheet, not knowing if he wanted to hear what was coming next, but unable to walk away or stop Baz.

Baz continued his story, "Well, the next day I was on my way to the gym and I stopped to buy a paper from the Spar. Charlotte was in there and immediately tried to hide from me. I found her skulking at the rear of the shop brandishing an angry looking black eye.

"I confronted her and she quickly denied that Wayne had hit her, telling me instead that she had slipped and fallen down the stairs. I didn't believe a word of it, of course. That's the oldest story in the book!" Baz grunted.

Next day at lunchtime, I went down to the school and had a chat with my nephew Shawn. I asked him to talk to Carrie and Josh separately to find out how things were at home. I didn't tell him to say anything else because I didn't want to put any ideas into their heads.

"I picked Shawn up from school later that day and he confirmed my worst fears. Wayne had hit Charlotte the night previous, and poor Josh had tried in vain to protect his mum but he wasn't strong enough. After being knocked to the floor a couple of times he had locked himself and Carrie in the bathroom."

Phil's face looked red and he seemed about to burst. Tears were already forming in the corners of his eyes. He ran his fingers through his hair, took a lung full of air then turned to Baz. "Why didn't you tell me?" he pleaded.

"Couldn't mate, you would have committed murder and you'd never have seen Carrie and Josh again." Phil glared at Baz, but said nothing more for the time being.

Baz went on addressing the now attentive group, "I went down to the house and clocking Wayne's car parked outside, I took out my Olympus 5 meg digital camera. Turning the flash off, I started taking pictures of the car, getting as close as I could without being seen and gathering as much information as possible. That evening when I returned home, I loaded the images onto my laptop, zooming in on every part of the car, studying and making notes."

At that moment, the starters began to arrive much to Phil's disapproval – he wanted all the information now. He didn't want to wait until after they had eaten, even though it did smell so wonderful. The waitress placed the dressed olives in front of Marco and Giles, while the remaining four waited for their scallops to arrive.

Baz couldn't resist a dig at Marco as they waited. "Those pink seats suit you!" he commented.

"Fuck off Baz," Marco replied. Marco was feeling light headed. The booze, need for food, lack of sleep from the early rise this morning and hearing about Carrie and Josh were all starting to take their toll.

Shortly after, the waitress arrived with four plates of premium scallops and Baz soon forgot about ribbing Marco, wolfing his down in seconds. "Fantastic!" Smiled Baz, before letting out a low belch. Phil remained quiet, thoughtful and more than a little angry, barely touching his scallops and pushing them around his plate in random circles.

Phil didn't have to wait long. Baz wiped his mouth with his napkin, placed it back on the table, cleared his throat and continued with his story.

"I'd already found a car we could use for the sting," Baz almost whispered. "An exact replica, apart from the garage sticker and of course the plates needed to be changed. I won't go into where I got the car from because I don't want to get you guys too involved in case anything goes wrong." Baz scanned the table gaining eye contact with each one of them around the table. They all got the message.

"The trouble is, nowadays you need a V5 document to have any plates made, which was a small problem, until I remembered someone owed me a favour – a big one!" He beamed. Taking a trip to an undisclosed garage Baz had collected on the debt and within ten minutes the plates were made up, even mirroring the exact type of lettering and having the garage name printed in small writing at the bottom.

After a long slug of cold beer and a quick check that he still had the group's full attention, the story continued. Sounding like a private detective Baz hunched forwards and spoke softly, "I had to know the exact route that he took to work each morning so I followed him for a few days, and luckily for me he went the same way every day.

"That evening, I collected the car," Baz recalled. "I changed the plates over in my garage, out of sight of prying eyes. It was as simple as that." Unbeknown to Wayne, on his trip to work the following morning, he wasn't alone. Baz and some backup were not far behind.

Several minutes into the journey, Wayne drove through the first of the usual speed cameras on his route to work. Baz grinned as he thought back and looked around the table. "I slowed my car down as we approached the camera, letting the bus in front move off into the distance. Behind me motors were jumping on their horns, but I didn't give a fuck." Marco stared at Giles knowing what was coming next. "When the camera came into view, I floored the mother fucker and went through a thirty limit at about sixty-five mph! I did the same routine at the second speed camera and saw the familiar two flashes in my rear-view mirror."

Another round of beers arrived and everyone took a moment to digest what Baz had said. Eagerly wanting more, Phil spurred him on. "Come on! Did he get done for it?"

"This is where it gets interesting boys," Baz replied. He'd gone out the next day with the intention of racking up more points on Wayne's licence but for some reason the camera didn't register his cloned speeding vehicle. "I thought I'd blown it!" Baz went on. "I was so pissed off that I floored the car. I must have been doing about 90 mph. I was driving like a maniac!"

Baz took a deep breath as the waitress removed the empty plate from in front of him. She cleared the rest of the table swiftly sensing the intrusion.

"I was flying down the road when I saw them. It was too late to brake and the police car that was sitting in a layby put its sirens on and began to chase me!"

"I pressed speed dial to tell my mate what was happening, although I don't know why. What could he do?" Baz was becoming visibly more excited as the story unfolded.

Breaking off for another swig of beer, Baz collected his thoughts. He had the guys eating out of his hand and he loved it! A deep breath and he started talking again. "Next thing I can remember was the crash as I whizzed by the T junction. My backup, ready and waiting, pulled out in front of the cop car and with an almighty crash the cop car had crashed into his pride and joy! I looked in the mirror and saw both cars spinning in the middle of the road."

"Was it John who helped you?" Phil demanded. By now he was standing leaning over the table towards Baz, insisting on answers.

Baz looked straight at him and reluctantly replied, "Yeah mate, it was. That's what put him in hospital! Little wonder that John said I owed him a drink when I went to visit him in hospital with two fuckin' broken legs!" Phil shook his head. Tears were now rolling down his cheeks. "He did that for me?" he asked Baz.

"He did it for you, me but mainly for Carrie and Josh. He'd heard the rumours too, mate." Baz tried to console a visibly upset Phil who was feeling more than responsible for John's injuries.

"I had to do it mate," Baz convinced Phil.

"I've got to ask. How come you disappeared and where did you disappear to?" Phil asked.

Baz explained that he had wanted to turn around and make sure John was okay but it would have been stupid. Car theft, careless driving and conspiracy were just a few potential charges.

Instead, he had turned off the main road and driven down a quiet alley, got out and peeled the fake plates off before chucking them in the back of the motor. A short drive home, including a cheeky stop by a roadside skip, and it was beer time.

It was Giles' turn to ask questions now. "What happened to Wayne?"

119

"The police swooped on his office in Chester, about ten cars loads apparently. They roughed him up a bit in the cells and checked his details," Baz laughed. "It transpired that he was still serving a driving ban and had also done time for beating up his ex-wife. Restricted access and visiting rights were still in place when it came to the kids."

"He had kids?" Phil asked in total disbelief.

"Yeah, the rumour is that their PE teacher noticed bruising while they were getting changed and reported it to the authorities. His wife and kids were quickly moved to sheltered accommodation and Wayne was promptly charged with assault."

"Shit," Phil said once more, rubbing his face and the back of his neck. "How do you know all this?"

"Mike told me," Baz murmured looking around before he said so. Phil nodded. He knew Mike was one of the coppers who worked regular night shifts around town.

"Mike told me Wayne had battered his own wife with a golf club and then beat up his eldest son of six with his fists, all because she had bought a new lip stick for herself and a Power Ranger toy for him." The wife had to have plastic surgery and although his son recovered from the physical injury, the mental scarring would with be with him for years to come.

"The downer is that he served two months on remand, went to court and got off on a technicality. Some of the locals and family chased him out of town, and that's how he ended up working in Chester and eventually ended up with Charlotte.

"He's serving time as we speak, and good riddance to him I say," Baz finished. His story was complete.

The table fell quiet and once again, Marco was the first to raise his glass, "I'd like to raise a toast to Baz because it takes guts to do something like that." Marco took a deep breath, eyes scanning the table, then carried on, "Baz you're fuckin' unbelievable and I hope one of my mates would do something like that for me if it was ever needed." Rockin raised his glass next and the rest of the lads raised theirs, except Phil.

Head down facing the floor, his pint of beer on the table with his right hand wrapped around it, he slowly lifted his head, dark brown hair falling forward in front of his eyes, tears streaming down his face.

Phil walked around the table squeezing past the General to where Baz stood and they embraced in the only way hard men can. Slapping each other on the back, tears falling in unison. Phil pulled back and whispered in Baz's ear, "Thanks mate." They pulled back further face to face.

Eyes locked, Baz held Phil's upper arms tight. "I wanted to tell you, but I couldn't. You have to understand!" Phil nodded, and they hugged again.

Chapter 17

The two silver Vauxhall Vectra's zoomed along the dark London streets heading towards the restaurant. Pulling up, the driver of the first car leapt out slamming the car door shut behind him as he ran towards the restaurant.

The driver of the second car stayed where he was, lit up a cigarette and breathed in deeply. Next, he picked up his radio microphone and spoke in a northern accent to the controller on the other end, who acknowledged him. Dropping his microphone onto his lap the driver continued to draw heavily on his fag.

The waitress gave the driver her courteous smile and asked how she could help. "Two taxis in the name of Jones," he replied.

"I'll inform our guests you're here," she said, turning her head back to the appointment book and watching him leave through the corner of her eye. When he was safely back in his car she went over to the lads and told them their taxis had arrived.

They each counted out eighty quid and placed it in the centre of the table to cover the bill, along with a hefty tip. They said their goodbyes to the General and his party, who all offered Rockin final bits of advice, assuring him it would work out for the best. Rockin took all the advice in his stride, and tried to look upset.

The party all moved over to where the waitress was standing and Baz said thanks for everything, she'd done to help them. She reached out and took Rockin's hand, taking him a little by surprise and looking deep into his eyes. "I'm sure everything will be alright. It may take a lot of time, but with your friends here to support you, you'll get through it," She told him quietly. Rockin nodded in the right places, but was getting fed up with all the advice. *It's bloody worse than being in the Sunday Sport,* he thought to himself.

Giles saw the taxi first and couldn't believe it. Laughing loudly, Giles turned to the lads and pointed to the waiting motors. The two silver Vectra's, with their engines idling and exhaust fumes gently drifting into the air, "It's got to be an omen," Giles managed to say in-between his laughter. "I hope it's a good fuckin' omen," Baz replied.

The driver of the second car watched as Phil, Baz and Giles eased themselves into the first taxi. The other three jumped into his and they moved away from the curb joining the stream of traffic ahead of them.

Unnoticed, a moped slipped in behind them, the rider being careful to keep a safe distance between himself and the two taxis ahead. The driver of the second taxi turned to the lads and asked, "Where are you from?" he spoke in a strong northern accent.

They all had the same thought and nudged each other in the ribs. Marco, trying to keep the laughter under control, was the first to answer. "Wrexham," he announced proudly. "I thought I recognised the accent," replied the driver, which stunned the lads.

"You know Wrexham?" Will asked.

"Used to work in Chester a while back," the driver said. "Doing a bit of this and that if you get me."

The lads all sat quietly for a brief moment. The look on Rockin's face confirmed what everyone was thinking. It was too uncanny to comprehend and anyway he was supposed to be in jail, wasn't he?

Rockin thought of asking some more questions, but deep down he knew they didn't really want to know that it was him. What good would it do? Considered Rockin. Wreck everything, most probably he concluded. Baz and Phil would want to hunt him down and would be looking to have more than just a chat with him, that was for sure.

Rockin decided to change the subject and discuss a subject which had been playing on his mind most of the day. Ever since he'd been nominated to be the groom, he'd suffered first with the panic of been thrust all over the pages of the national newspapers, the consequences of which could end his relationship with Lara, and second having to act upset and listen to endless relationship advice when all he really wanted to do was party.

He didn't want to sound like a spoilt school kid, who didn't want to play anymore, but something had to be said before they arrived at Stringfellow's.

Tentatively, Rockin asked, "Does anyone else fancy being the groom?" He didn't have to wait long for an answer. "I'll swap with you if you want!" Marco beamed. He'd been secretly jealous of all the attention Rockin had been receiving, especially from the gorgeous Abigail!

They headed up towards the centre with the bright lights of the city beaming down on them, watching as people rushed back and forth with bags brimming full of Christmas shopping. The taxi carrying Baz indicated and pulled over to the left, quickly followed by the second carrying a now visibly animated Marco who was already embellishing his version of being jilted at the altar.

Marco was the first out handing twenty quid over to the driver telling him to keep the change. Before Baz got within earshot, Rockin turned quickly to the rest of the lads. "Keep this quiet," he whispered. "If he is Wayne and Baz finds out it'll wreck the night, so don't say anything." Nods of agreement came from everyone.

As the group headed towards the lights and noise of the action, the moped rider pulled up and switched his engine off. Without removing his darkened helmet, he watched Baz and the lads walk on before contemplating his next move.

Chapter 18

The lights shone brightly in the dressing room reflecting the image of a naked beauty against the large mirror. Removing the last heated roller from her long blonde hair, and letting the curls drop lightly, she placed some serum on her fingertips and gently rubbed her hands together. Running skinny fingers through her hair, Kate turned to her friend Sarah. "I need a rich man!" she stated as she admired her slim, toned, naked reflection in the mirror, slowly twisting her body and watching the outline for any signs of imperfection.

"You're not going to find any you know!" remarked Sarah smiling.

"Thanks for the vote of confidence," scowled Kate.

"No, I mean cellulite silly!" Sarah laughed.

Sarah lifted her arm and took a deep drag on her cigarette. Tilting her head back she exhaled the smoke watching it rise slowly towards the ceiling. "You must be going for the wrong type of men," she added.

"I've been here for five years now and not so much as a date!" moaned Kate. "All they want to do is meet me after work and shag me, the cheeky fuckers!"

"You always go for the oldies. Why not try someone younger?" asked Sarah.

"Yeah but the older ones have the money!" Kate replied.

As Sarah began to 'enlighten' Kate on the attributes of the younger man, the dressing room door swung open and a beautiful redhead girl called Keira walked in and sat down next to them. A few pleasantries were briefly exchanged before she proceeded to unpack a small travel bag and emptied an array of makeup and various other beauty products. Next, she carefully removed her dress, hanging it up on the chrome rail behind her, before reaching for a skimpy outfit nearby.

Kate turned to face Kiera allowing her eyes to wander down her perfectly formed body, lingering briefly on her navel which held a tear drop size diamond encased in platinum. A gift from a wealthy Saudi prince, who had taken a shine to Kiera and showered her with expensive gifts over the years.

Her eyes drifted down to Keira's perfectly waxed bikini line leaving only a sliver of short, dark pubic hair. Kate envied Keira's body and Keira knew it.

"Kiera, do you think I'm going for the wrong type of men?" asked Kate.

Kiera looked up as she applied the finishing touches to her nail polish.

"I always say you've got to think what they are going to look like in ten years," she replied.

"There you go, Kate. All the men you go for will be collecting their pension in ten years!" remarked Sarah.

Meanwhile, Baz and the crew were crowding around the strip club's entrance eagerly handing over their £15 and looking forward to the entertainment to follow. Passing a row of smartly dressed bouncers, Marco asked whether the £15 included any free dances. A stone-faced hulk of a bloke shook his head and ushered them quickly through.

The entrance to Peter Stringfellow's was nothing to shout home about. Dark carpets and darker walls, with a cashier's desk at the end, greeted the punters as they arrived. Even so, it was a lot cleaner and more up to date than the previous establishments they had been in that day and to be fair, the décor was the last thing on most people's mind as they crossed into this famous club.

The same dark carpet that was in reception covered the floor of the club, but that was the only similarity. Straight ahead of them on a raised platform lay gold-framed chairs upholstered with leopard skin-style material, all neatly placed around oak tables.

To the right was the bar. Continuing the oak and gold theme it was stocked up with the best beers and the most expensive Champagnes money could buy. In front of the bar was a double podium with two chrome poles reaching up to the ceiling. Two stunning ladies were moving their bodies slowly to the music. Around the bar stood a dozen or so beautiful and very glamorous ladies, their dresses glittering as the lights bounced off them.

The lads pushed past each other jokingly and made their way to the bar. As they looked around it was Baz who broke the silence. "Wow!" was all he could manage as various images of beauty passed by smiling. The smell of sweet perfume filled his nostrils and he knew this was definitely a good choice of venue.

Will and Giles looked just as glad to be there and now Rockin was no longer 'the groom', he appeared raring to go! Marco, already eager for the attention and sympathy votes, pushed to the front of the bar. *Make an impression,* he thought to himself as he leant over the bar and asked the barmaid for two bottles of Dom Perignon and six glasses.

Marco turned to the lads and as he handed out the flutes, he noticed some curious looks from the ladies nearby. *No doubt they were wondering what a wedding party was doing in a strip club,* he guessed.

Marco knew exactly how to open a bottle of bubbly without spilling a drop but that wouldn't bring him the attention he was after. As he shook the bottle vigorously, the cork popped and went hurtling across the bar nearly hitting one of the girls on the podium before landing on the floor in front of them. Champagne spurted and bubbled onto the carpet and with a big grin, Marco started pouring.

The lads made a toast to the night and all took a hit of champagne. It wasn't long before a couple of the ladies wandered over to them and introduced themselves as Jane and Helena. Jane could have been a Miss UK contender with her beautiful looks, long flowing chestnut hair and silver sequined dress split up to her hip on one side, revealing a bronzed leg.

As Helena spoke, Marco exchanged glances with Giles and Will. She had long blonde hair and a very sexy Swedish accent. Marco appeared visibly elated at the thought of the forthcoming sympathy. After a bit of small talk, came the question that Marco had been waiting for, "Aren't you supposed to be at a wedding?" Jane asked the lads. Before Rockin could even open his mouth, Phil stepped forward placing his hand on Rockin's shoulder. Gripping tightly, Phil announced to the ladies that, "This poor guy's been to hell and back today!"

That was that then, thought Marco. His plans were dashed in an instant and Rockin was in for a hell of a lot more advice and sympathy!

Phil filled the girls in with all the fictitious details and they both immediately wrapped their arms around him. Rockin was soon dragged away to the waiting arms of the rest of the ladies who lavished attention on him, hugging him close and buying him drinks. He was in his element!

The other five lads were left standing alone drinking their champagne with not a single lady to talk to amongst them. The same also applied to the other members in the club, made up mostly of businessmen charging everything they could on expenses.

Meanwhile the DJ cranked up the volume and pumped out some tunes. A few of the girls who couldn't get close to Rockin moved across to talk to Marco and the rest of the gang. The atmosphere quickly improved until it became clear that they were only interested in talking about Rockin and his failed marriage.

This conversation wasn't a problem, however, as the lads relished the chance to captivate these girls. After a few minutes one of the corporate types approached a very sexy looking girl who was chatting to Baz and asked if he could have a dance with her. This could quite easily have ended up being a problem, as Baz looked up menacingly, but she very politely told him she was busy and turned and continued talking to Baz, fascinated by today's events.

The disgruntled businessman returned to his colleagues and muttered something inaudible, turning several times and staring across towards Baz. Shortly after, a geeky looking man, who was about 34 years old and balding, took it upon himself to try to sort the lack of women issue out.

He marched over to the reception like a spoilt school kid and demanded to speak to Peter Stringfellow's. Little did he know that Peter rarely arrived until 11 pm and only then if he was even in the country. Beautiful girls, usually twenty years his junior, sailing the warm waters of the med or lazing on a beach in the Caribbean was quite a regular occurrence for Mr Stringfellow's.

The receptionist tried in vain to explain the situation with Mr Stringfellow's but the now visibly frustrated man was having none of it. A burly bouncer appeared and after asking the receptionist if she was okay, politely told the gentleman to quieten down. Amazingly, given the fact the geeky looking chap was dwarfed by a 20-stone bouncer, this seemed to make the situation worse. He started to stamp his feet like a child, challenging the bouncer and asking if he knew who he was. Unsurprisingly the bouncer didn't and having dealt with these sorts many times before, he quickly and professionally ejected him without a second thought. *Idiot,* thought the bouncer as he walked slowly back into the club.

Chapter 19

Sabir lifted his moped onto its stand watching intently as the lads walked into Stringfellow's. He opened the lid on his pannier and after removing his suit jacket, he placed his helmet inside and locked it.

He crossed the road, carefully dodging the slow-moving traffic as he went, and made his way into the McDonalds opposite the club. A quick glance at the menu and he placed an order with the spotty girl behind the counter. "Chicken burger and a large coffee, but no fries," he requested.

Sabir found a table by the window giving him a good view of the entrance to Stringfellow's, and wrapped his ice-cold hands around the steaming coffee.

He wondered if they would be in Stringfellow's for the whole night or whether they had to escape back to the wedding before someone noticed. Sabir doubted this and was now sure that these lads were up to something. He wanted to know what it was, and was hanging onto the notion that they might lead him back to Charlotte. *Maybe she was staying at the same hotel?* he thought.

His mind wandered, remembering the sweet smell of her perfume in the night air and the soft touch of her skin against his body. Sabir's mind drifted on, and his hands started to thaw as he half watched shoppers rush by laden down with over loaded bags.

He took a of bite of his burger leaving threads of lettuce dangling from his mouth and mayonnaise dribbling over his chin. Looking around embarrassed, Sabir wiped the mess off with a handful of paper napkins and took a long slug of hot coffee. Next a trip to the toilet was needed.

A gang of five teenage boys, each wearing a loose-fitting tracksuit, loitered outside the toilet with a single fag, taking a quick drag before passing it on. Spotting Sabir heading their way, they soon dispersed with their hoods up and mobiles in hand.

Once inside, Sabir relieved himself, spraying piss like a watering can in the urinal and all over the floor with his mutilated and battered cock. Moving across to the sink, Sabir began to wash his hands and clean his face, but then he stopped. Starring at the image in the mirror, he slowly combed his hair into place finishing with a forced smile as he still struggled to get used to the now disfigured face looking back at him.

Sabir left McDonalds and made his way back across the street, stopping about a hundred yards away from Stringfellow's and stepping quietly into the shadow of a shop entrance. Keeping his head down, Sabir scanned the street ahead for his target. He didn't have to wait long as five business-looking types rounded the corner. Sabir moved quickly and tagged on at the back of the group blending in nicely.

He needn't have worried, as the bouncers were preoccupied with calming a disgruntled punter that they had just ejected from the club. Sabir busied himself with his Nokia and tried to look like a businessman out for a night with his colleagues. On entering the club, he casually left his new 'friends' and scanned the room for Phil and his party, who were surrounded by women. He felt a pang of jealousy watching them getting the attention he had always yearned for. He moved slowly, keeping to the shadows as much as he could, while scanning the room for all the emergency exits.

After buying himself an orange and passion fruit J2O from the bar, he made his way downstairs but noticed it was empty, except for one bouncer who was fiddling with his mobile phone and looked extremely bored.

The basement consisted of lots of tables and chairs tightly packed together and a dance floor with an array of flashing lights above. On the far side lay a roped off area, with more tables and chairs, but these weren't half as cramped and were considerably more luxurious. The VIP area he concluded.

He made a mental note of the two fire exits and the positions of the toilets then made his way back up to the main floor. Deciding not to sit in the corner and watch from afar, he made his way over to the lads, blending quietly in.

His eyes flitted from girl to girl admiring their sexy curves, the silkiness of their skin, glossy hair and perfect makeup. One girl, in a very elegant red dress with flowing blonde hair, led a businessman in his forties to a chair a few feet from the bar. Sitting him down she graced his lap with her body. In a normal bar, they could have been lovers, with him being the sugar daddy.

An Oasis song came to an end and the girl stood up and caressed his face gently with the palm of her hand. Madonna's voice bellowed from the speakers as the girl began her routine. Moving her hips to the music, she seductively removed her dress, revealing her small but perfectly formed breasts.

Sabir watched as she twisted and turned. He glanced over to where Phil was standing chatting away, oblivious to his stalker. Sabir's eye darted back to the happy couple, and he noticed the girl's slim, taught body and small yet firm breasts. Her long blonde hair reminded him of Charlotte.

Meanwhile, Will and Giles had cornered a couple of beauties about five or six years their junior. Giles was supposed to be hunting birds today anyway, seeing as he had passed over a pheasant shoot. A completely different type of bird, of course! Little did he know that in fact he was being hunted, or soon would be!

Marco was over by Rockin now and not wanting to miss out on anything, he let the girls run their hands through his long dark hair. One even asked if he was a Chippendale! This made him feel like the king of the club and he was soon pretending to be the rock star he always dreamt of becoming. Oozing confidence now, he recited tales of how he had been asked to be a member of a famous rock band. The only one problem was that he couldn't play the guitar – or any other instrument for that matter.

Rockin had the full attention of a dancer called Chloe. She was a couple of inches taller than Rockin and was wearing a short blue dress with a plunging neck line finished off with a diamond necklace, which drew his eye purposely down to her ample cleavage.

Chloe rightly surmised he'd probably had enough of wedding talk so she decided to talk about what hairstyle would suit her best. She kept noticing his eyes drifting to her breasts and leaning forward, she placed a hand on his shoulder. "Would you like a dance?" she whispered seductively.

Rockin smiled and without waiting for the song to end, she guided him to a chair in a quieter part of the club and told him to take a seat. Chloe moved forward, placing herself closely between Rockin's legs and looked into his eyes. She mouthed, "I want to get close to you."

Chloe held his gaze momentarily as he looked at her profile. A chance to fully appreciate her amazing body was not wasted on Rockin, who was smiling and reminding himself what a lucky man he was.

Chloe stood with her legs shoulder width apart and slowly started to run her hands down the side of her body, moving sexily across her stomach then over her breasts.

131

Next, she knelt down in front of him placing her hands together as if to pray. Looking up, she placed her hands on his knees and caressed the inside of his thighs before slowly moving up to his crotch. Holding them there for what felt like an eternity, Chloe teased Rockin who by now was feeling more than a little turned on.

Moving over his legs, she embraced the sides of the chair and gracefully pressed her chest up against his. The smell of her perfume filled his lungs, increasing the tension between them.

Their chests met and the perfume intensified. She whispered in his ear, "Touch me!" Her breasts swept under his nose, he breathed deeply taking her natural scent into his body. He curved his hands around her bum touching her ever so gently, as she pulled back, giving him a look of passion.

She slipped one strap off her shoulder, then the next, letting her dress float gently past her waist and finally allowing it to drop to the floor. Chloe placed a hand over each nipple and lowered her body once more, her head hovering closely over his crotch. She moved slowly from side to side, swaying in time with the music, before arching her body back and moving up Rockin's now quivering body.

Rockin inhaled deeply as her breasts became level with his lips. He moved forwards gently kissing her left nipple. Chloe swayed her body to the left, bringing her right nipple in direct contact with his lip, and Rockin bit softly down thinking he was in heaven!

By now, the lads had cottoned on to what was occurring and watching Rockin take her nipple into his mouth, they waited for the powerful slap that they knew would come Rockin's way. It was well-known that there was a no touching policy in clubs like this.

Unbelievably, instead of the expected scream, she flung her head back and stretched her neck as if in sexually ecstasy then slipped her hands around his neck. "Lucky bastard," grinned Baz.

Chapter 20

Sabir toyed with the idea of asking the dancer who reminded him of Charlotte to come over and dance for him, but then he remembered his disfigured face. She would most probably take one look at him and scream, quickly running off to the bouncers to have him ejected from the club.

Apart from his formative years, most of his life now focussed around rejection of some sort. Sabir had grown up in the dusty suburbs of Baghdad living in a modest house, perhaps not in the best part of town but also not in the worst. His father had been fortunate enough to have a good job with the interior ministry that enabled them to send him to one of the better schools in the area. Despite the harsh climate, they had a luscious green garden, which his mother took care of daily with a passion.

His mother hadn't needed to go to work and happily stayed at home to raise their pride and joy. Sabir always had a clean uniform for school each day, his homework was checked by both parents in a helpful way and he was allowed to have his friends around to play as often as he liked. He had been lucky having lots of friends and remembered frequent parties and sleepovers. Looking back, he was 'pretty cool', as the Americans standing by the bar would say.

As the music's hypnotic beat began to relax Sabir, he continued to reminisce over the years gone by. "How did it all go so very wrong?" He already knew the answer of course, it wasn't the alleged rape of the two college girls which he had been found guilty of, nor being expelled from school at the age of fourteen.

As his mind wandered, Sabir relived the years before his life had changed so dramatically, remembering the happy times. Playing together with his father, endless ball games in the garden, the running races which his father would always let him win. They did it all and he had loved every moment of it.

Then came the moment when everything changed. Teachers at school took him out of classes for no reason, physically abusing him and often beating him with a cane until his backside was covered in bleeding welts. Sabir recalled the confusion and hurt as he went from teacher's pet one moment to the target of their hatred the next. Suddenly his best friends, the same friends who had shared his life for many years, turned their backs on him shunning him in the playground and in classes. Sabir knew he had done nothing wrong, nothing at least in his mind to warrant what happened next.

When Saddam's men came, the family were eating their evening meal on the garden patio. They smashed the front door down and swarmed through the house like a pack of wolves, punching his father to the floor and viciously kicking him in the stomach stopping only to stamp on his unprotected head. Sabir remembered painfully how his mother had tried to stop them, flinging herself over her bleeding husband only to be dragged off and raped repeatedly in front of his crying eyes.

Sabir never saw his parents again. Years later he discovered what had caused so much pain and suffering. His father had ordered the wrong colour leather upholstery for one of Saddam's many yachts! Such a seemingly innocuous mistake had been responsible for the death of his parents and had left Sabir with a burning hatred deep inside.

Chapter 21

Chloe leant forward and kissed Rockin gently on the lips at the end of the dance leaving a shimmer of colour on his lips. She looked into his piercing blue eyes and told him she would see him later, turned and walked towards the stairs at which point Rockin lost sight of her elegant figure.

Looking around the club, Rockin failed at first to see the lads through the darkness. Standing up he went for a wander and soon spotted Marco, with his distinctive long, dark hair, talking to a very pretty red head. As Rockin got a little closer he began to pick out the familiar silhouettes of his mates dotted around the far corners of the club, each of them sitting on chairs, just as he had been, with a dancer moving erotically over them.

Marco saw Rockin coming and swung his head round. "A face without freckles is like a night sky without stars!" he proudly recited. The redhead told Marco that he was full of shit, but with a smile on her face.

She introduced herself as Keira and held her hand out for Rockin to shake. As he took her soft hand in his, she told him how sorry she was about today. He replied with a well-rehearsed sigh and assured her that he was okay. Marco quickly tried to change the subject but it was too late and Keira was already moving off him and making her way to the rejected groom.

Marco knew there was no point in hanging around and slowly pulling himself up, he headed towards the bar. With a slight pang of jealously, he thought to himself, *That should have been me,* just as Baz came barging in nearly knocking him clean over. Keira turned, giving Baz a look of disdain over his boyish antics, re-adjusted herself and continued to offer her support to the ever-grateful Rockin.

"This place is unbelievable!" Baz exclaimed. "Just had a beauty. She milked me for thirty quid, but a tenner a dance was well worth it! How much did you pay, Rockin?"

Keira, now outnumbered, made her excuses and left, at which point Rockin replied, "Nothing."

135

"You're a smarmy bastard!" Baz grinned and asked the same of Marco. Before he could manage a reply, Giles came bounding over acting like an excited puppy.

"I'm in love!" he beamed and proceeded to dance about. Smiling knowingly, Marco and Rockin both shook their heads slowly. People always fancied, or even fell in love with, a lap dancer the first time they had a dance. The dancers worked their charm for cash, and only cash, and they were very good at it. By the end of most dances, the punter would be convinced that she fancied them, persuading them to pay for more dances. This was a business after all!

Keira worked the floor looking for likely punters and quickly spotted a likely 'victim' sitting with his head slightly down and facing away from his group of friends. *Perfect,* she thought. She made her way over to him and slipped her hands confidently around his firm waist.

Sabir flinched on feeling her arms tighten around his waist. No one had touched him like this since he was about eight years old and he instantly flashed back to his childhood, when his mother would hug him warmly as he ran out of the school gates and hold his hand all the way home.

Keira moved around to introduce herself and forcing Sabir to look up and face her, she hoped he was good-looking. She instantly saw the scarred and mutilated face, now just inches away, and instinctively took two steps back bringing her hand to her mouth as she sucked deeply in.

Keira saw Sabir's face drop and turn away. He wanted to run out of the club before he was chucked out for frightening the girls but to his amazement as he moved to leave, the red-headed lady lowered her hand from her mouth and took his.

She introduced herself as Keira, apologising quickly for her behaviour as she sat him back down and rested herself on his lap. His mind whirled with emotion but her eye contact kept him from collapsing in a heap on the floor. He couldn't think how to respond. Sabir wasn't used to people being this nice to him – even if most were polite, they always kept their distance and tended to avoid eye contact at all costs.

Keira seemed somehow different, as she happily held his gaze and asked if he was enjoying himself, and what he thought of the club? Sabir responded in perfect English beginning to relax a little as they made polite conversation. Sabir nervously brought the conversation around to Keira.

It transpired that Keira had started this year having enrolled on a college course in nursing in her home town, when a scout for a model agency had approached her as she sat in a coffee shop. Unlike many, they were quite genuine and had initially managed to find her some work, which had prompted Keira to leave college and travel to London on the promise of bigger and better jobs.

A couple of months later, her bubble had burst. When no more work or contracts came her way, Keira was forced to make some hard choices. The rents in London were astronomical and her meagre savings would soon run out. She couldn't face going home, admitting defeat to her friends and family, so taking some advice from her housemate who already worked at Stringfellow's, she had decided to give dancing a go. "The rest is history," Keira mused.

Keira asked Sabir if he'd like to join her somewhere more comfortable. Taking his slightly astonished look as a yes, she guided him to a nearby booth. They both took a seat and continued chatting, while Sabir couldn't believe his luck! Shortly afterwards a waitress came over dressed as a naughty schoolgirl, with her hair divided into two pigtails, and asked if they would like a drink. Sabir ordered another J2O and Keira asked for her usual. The drinks arrived at the table a few minutes later and much to his surprise, the bill was very reasonable. In fact, the J20 was the same price as it had been at the bar and Keira had only ordered a dry white wine.

Pleasantly surprised, Sabir placed an extra tenner on the silver tray and told the waitress to keep the change. Keira did most of the talking, adding the odd question to try and encourage Sabir to open up a little more.

Sabir struggled to make conversation after all the years he'd spent avoiding it, and the fact that the woman he was talking to was stunning made it doubly difficult. He'd often dreamt of spending time with a beautiful woman, laughing together and enjoying each other's company. The truth was that his mind was blank as he tried in vain to find something interesting or funny to say to her, and he clumsily mumbled through the next few minutes unsure of how to act.

In a quiet corner across the club, Giles stopped a waitress on her rounds and asked if they could have two more bottles of Champers with fresh glasses. Will was the last to arrive back in the pack. He'd been cornered by a Chinese girl who had, apparently, pinned him down in a chair and forced herself on him. Everyone smiled.

The waitress arrived with the Champagne, somehow balancing two bottles and six glasses on her tray with a stash of cash in used notes clipped to the side.

Marco took the glasses and handing them around, he watched as Giles thumbed his wallet counting out the cash, folded it up and slipped it into the top of her push up bra which was protruding slightly from her white, half open shirt. She didn't smack him as Marco thought she would, but then he realised that Giles must have tipped her. He knew he was right when he saw the waitress remove the extra £20 from the bill.

Giles poured the champagne like a true professional, creating just enough bubbles to let everyone know what they were drinking, but not too much as to overflow the slim flutes. Marco's phone vibrated in his trouser pocket and after checking the caller ID, he lifted the Nokia to his ear pressing the answer key as he did. It was his wife.

Meanwhile, Keira, tiring of a slightly one-way conversation, decided to step things up a bit. Without a word, she stood by Sabir's side gesturing him to turn his body towards hers. She leant down, placed his hands on his knees and gradually opened his legs. He showed some resistance at first but soon gave way.

The beat of the music increased as Sabir's heart pounded against his chest. Keira lifted her dress revealing her soft, flawless skin. He breathed deeply, taking in her essence, just as Rockin had done with his lap dancer. Keira twisted and turned her body, eventually letting her dress slip to the floor leaving just her skimpy black G-string.

Marco finished talking to his wife, pressed the end button and looked at the time. It was 9 pm. "Is everything alright?" Rockin asked.

"Yeah, she's just checking that we are still alive!"

Rockin felt a hand touch his shoulder and slowly turned his head until he could see the vision of beauty at his side. Word had spread throughout the dancers by now and this lap dancer asked him how he was feeling. Rockin replied, "Getting through, just about." She leant forward and whispered in his ear, "Would you like a free dance?"

Rockin just nodded calmly and flicked a cheeky glance towards the lads, following her over to a nearby booth where he sat back to enjoy the erotic dance routine. Marco and the rest of the lads looked on once again. All of them were slightly envious but still didn't pass up the chance to watch the gorgeous dancer move around a visibly content Rockin. Marco got lost in the ambience of it all, enjoying her beautiful features, the way she moved her body to the pulsating sounds of the music. *Oh well,* he thought to himself. *Next time.* Giles, too, felt himself being drawn to her. He could feel himself being hypnotised just by her presence in the room.

Meanwhile Keira brushed herself softly against Sabir's crotch, instantly arousing him, his cock started to swell. He hadn't felt sexual excitement for years! She brushed her arse cheeks against his rock-hard penis her hands slipped behind her and sensuously caressed his cock through his trousers.

She spun around and placed her hands deftly on Sabir's shoulders, kissing him tenderly on his cheek. He could feel her moist lips touching him. No girl had ever done this voluntarily before.

Keira slipped her dress elegantly back on and sat down beside him. Sabir went to reach for his wallet, hands shaking, but as he fumbled for some notes, Keira placed her hand on top of his and said politely, "That dance was on me." Sabir's head was still recovering from it all and he couldn't even look at her now, which made him feel ashamed. Keira was so beautiful and she was being so kind to him like no other had ever been.

"I've got to go and do some work now, but I'll be back later," Keira whispered in his ear as she got up and made her way to the bar.

As Rockin's dance ended, he too went for his wallet out of politeness more than anything – he never liked parting with money unless he had to. His money was refused, "We can give a free dance on the hour," smiled the dancer. Rockin nodded and slid his wallet back inside his jacket pocket.

Marco had made a beeline for Keira now, as she finished with the creepy looking guy in the booth, and they were soon chatting together at the bar. Sabir looked on, the hatred and envy burning through his body, watching as the good-looking Marco ordered Champagne for them both. His confidence, and the way Keira responded with smiles and laughter to everything Marco said, made Sabir even more jealous and he felt his hands clenching and jaw tightening uncontrollably. The dancer with Rockin introduced herself as Kate as she sat down next to him. Before Rockin could excuse himself – after all there were a lot more beautiful ladies in the club and another free dance could be on the cards – she began chatting happily away to him. "Tell me what had happened today?" she enquired. "Had he not realised that his fiancée had been sleeping around?" Rockin half-heartedly replied that he'd been blissfully unaware and how much of a shock the whole morning's events had been.

Kate asked what he did for a living, to which he told the truth about being a hairdresser and working for Marco. She gathered from this that he was not going to be her knight in shining armour, able to whisk her away to her country retreat that she'd always dreamt of having. She asked what the rest of his party did for a living, hoping to gain some useful information from a slightly drunk Rockin. Most of the girls dreamt of finding a rich husband who wanted to shower them with gifts and take them away from all of this. It was a nightly ritual for the girls to work the club looking for potential targets and tonight was no different for Kate. Rockin, sensing that this might be case, started with Marco. He described how he'd made a small fortune and was somewhat a local celebrity with a large house in the country. He watched her face light up briefly and then drop suddenly crestfallen as he added, "He's married with two gorgeous kids.

"Baz was supposed to be worth a fair bit," Rockin went on. "He's done well for himself, owns a gym and a large security firm." This got Kate's full attention and she asked Rockin to point him out. She glanced over to where Rockin was pointing. "You mean the one who looks like Phil Mitchell from EastEnders?"

"Yeah that's the one!" Rockin laughed. It wasn't the first time that this similarity had been brought up in conversation.

Enjoying the game, Rockin moved on to Phil, giving a not very complimentary summary of his worth. Kate simply said, "Too poor, move on."

"Who's the tall dark-haired guy?" Kate asked Rockin. "Oh, that's Will. He runs the coffee shop at the Plassey. Does alright for himself, and he's got a nice black beamer and a sizable house with a massive hot tub."

"I'm not into swinging," came the swift reply. "Who's the blonde version of Hugh Grant?" Rockin nearly choked on his drink. "Hugh Grant, you must be joking?"

"He does look like him. Anyway, who is he?"

"His name is Giles, and his family owns the Plassey Leisure Park which is worth a few pounds. Nice lad too."

"What is the Plassey?" Kate enquired.

Rockin started going into great detail about the array of the shop and the business and how many caravans the site could hold. Then he mentioned the golf course. Kate's eyes nearly popped out of her head. She excused herself by saying she needed the bathroom and left Rockin's side.

Chapter 22

Sabir was a master at reading body language, or so he thought, and he watched Keira intently. Observing her running her hands through her long flowing hair then checking her make-up in the mirror behind the bar, she was grooming herself effortlessly trying to make herself attractive and ready for the next punter, he concluded.

Keira had other ideas though and the object of her attention was Marco. Sabir watched with resentment as Marco flirted with her, flicking his long black hair from side to side, with a cigarette hanging out of his mouth as he spoke. Holding out a packet of Silk Cuts, Marco offered Keira one, at the same time bringing up a Zippo and flicking the wheel with his thumb. *Cool bastard,* thought Sabir.

In another part of the club, Kate had found Sarah. She was surrounded by a bunch of stockbrokers all trying in vain to keep her attention, all extremely drunk and getting louder as they drank their way through copious amounts of top end Champagne.

Kate recognised the type. They were always the same – too much money, drinking the best Champagne money could buy and assuming they could buy any of the girls who worked in the club. Why pay for a dance when they thought their power, money and supposed good looks entitled them to grope and make sexual advances towards them without recourse?

Kate had grown tired of the likes of these men over the years. "All big-headed twats," she muttered to herself and pushed her way towards her friend. That's why she generally headed for the older types who would, on the whole, treat her with respect and appreciate the attention of a young beautiful girl half their age. Their sexual appetite had also diminished making them easy work.

As she reached her friend, Kate felt one of the men pinch her bum. This was another thing that annoyed her but she pretended not to have noticed this time, more interested in telling Sarah about her new 'soul-mate'. Sarah immediately clocked her cheerful expression and demanded an update of the evening's events so far.

"Who is he?" she asked excitedly.

"He's a blonde version of Hugh Grant and get this, he owns a golf course and everything!" blurted Kate. "I haven't even spoken to him yet," she continued, her eyes wide and bright.

"You live on a different planet!" Laughed Sarah.

Sabir dragged his eyes away from the happy couple and decided to have a real drink. He rarely drank but felt this was a good time to make an exception, as he got the bartender's attention. Opening his snakeskin wallet and removing a fifty-pound note, he held it up in-between his fingers like they do in the movies. The barmaid immediately came over, giving him a welcoming smile and asking what he would like to drink.

"What can I get you sir?" a smart-looking barmaid asked Sabir. He hadn't thought what type of alcoholic drink he wanted, causing him to pause momentarily before deciding on whisky. "Any particular one sir?" replied the barmaid as she reached for a shot glass.

Sabir shook his head and said, "Whatever you recommend love."

There was an impressive range of over thirty different whiskeys to choose from, ranging from three pounds a shot to over four hundred for a double. It wasn't in her interest to rip off the punters as she'd only end up with fewer tips. This guy obviously wasn't a whisky connoisseur, which was another reason not to give him the expensive stuff. At the same time, she had to be careful not to insult him by giving him the cheap stuff, just in case he was. Finally, the barmaid opted for a twelve-year-old malt which, at seven pounds a shot, was half decent but more importantly, it often resulted with a three-pound tip from the customer. That was exactly what she got.

Sabir lifted his glass and took a slug of Scotch. His mouth felt like it was on fire and the burning sensation continued down his throat as his memory flashed back to his days locked up in prison in Iraq. The guards had deprived him of water for days on end, eventually giving him some after the tears and begging. Sabir remembering accurately the intense burning sensation in his throat and stomach as soon as the cool liquid had flowed into his mouth – they'd mixed in a quart of battery acid for good measure.

The barmaid noted his expression and gave him a caring smile. She removed the glass from his hand pouring the remaining Scotch into a long glass and filling it to the top with lemonade. "Try it now," she suggested.

With some apprehension, Sabir took a small sip and to his surprise, it tasted quite refreshing. He thanked the barmaid, glass in hand, and turned with a little apprehension to the crowd that had gathered to watch the girls pole dancing.

Sabir couldn't see Keira anywhere at first, which made his heart jump, but then he caught the sight of her long red hair gently swishing from one side to the other as she danced for a client.

He swept around the perimeter, keeping to the edges to make sure he never made eye contact with anyone. He didn't want to draw attention to himself. After doing a half circle, he found a perfect observation post, from where he could watch her without anyone noticing him.

He wanted to be able to scrutinise her without being caught, and his spot was perfect. He had a good view of the podium and several other girls and, of course, he could watch, or pretend to watch, the packs of males also hunting their prey.

Marco sat with his legs parted as Keira wiggled her breasts in his face. Sabir's eyes absorbed all the images, and all he could feel inside was anger and hatred.

Baz came over and by coincidence stood next to Sabir. He saw him watching Keira dancing for Marco. In his Welsh accent, Baz said, "She's nice, isn't she?" He nodded in the direction of them both. Sabir felt a sudden rush of adrenaline as he realised he'd been caught watching her.

He acted as if he'd not heard Baz's remark, biding his time while he decided what to do next. Thoughts raced across his mind. *Would he be recognised from Wrexham?* He doubted this on reflection because he had changed his image so much since then. The only thing that could give him away were his scars.

Baz tried to make conversation again. "I like a ginger nut, and she's a hell of a beautiful one." Sabir had to answer as there was no way out, except to pretend to be deaf, but if Baz saw him talking to Keira afterwards, he might smell a rat!

"Yes, she is very beautiful, but they all are." Sabir used his poshest accent as another disguise to cover his past.

"You come here often?" asked Baz.

"No, it's my first time."

"It's paradise, isn't it. This must be like the place that you go when you die, except there are no virgins."

Sabir's head and body swung around until he was face to face with Baz. Sabir had taken many lives in time and he was not scared of taking another life, even this gorilla's.

"What did you say?" Sabir spat onto the floor by Baz's feet as he spoke. Baz held his hands up and backed off a few inches.

"Sorry mate just trying to be friendly. I've had too much of this stuff," he said pointing to his glass of Champagne.

It was after Baz had backed off that he had noticed his scar-ridden face and Sabir noticed his expression change. Was it the sight of his face or recognition of a face from the past?

Baz lowered his hands slightly in case there was a fight. He needed to be sure he could drive his fist into this crazy man's face if need be. He paused and held his ground for a few seconds not sure what would happen next. Would the bouncers come over and chuck both out or would this mad man try something?

Nothing happened, so Baz edged away not turning his back on his aggressor until he was at a safe distance. He quickly found the rest of the gang and explained what had happened. "You've got to be careful what you say to the cloth heads," Phil offered.

They all seemed to agree. "I can look after myself, but we should keep an eye out for each other, and you never know what he could be carrying. He squared up to me pretty quick!" Baz commented. "But I'll rip him to shreds if he tries that again," Baz added.

Letting this piece of info sink in, Baz added, "He was watching Marco with the ginger one."

"Perhaps he fancies Marco," Phil remarked with a cheeky grin.

The lads settled down after about ten minutes, their minds firmly focused on all the naked and semi naked girls strutting around them. Marco eventually emerged from Keira's grasp with his wallet fifty quid lighter and Rockin explained what had happed to Baz. Nothing seemed to register with Marco though. He was fully in women mode and nothing else counted. After a quick refreshment of Champagne, he was off again, this time with a dark-haired dancer with big tits.

At that moment, Kate came over to Rockin. "I want you to meet me at the top of the stairs at ten to eleven," she told him.

"Why?" Rockin asked.

"You'll have to wait and see, won't you," she replied sliding her index finger slowly under his chin then placing it on his lips to stop him asking any more questions.

"Anyway, who's his fine figure of a gentleman?" she added, pointing to Giles.

Rockin introduced them both, winked at Giles and made his excuses to leave.

Giles was the perfect gentleman and he immediately ordered another bottle of Moet with an extra glass for Kate. One thing that astounded Kate was that he wasn't like all the other boring bastards in this place – he wanted to know about her. Not once did he boast, and best of all he never asked how she'd got into this business. Not that she really minded, but sometimes it felt a little degrading.

Chapter 23

Rockin glanced down at his watch. It was quarter to eleven. He held his glass out to Will to top up, looking around for Kate and Giles, but they were nowhere to be seen. He hoped that he hadn't distracted her too much and that she would come back to collect him for whatever it was she had planned.

Baz, Marco and Phil were standing a few feet away vying for the attention of a petite blonde, who seemed to model herself on Kylie Minogue.

Rockin moved to the top of the stairs and began waiting for his escort to arrive, pondering on what she might have planned for him. *Surely it must be good,* he thought to himself as he sipped from his glass.

He watched the dancers and their clients walk up and down the stairs. He'd kept an eye out for this Arab man who'd had a confrontation with Baz, but hadn't spotted him at all.

At five to eleven he began to think he'd been stood up, but just as these thoughts passed through his mind, there she was standing right before him. It was as if she had been teleported in. Eyeing her from top to toe, Rockin decided she was one of the most beautiful creatures he had ever set eyes on.

Kate linked her arm through his and they made their way down the stairs. Crowds of people stopped to watch, and Rockin felt like he was in one of those old fashioned black and white movies, when the leading couple would sweep down the ornate staircase while people gazed on in awe.

The crowd carried on watching as Rockin and Kate made the last couple of steps and walked across the carpet to the VIP area where a huge burly bouncer stood on guard. As they approached, the bouncer lifted the thick red rope from its resting position.

Kate turned her head towards Rockin as he passed through into the VIP area, and guided him to a table where five stunning young ladies stood up to greet him. They held out their hands as they introduced themselves, and he didn't know whether to kiss them on the cheek or hand, so in turn he tenderly kissed each one on the back of the hand.

Kate brought him around to the other side of the table, so that he faced the watching crowd in the commoner's area, and pulled a heavily upholstered chair for him to sit on. As she took a seat next to him, Rockin wished the rest of the lads were watching from somewhere.

One of the girls, who introduced herself as Cameron, had dark olive skin and thick black glossy hair. She was wearing a deep red dress which seemed to float on her skin as she began pouring the Champagne.

Kate explained that all the girls in the club had chipped in to buy him this bottle of Champagne. One of the girls, whose name Rockin had already forgotten, raised a toast to his future happiness and the glasses all clinked together.

Rockin tried to scan the crowd for the lads as the girls chatted to him, but none of them were in direct sight. He gave up after a few attempts, as he began to feel discourteous. After all, they were talking to him and it was rude to break eye contact and look around for his mates.

Half way through his glass of Champagne, a Europe song came on. It was 'The Final Countdown'. Kate and the rest of the girls stood up and guided him to an even larger chair – more like a throne. Doing as he was told, Rocking sat down and all six girls started to dance for him and him alone.

Each one of them took it in turns to shake their beauty in front of him, starting with Kate while two of the other girls massaged his shoulders, all the time dancing their best dances and getting in as close as possible.

Rockin inhaled their perfumes and natural essence, which changed as the girls rotated. He wanted to close his eyes and stay in this dream world forever, but he knew he had to live this moment using every sense he could as it wouldn't last forever.

He placed his hands on the sides of his legs so that he could feel the silky-smooth skin of each girl. Doing this was usually a big NO but he knew he'd get away with it – and he did.

As Kate came around again and moved in even closer than the other girls, the song came to an end and so did his dances. Kate gave him a long, lingering kiss on the lips and the rest of the girls came in turns and pecked him on the lips as well, wishing him all the best for the future. Then, making their excuses, they upped and left.

But Kate and Keira stayed at the table and carried on drinking the remainder of the Champagne, chatting together quite happily. They spoke mostly about his friends but the subject soon came around to Giles, and Rockin got the impression Giles was being hunted for marriage. The chances of them seeing each other would be pretty slim, so he decided to lead them on.

Rockin glanced around the dispersed crowd to see if any of the lads were hanging around after witnessing his VIP treatment. There was no sign of anyone, but he kept on getting a sixth sense that he was being watched.

Keira made her excuses to leave and they both watched her climb the stairs and disappear around the corner. Rockin thanked Kate for organising this for him. "It was a pleasure and the least I could do for you," she said winking at him.

Rockin and Kate sipped the last of the Champagne and watched the mingling crowd casting envious glances as they passed by.

They stood up and Rockin turned to face her. As he started to thank her once more, much to his surprise, she took hold of both of his hands and said, "You'll be alright you know. You're a genuine guy, but shit happens, and sometimes these things are probably for the best. Hopefully one day you will find your soul mate, and maybe I'll find mine, too." Then she winked at him and said, "Let me escort you to your friends."

"Giles, you mean," replied Rockin, but Kate ignored this comment, and taking his hand, she led him back upstairs. The first thing that caught his eye was Keira dancing for Marco. Marco managed to raise his head and glimpsed at Rockin, "You lucky bastard," he mimed and then returned his attention to Keira's chest.

Chapter 24

Will eventually found Baz and Rockin propping up the bar. "Tony's just phoned," he informed them.

"Who the fuck is Tony?" Baz asked.

"The limo driver!"

"Oh him."

"He wants to pick us up at one!"

"That's a bit early isn't it?" Rockin piped up.

"I tried later, but he said he'd go without us otherwise."

"I'd kill the fucker before he'd do that," Baz demanded.

"Where is everyone anyway?" Rockin asked Will.

"Phil's over there with some ugly bird and Giles is with Kate in the VIP area."

"Lucky bugger," Baz muttered.

"Haven't seen Marco for ages."

Everyone looked around at each other and shrugged. "I'll go and find him. No doubt he'll have his hands over some bird's tits," said Rockin wandering off. He rambled over to where Phil was sitting chatting to a good-looking girl. If you met her in a local club, you'd be more than happy to be with her, but here at Stringfellow's she just didn't stand out.

Rockin asked Phil if he'd seen Marco, but Phil just shook his head and carried on talking to his bird.

Rockin did a full circuit of upstairs, but to no avail, so he sauntered downstairs clocking Giles in the VIP area being the perfect gentleman to Kate. He asked Giles the same question, but the answer was just the same. It seemed no one had seen Marco.

Lapping the whole downstairs twice, Rockin could still see no sign of Marco, so he pulled out his phone. No signal. "Crap phone," he muttered under his breath, and then made his way back upstairs. Still no Marco.

"Trust him," said Baz. "Why don't you just phone him?"

"No signal."

Baz flipped open his phone and speed dialled Marco's number. He held the phone to his ear for a while until the answer machine kicked in.

"He's not answering."

"I wouldn't worry, he'll turn up," said Rockin.

"Well I'm going to get myself a wench. Anyone coming?" asked Baz.

"Ah I'll come," Will said following him at once. Rockin looked around and discovered he was by himself, so he pulled up a bar stool and sat down. Scanning the area just in case Marco appeared, Rockin sat quietly enjoying some time to himself and reflecting on the day's events.

Kate wanted to know everything about Giles – where he went to school, where he worked, even though she knew this already from Rockin. Giles told her about the Plassey Leisure Park that he and his parents ran, and how he went pheasant shooting. This was her chance, she decided. "That's one thing I've always wanted to do!" she exclaimed looking directly into his eyes.

"You should come up to stay and then I could take you."

"That would be amazing! I really fancy a weekend in the country, as I am tiring of the city life."

Before Giles knew what had happened, he was entering Kate's mobile number into his phone and she checked he had entered it correctly before saving it to SIM.

"You will phone me, won't you?" Kate asked Giles.

"Of course, I will, I'm a man of my word."

"There will be no point giving you my number if you don't."

"I will, I promise."

"And for another thing, you're the first person I've given my number to, so don't take it for granted."

Giles looked at her, and thought what Muppet wouldn't phone this girl? He couldn't quite believe his luck.

Baz and Will strolled around the club and for the first time that day, they didn't have a drink in their hands. The punters were thinning out and by the look of things the girls were, too. Or at least they seemed settled with the punters they already had, milking them for every last dollar. Noticing Giles with Kate confirmed this.

Baz and Will sat down adjacent to a couple of stunners who were dancing for some business types. "Hey, this is the way," said Baz. "You get to see everything without having to pay." They both made themselves comfortable and settled in for the rest of the night.

Rockin dialled Marco's number once more, but there was nothing except the nice lady from Orange saying, "The caller is unable to take your message right now." He did think of leaving a message but couldn't be bothered.

Kate felt quite comfortable with Giles' arm around her shoulder as they walked upstairs. She'd always gone for the wrong type and even in school she'd always liked the rogues because they were a lot more exciting. You never knew what they would get up to next. Drinking the cheapest and strongest cider they could get their hands on, staying out until the early hours worrying her mum and dad to death.

In college, she had progressed onto the pub and club scene but still liking the wayward boys, partying until daybreak sometimes, she'd dabbled with a bit of speed and ecstasy.

One night she had gone to an all-night rave and then back to someone's dingy flat in Moss Side, Manchester, to carry on with the party. She had caught her mates dabbling in heroin and when she confronted them, they told her not to be such a wimp and to try some for herself. "It was good stuff," they promised her. The party was in full swing, the music screeching in her ears, and she could hear shouting and screaming in the background as the neighbours argued.

Glimpsing around the room, Kate saw losers smoking joints on the sofa, passing it along as if it were sacred. On the coffee table lay a mirror, with the remains of lines of cocaine and cigarette butts all over it, and the carpet was filthy and peppered with burn holes. Dirt encrusted wallpaper hung off at the corners, there was a gap where a dado rail once was and all the furniture was well used and battered.

Needing space, Kate made her way to the bathroom passing an open bedroom door on her way. She glanced in and momentarily watched three men working on a girl who had a denim mini skirt pushed up to her waist.

She closed the bathroom door behind her, if you could call it a bathroom. The bath was smashed, the shower curtain was ripped down and the toilet was brown and encrusted with years of neglect.

Leaning against a wall, Kate silently cried into her hands. She had no way of escape until one of her so-called friends was sober enough to drive, which would be hours and hours away.

She can't remember how long she cried for and wondered whether this was what her life was about from now on. This made her cry again, until eventually she pulled her mobile from her pocket and dialled for her dad to come and rescue her.

Her parents were middle class, loved her to bits and would do anything for her. And now, for the first time, she realised how much she loved them, too.

Her father arrived about forty minutes later. He'd broken every speed limit to get to her – to save his little girl. When he arrived, Kate was standing on the pavement. He asked her if she was alright and Kate just nodded as she fastened her seat belt, still wiping the tears away.

Kate's Dad then placed the blanket he'd always kept neatly folded on the back seat on her lap, gave her a huge embracing hug, which they hadn't done for years, and drove off. They never spoke of that night again and she never saw those friends again either!

Chapter 25

"Have you found him yet?" asked Giles as he approached Rockin at the bar. Rockin shook his head, "You know what he's like."

Baz and Will suddenly appeared from nowhere. "What's everyone drinking?" Baz asked. "I've just got myself a coke," Rockin replied.

"Can I have six beers please love?" Baz asked the barmaid, shaking his head at Rockin. "No, actually, make that five because Marco's not here. And what would you like to drink my dear?" Baz asked, turning towards Kate.

"Nobody's found Marco yet then?" asked Will. No one replied, but they all shook their heads.

"Where's your mate with the red hair? Marco was with her for a time," Will asked Kate.

"She's had to go home as some weird guy was giving her the creeps."

Baz stopped in his tracks, "It wasn't that Arab with a scarred face, was it?" he asked.

"I think so. The bouncers wouldn't chuck him out, so she went home instead."

"Phone her now!" Baz demanded.

Kate suddenly looked concerned, "Why?" she asked him.

"I had a bit of a run in with him earlier and caught him watching your mate dancing for Marco," Baz explained.

Giles handed his phone over to Kate and she dialled her friend's mobile number from memory. The phone rang for about twenty seconds until the answer machine cut in. Leaving a message, Kate hung up.

Baz started to bark orders to the rest of the lads. Giles to go and get Phil, Rockin to phone Marco "and make sure you leave a message this time," and Will to send him a text message telling him to get in contact.

At that moment, Phil came rushing over. "What's up mate?" Baz explained the situation to him.

"After you had a run in with that cloth head, I kept an eye on him," Phil explained.

"Well?" Baz demanded.

"He watched the girl with the red hair a lot, but always from afar. And I caught him keeping an eye on Marco too."

Kate grabbed the phone from Giles once again and pressed redial, but again it went to answer phone. Next, she tried Keira's home number, but still no luck. "She always answers her phone," Kate said with a frightened tone to her voice.

Kate, looking panicky, stood up and quickly made her way over to the entrance to speak to the bouncers.

"Will, phone the driver and see if Marco is with him," Baz said, looking down at his watch and realising that it was twenty to one.

After a few minutes, Kate came back looking pale and frightened. "The bouncers said she was going to get a black cab from the rank just down the road."

"Don't the club pay for the taxis?" asked Phil.

"Yeah if you work till the end of the night, but she went early."

Baz said "Shit" and rubbed his forehead. "I've explained the situation to Rob, the head bouncer, and they're going to keep on phoning her. Also, he's sending one of the other guys around to her flat."

Suddenly they all felt very sober as they fell silent and went into their own thoughts.

Rob – an ex-military man in his early forties with a goatee, hair cropped short and greying at the sides – came over. "The guy's downstairs removed a foreign looking guy from the club at about the same time as the girl went home." He carried on, "I've sent Dave and Mike to her flat. We'll be able to cope here with fewer men."

Baz looked at Rockin and Will and told them to check all the toilet cubicles, in case Marco was in there puking up. "And check all the corners in the club as well!" Baz shouted after them.

Their eyes flitted around the edges of the club but they found no sign of Marco or the Arab. Will pushed open the door of the ground floor gents' toilet and they both scanned the urinal area. Nothing. The room was silent except for the trickle of water washing out the urinals.

Two closed cubicle doors faced them. "Marco, are you in there?" asked Rockin. No reply. Will slowly pushed the door of the first cubicle and it smoothly swung open – empty. He moved on to the second door. "It feels like we're looking for a dead body," he commented. The door opened revealing another empty cubicle, except for sheets of toilet paper littering the floor.

Leaving the toilet, they made their way downstairs again, scanning all the corners as they did so, and made their way to the gents in the basement. Inside a couple of guys stood pissing into the urinals, but as Rockin pushed open the first cubicle door again he found nothing! Will noticed the two guys watching them as Rockin opened the next door.

Rockin was the first to notice the gold cravat on the floor with blood surrounding it. "Will!" he shouted. Will came rushing over.

"Fuck shit!" Will whispered under his breath. Then Will noticed that the lock on the cubicle door had been forced.

As Rockin stepped back, he could see small trickles of blood running from the cubicle to the door back into the club. Will picked up the cravat and looked at it. "Should you touch it?" asked Rockin.

"There's hardly any blood on it," Will replied.

"No, I mean for forensics."

Will held on to the cravat and the said, "Well, it's too late now."

Rob came back over to Kate. "The bouncers are at her flat, but she's not answering the door!"

The colour drained from Kate's face and she looked panicked. The girls had always vowed to stick together, and she shouldn't have let her go by herself.

Will and Rockin came sprinting up the stairs with the cravat in hand and explained to everyone what they had found. At this stage, Kate began to shake with fear, so Giles placed his arm around her to try and give her some reassurance, although he was also feeling the pressure.

Rob rubbed his forehead, "My men would have seen something," he said. "But what if Marco was drugged?" asked Giles.

"In that case, they probably would have walked him out of the club as if he'd had too much to drink," Phil added.

Rob's face went grey. "Our guys are taught to look out for possible drugged girls, but not guys."

"This is becoming serious shit, we're not jumping ahead of ourselves, are we?" asked Rockin.

"Look at the evidence."

Will's phone started to vibrate in his pocket. Pulling it out, he glimpsed at the caller display. 'Tony limo' appeared on his screen. "Hello," he said.

"He's just pulled up outside," Will reported back to the lads.

"Is Marco with you?" he asked Tony.

Will hung up and informed everyone that Tony was by himself.

"I think we should call the police," Kate said firmly, finding some strength from somewhere.

Chapter 26

Tony watched the clock on the dash board. It was 1.10 am and he was growing impatient. He lifted his phone and dialled Will for the final time. He told Will that they had five minutes and then he was going. If they wanted to go home, this was their last opportunity. As Tony hung up, he heard the back door open and someone climbed in. *At last,* he thought to himself. Tony pressed the button to wind down the partition window and turned his head to give them an ear full.

"What are we going to do?" asked Giles, but just silence followed. They all knew the dilemma. Either go home in the limo and leave Marco behind, when he could be lying in a gutter somewhere, or stay, miss the ride home and then possibly discover that Marco was sitting in a plush hotel somewhere.

They had made a pact on the way down, "No one gets left behind." And they were going to stick to it.

Rob's phone rang. "What's happening?" He waited before answering, "Thank God for that!" Lowering the phone, he told the group, "She's safe. She went for a pizza and left her phone in the taxi. She's been trying to track it down."

Kate let out a huge sigh of relief and grabbed the phone off Rob, sobbing and talking to her friend.

"One down, one to go," Baz said. "We'd better get to the limo, before Tony pisses off, and decide what to do then." After Baz and Phil had a quick word with Rob, they all filed out of the club except Giles who waited behind with Kate and promised to be in contact with her soon. They kissed on the lips and Giles squished her hand reassuringly, finally letting go and following the rest of the lads.

Rockin opened the door and started to clamber into the limo when he felt a blow to the back of the head. He lost his grip on the leather seats and fell, his head hitting the foot well. Before he knew what was happening, he felt himself being lifted and dragged inside.

Rockin twisted his head around and saw Marco staring down at him. "Sorry mate, I didn't mean to hit you so hard."

Pulling himself onto the seat, Rockin asked, "And where the fuck have you been?"

Will was the next to get in. "Marco's in the limo!" Rockin shouted to the lads happily, and they all piled in.

"Fuckin' hell, we've been looking for you everywhere," Rockin said.

"I had you dead and buried," added Baz.

"Yeah and what's with the blood in the toilet?" asked Will.

"Oh fuckin' hell I've had a wild night!" Marco exclaimed.

"Where's your phone?" asked Will.

"It got smashed."

"So, what happened to you?" demanded Baz.

"I was into Keira, the red head, but she buggered off somewhere so I went for a piss."

There was silence, and Rockin knew what was coming.

"I went into the women's toilet by accident and there was no one in there, so I decided to have a piss in one of the cubicles. While I was doing my business, loads of girls came in and I was trapped. After a while I put my phone under the cubicle to have a look at what was going on."

The lads gave him a few dubious looks.

"Come on, you must have always wondered what these girls do when they go to the toilet together?" Marco looked around for encouraging signs, unsure whether to carry on.

"What do they do then?" asked Phil.

"Well, they do a lot of talking and have a piss."

"Is that when your phone got smashed?" asked Rockin.

"I was alright for a while, as I got a right eye full if you know what I mean. There was this one girl with a beautiful arse and I managed to record it as well."

"You're a fuckin' pervert," Phil remarked.

"Did they see the phone?" asked Giles.

"No, I wanted a proper look, so I tried to look under the cubicle, but some of my hair fell onto the floor and one of the other the girls copped it. I didn't see her foot coming, and let me tell you those Jimmy Choo shoes fuckin' hurt. She kept kicking as well the stupid bitch."

"I know this is a daft question but why didn't you move your head?" asked Baz.

"Because my head was wedged against the toilet," Marco looked around for sympathy but none came, so he carried on. "So, I legged it into the men's bogs and tried to stop my nose from bleeding," he added.

"The bouncers came rushing in, smashed the door open and punched me on the nose. Then they stamped on my phone."

"So, you were the one they chucked out!" Will commented as it all made sense.

Baz explained how they had all thought some nutter had done him in, and how they had nearly phoned the Metropolitan Police.

"Then I went to the Windmill, another lap dancing bar. It's awesome in there!"

Tony was already guiding the stretch limo through the streets of London, glad to be on the move, and in less n than seven hours he would be driving a school bus.

Chapter 27

The lads all exchanged battle stories from the eventful day as Tony drove the limo up the motorway heading back towards North Wales. He'd been trying to do a head count while driving through London, but his main priority was keeping an eye on the road.

Now that he was on the quiet motorway, he studied the passenger compartment and he was right. There were still six of them. How come the groom was still in the limo and not with his bride? He counted once more, just to be sure, but he was right first time.

Tony pondered on this matter as he cruised up the motorway at eighty miles an hour. Perhaps something had gone wrong for the poor lad. Perhaps they were just the ushers, but he could have sworn the one with the spiky hair was supposed to be getting married.

If they had been to a wedding, why had he picked them up from Peter Stringfellow's? Unless, of course, they had all sneaked away from the evening do, which he somewhat doubted. He couldn't fathom what was going on, but if there had been a wedding it was an awfully strange one.

Rockin tried to get some shut eye but without much success. With the endless chatter and loud laughter, he stood little chance. Baz and Marco had no intention of sleeping. Instead, they were trying to plan their next expedition.

They had one stumbling block. How could they go one better than they did today? Will came up with the suggestion that they should find a camera crew from somewhere and pretend they were doing a documentary. Everyone always wants to get on camera and it would draw a lot of attention to them.

Marco and Rockin weren't too sure. It would be bad enough having witnesses never mind having the evidence in full colour and preserved forever. That idea was dropped for now.

At about three thirty, Tony decided he needed a break and some fuel, so they pulled into one of the service stations. He managed to stop right outside the automatic doors and the lads piled out. Locking the limo, Tony followed them inside.

The strip lighting glared harshly as they all walked into the deserted service station. Most of the areas were closed for the night apart from one small section of the cafeteria, which served hot and cold drinks and film wrapped muffins and chocolate.

They ordered some take out drinks to quench their thirst then moved to the arcade section, which consisted of the usual fruit machines promising winnings as high as twenty-five pounds.

Bypassing these, the lads made their way to the driving games and the shoot 'em up machines. Giles dropped a quid coin into a 'Hell raiser' and took arm with his machine gun. He blasted every vampire that crossed the screen, sending electronic blood splattering across it.

Will and Baz watched over his shoulder, and suitably impressed, Baz resolved not to challenge him. Gun totting games were never his forte – he preferred to show off his driving skills.

Marco floored the accelerator on his red 911, not even touching the brakes as he slammed into the barriers of the race track. He never believed in brakes, not on these games anyway, just foot to the floor. Phil couldn't believe what a crap driver he was. "I'm glad you're not driving the limo," he told Marco.

Will drained the last of his diet Coke from the chrome can and strolled out of the arcade section eyeing up an aircraft simulator. "Anyone want to have a go at this?" he asked, pointing to the yellow machine.

"Need someone to hold your hand?" Rockin shouted, as Baz wandered over, eyed up the machine and clambered in. "Come on then Will," he challenged.

They both place a pound coin in the slot and pressed the green button, but nothing happened. Baz banged on the button a couple of times until he saw the message on the screen. 'FASTEN SEAT BELTS', which they both did immediately.

The doors on each side slid forward and locked them both in the capsule. Three, two, one and they were off. The simulator lurched backwards as the stunt plane accelerated off the runway and climbed steeply into the sky. Then the lads began a steep descent, twisting and turning, and sending the simulator into overdrive. As the machine worked its magic and went through its daredevil routine, the lads' heads banged the sides of the plastic seats.

Baz immediately began to feel sick. All the alcohol, lack of sleep and the motion of the simulator made the confined area begin to spin.

Will screamed with delight, until he saw the colour of Baz's face. Baz looked yellow and was drooling at the mouth. Will didn't want to wait to see what might happen next. He quickly pressed the red emergency stop button and the machine came to an immediate halt, gently lowering itself down.

Baz started pulling at the door handle, but nothing happened. He could feel the vomit trying to push its way up his throat. He swallowed hard, but didn't know whether he would be able to keep it down.

Will tried his door with the same result, so Baz looked around for another exit. He saw an emergency hatch on the roof. 'PUSH IN CASE OF EMERGENCY' it read. But Baz didn't push – he punched it so hard that the hatch went flying a couple of feet into the air before crashing down on the floor. Breaking free of the seatbelt, with a little help from Will, he launched himself through the roof and then vaulted to the floor.

Baz stumbled, trying to balance himself, before an explosion of sick projected onto the Marble floor tiles. Some of it ricocheted off the floor and landed a couple of feet away, making Marco leap out of the way. The lads looked in shock and no one ventured near him or offered him any help.

Baz remained bent over until he regained control and then wiped his mouth with his sleeve. By now he could feel a load of snot dripping from his nose, so he wiped again.

Straightening himself up, without looking at anyone, Baz made his way to the gents' and Phil followed him.

The rest of the lads made a sharp exit to the limo before anyone came to give them a bollocking and asked them to mop up the sick. Tony was already back at the limo totally unaware of Baz's health, which made things a lot easier.

Tony felt like asking what had been going on today, but had already decided not to. After all, they had paid him, the limo was still intact and they all seemed to have enjoyed themselves, whatever they had been up to.

"That was fuckin' disgusting. I feel sick just thinking about," Marco said.

"I was next to him. I thought he was going to puke all over me," said Will, pulling a face. "I hope he doesn't stink when he gets back in."

Baz and Phil arrived a few minutes later and Phil got in first. Then Baz looked behind him and handed Phil the emergency hatch. Phil hauled it in and placed it on his lap.

"What the fuck are you doing?" asked Rockin. "Fuckin' bad health and safety that. I'm doing the country a favour," Baz replied. They all looked at him in amazement.

Tony looked in his mirror and asked if they were ready to go. "Burn rubber!" Baz shouted, and with that Tony pulled off, as Baz and Phil went into a fit of laughter.

"At least you don't stink," Rockin said. "What happened anyway?"

The limo pulled into the Plassey at five thirty in the morning. Marco and Rockin would be back at work in three and a half hours.

Chapter 28

Marco and Rockin rolled into work at five past nine, having consumed three cans of Red Bull each for breakfast. The salon was situated in the old hay barn with vaulted ceilings, Ruabon brick walls and the finest Italian floor tiles money could buy.

Their clients waited patiently for their arrival on the plush leather sofas as they both came bounding through the doors, after stepping over the emergency hatch which Baz had left behind in the hall way.

Will and Giles stayed absent from work all morning with Will arriving just after twelve to open his coffee shop and Giles staying in his office not daring to venture outside.

Marco and Rockin retold their stories to anybody who would listen, namely their clients who were a captive audience as they were unable to get away while having their hair attended to. By the end of the first day, the emergency hatch had turned into Peter Stringfellow's sunroof from his Ferrari as the lads elaborated on their story.

Baz and Giles purchased the Daily Sport every day, but each day brought disappointment. Not a mention of their story, even on the inner pages. There were no photos of the girls they had posed with and the day's events were quickly becoming nothing more than a happy memory.

The following Tuesday – just four days after the trip – Marco received a phone call from Tony.

"Hi, Marco, I've got to ask you a question," he said.

"Yeah, go on," Marco replied.

"What was really going on when I took you to London because my wife thinks I've lost the plot?"

Marco gave him the real lowdown, and Tony couldn't believe his ears.

"There's just one more thing you should know." There was silence then Tony continued, "I've had the police on the phone."

Marco's heart missed a beat. "A hatch has gone missing from a service station and they want it back. I had to give them your name."

Marco rubbed his temple after replacing the receiver and then walked over to Rockin. Baz arrived at the salon twenty minutes later. "I'll just post it back to them, say it was a joke, which went wrong, and no harm is done," Baz suggested, but Marco and Rockin doubted the manager at the service station would see it that way.

Baz went to Wrexham post office, bought everything he needed to package his item, wrote a note saying, 'Sorry for any inconvenience Burger King' and sellotaped it all together. Finally, he addressed it to Crawley Service Station. When the cashier at the Post Office asked for £26 to post it, Baz nearly dropped in a heap, but he paid without arguing, just wanting to get rid of the thing.

The following Saturday morning at about ten o'clock, just as Marco was doing a colour consultation, in walked the police. Marco spoke to the officers at the reception desk and tried unsuccessfully to make it look like they wanted to book an appointment. He didn't last long under interrogation as he wanted them out of the salon as quickly as possible.

Rockin was called over to back up Marco's story and give Baz's details, which Baz had already authorised. "I don't know where Baz lives but he's got a gym just outside Wrexham," explained Rockin, giving them the rest of the details.

The officers pulled into the small industrial estate, where Baz had his gym, and parking next to a fork lift truck holding a pallet of Welsh slate, they made their way into the gym.

Baz instantly recognised them from working on the doors, although he wasn't on first name terms. "Can I help you?" he asked them.

"Yes, we're looking for Baz," one of the officers replied.

"You've found him."

"We'd like to ask you some questions about a missing hatch from an arcade machine."

"I'm sorry about that officers. I had a few too many beers, but I posted it back to the Crawley Service Station this morning."

"Which service station?"

"Crawley, just outside Birmingham."

One of the officers shook his head. "You didn't take it from Crawley. You stole it from Warwick Services."

Baz could feel his heart sinking. As soon as the officer had said it, he remembered.

"Have you got any proof of posting?"

"No."

"So, you admit stealing the hatch?"

"Err, I didn't steal it, I took it as evidence. The machine we were using locked us in and we had to climb out of the emergency hatch, which was no mean feat."

"So, you admit taking the hatch?"

"Yeah, but I should sue the company."

The officers both looked at each other. "I'm afraid we're going to have to continue this conversation down at the station," one of the officers informed him.

Baz looked shocked and said, "I want my solicitor present." The police both sighed. "OK, well come down to the station tomorrow at 9 am with your brief."

Chapter 29

While they were in London, Phil had made a resolution to patch things up with Charlotte, and on the Sunday morning after the trip, he found himself standing on her front step. He tenderly pressed the door bell, as if not wanting to disturb anyone, and after an agonising forty seconds or so, Charlotte answered the door, only opening it a couple of inches with the chain still in place.

A smile crossed her face when she saw Phil standing nervously in front of her. Unhooking the chain, she swung the door open and immediately hugged him. The beautiful memories of what they'd had before she'd mucked things up came flooding back to her and with it came the tears of emotion.

They stayed hugging for the best part of a minute minutes until Carey and Josh spotted them and joined in with a group hug.

"Are you staying Dad?" asked Carey, with her large blue eyes beaming up at him.

How could he answer this question? Moments earlier he was expecting an argument, not big smiles and not embracing hugs. He smiled at her, laid his hand on top of her platinum blonde hair and pulled her in close.

They all sat chatting for about three hours, with Charlotte doing most of the talking. Phil listened intently as she unloaded all the trauma and emotion of the past few years, explaining how Wayne Williams had treated her. Phil didn't judge her – or Wayne for that matter – and never let on about Baz's involvement. They held hands for the first time in years and looked into each other's eyes as the emotion flowed seamlessly from one to the other.

Carey and Josh wanted to play with their dad – their real Dad, not an imposter – but they sensed their lives were about to change for the better, so they let their mother and father talk. As time slipped by, they grew more and more hopeful, with their ears pinned to the closed door straining for a hint of their father's return.

"So, what happens now?" asked Phil.

There was no pause. "I want you back and I want you back for good." Phil thought he'd never hear these words flow from Charlotte's mouth and right at that moment, the kids burst through the door and piled on top of them as they both embraced their new-found commitment.

Phil wanted to go and get some of his things from his flat – nothing heavy just a tooth brush and a change of clothes – but Charlotte and the kids didn't want to lose sight of him.

Playing Power Rangers with Josh and pretending to be a horse, with Carey riding on his back, Charlotte watched Phil and their children with love in her eyes and with the occasional tear drop trickling down her cheek. She wondered how she could have given him up.

Phil read his precious children their bedtime stories, kissing them good night and watched their breathing gradually slow as they fell quietly to sleep. He sat and watched as their little chests barely moved up and down, pinching himself several times just in case he was in a dream. Then he stopped and realised that this was his world again now and he was going to treasure it, every second of it.

Phil woke in the morning. With his eyes still closed, he felt next to him for Charlotte, reaching his arm further and further out, but she wasn't there. He felt sick inside. *It must have been a dream after all,* he thought to himself. He could feel his new world come crashing down around him.

Bringing his hands up to his face to shield the tears from the outside world, he rolled over onto his side. As he sobbed, he took a gasp of air deep into his lungs and there it was. Charlotte's perfume was on the pillow beside him. His head whirled with emotion, and confusion rattled through his brain.

There was only one thing for it – he had to open his eyes. Just as he did, he heard a bang in another room and a scream from Charlotte and Carey. Phil sat bolt upright, his eyes focusing on his surroundings. The walls were painted a soft yellow and there they were – the fitted wardrobes that he had assembled himself a good few years earlier. The curtains were still closed with no light creeping through them, just the light from the hall filtering through.

As he slipped his jeans on, he heard something coming from downstairs. He stopped and listened and realised that it was Carey crying her heart out. He bolted from the bedroom past the kids' rooms and flung himself down the staircase. As he reached the downstairs hallway, he could still hear Carey and a mumbled voice.

Phil pushed the kitchen door open and all he could see was orange liquid splattered everywhere, with Carey's sobbing still audible from behind the door. He pushed further into the kitchen and there she was standing next to her mother.

Charlotte was knelt beside her, wiping away the tears. "What on earth has happened?" Phil asked.

"I, I wanted to," and the sobbing continued as she looked up at her dad with those big blue eyes. Charlotte continued, "Carey got up by herself and wanted to make breakfast for us both. She'd managed to open a can of beans when I walked in. I don't know who jumped the most!"

Phil bent down and taking Carey into his arms, he held her tight.

Chapter 30

Sabir paced back and forth from his bedroom to the small kitchen in his one-bedroom apartment in the East end of London. He'd never been distracted like this before in his life.

He was torn between two women – Charlotte and Keira – as they both fascinated him. The light had been ignited again after seeing the strange wedding party from Wrexham, who by some strange twist of coincidence had introduced him to Keira. Keira had showed him humanity like no other human being had ever done before.

As he paced, he knew deep down that Charlotte would never give herself voluntarily to him, but perhaps Keira might. He imagined what it must be like for a beautiful woman, or any woman for that matter, to give herself to him, to embrace him, hold him and to kiss him.

His bag lay half packed on his double bed and his open wallet sat on the pine bedside cabinet, displaying various debit and credit cards although not one of them was in his name. The introduction of pin numbers had not stopped him. In fact, if anything, it had made life easier. No more practicing signatures. He would stand in the queue at the cash point, behind young and old people – it made no difference – and watch them type in their pin numbers. Then there was the simple task of pick pocketing these poor, unsuspecting souls. Best of all, he kept hold of the card and the cashier never even bothered to look at the name.

Sabir's apartment was in a dead person's name – an Egyptian with papers to stay in this country, who had died while working on a building site somewhere in London.

Sabir claimed the name after reading about the accident in the London Standard – he'd been waiting a while for a new identity. The nationality had to fit his description, and there was no point claiming to be a Jones or a Williams – popular names in Wales – as it would just draw too much attention to him.

By chance, they were of similar age and height, and on checking the Egyptian's police record, he was delighted to discover it came up clean. It didn't take much more digging to find out his national insurance number, not that Sabir really needed one, but it just made him feel better and added to his authenticity.

Sabir even went to the coroner's court to see if he could learn any more facts and in case some family had suddenly materialised. But the Egyptian had no family in this country, which helped to keep things a lot simpler.

Sabir stood in front of his wall of fame, trying to find what he was looking for, but he knew deep down that he would have to look elsewhere. This wall consisted of newspaper cuttings of all the girls he had taken, with added extras of some he wished he had.

Pride of place, right in the centre of the wall of fame, was a large digital picture of Keira as she waited for a cab on the very night that he'd met her. Even though she looked cold and tired, her radiance still glowed, seeming to lift her out of the photo.

His mind slipped back to Charlotte. The only image he had of her was in his head, which sometimes was best. He could bring her close or watch her from afar, smelling her scent.

On each of the newspaper clippings he'd sellotaped a lock of the girl's hair to bring him closer to them. He'd even purchased the perfume that they had been wearing the night he'd taken them.

He had made mistakes with the first couple of girls, as he'd scanned the perfume counters trying to pin point the fragrance yet failing dismally. So, after that he simply asked them what perfume they were wearing. Generally, they got it right, but sometimes they were too scared to think properly and got mixed up.

Sabir carefully folded the rest of his clothes into his holdall and zipped it up, securing it with a small but strong padlock. Carefully removing Keira's photo, he folded it and slipped it into a side pocket of his black leather wallet.

He'd followed Keira wherever she'd gone since the day that they'd met. He'd discovered that her real name was Kelly Hanson and confirmed that she came from St Helens, which she had already told him in the club anyway.

Keira had made one move that Sabir had not been expecting. On Wednesday morning, she had appeared with a small suitcase and took a taxi to Euston train station where she purchased a train ticket.

Sabir watched her buy a Latte and a paper then walk to platform 13 for Liverpool. Just to make sure, he bought a platform ticket and studied her as she boarded the Virgin Express train. The only conclusion he could come to was that she was going home.

Sabir raced back to his flat on his moped, burst through the door and fired up his computer. He checked the Stringfellow's website, which informed which girls were working in the forthcoming week. Keira's column was marked up as on holiday for one week. Next, he went on to BT's website and searched for the name Hanson in the St Helens area.

Only two results came back, so he searched the same name for the entire Liverpool area ending up with twelve results. Most of those were in the same post code area. *Relations,* he thought to himself. He printed off the results with the names and addresses and the location of each on a map.

Just as he was about to turn his computer off, Sabir had a thought. He logged onto www.getmapping.com and typed in the postcodes for all the St Helens addresses. Next, he clicked on the button for aerial photos and noted that both houses in the St Helens area were in a village on the outskirts of the town.

Sabir then used one of the credit cards to purchase a high-resolution image and downloaded it onto his computer. Both houses were situated next to each other in what looked like converted barns, with plenty of greenery where he would be able to sit and watch. He smiled to himself with great satisfaction, remembering faintly that she had told him she had grown up on a farm.

He lifted his bag from the bed and glanced around the flat to make sure everything was in its correct place. Sabir would know if someone moved even the smallest of items from his flat.

Double locking his door, Sabir made his way out, walking about half a mile before hailing a cab to take him to the station.

Chapter 31

Baz exited the police station, with his solicitor in tow. Clearly wound up, he was swearing a lot. He kicked a stone, which went hurtling towards an unmarked police car, impacting on the side window and sending the alarm screeching.

Baz carried on walking, forcing his hands deep into his pockets and keeping his head down, until he realised his solicitor was standing watching the cop car light blazing.

"Come on!" Baz demanded, but the solicitor stood routed to the spot not sure what to do. He stared at the police car but there was no visible damage. Turning his head towards the police station, he noticed that there weren't any officers racing towards them.

He took a deep breath of the cold, damp Wrexham air and started walking towards Baz, who looked like he was about to explode at any second. They made it into the solicitor's office without any conversation taking place, and Baz's solicitor, who was called Mr Hughes, was more than pleased to have arrived safely.

The receptionist, who was carrying a pile of red files, greeted Baz with a warm smile. Baz eyed her tight knee-length skirt and dark tights, and he found himself wondering whether she was wearing suspenders. This brought a smile to his face as he turned to face Mr Hughes, who suggested they take a seat in the conference room. "We'll sort things out in here," he told Baz. As they sat down, the receptionist brought in two cups of fresh filtered coffee and lay them down on the table in front of them.

The solicitor took a couple of sips of coffee trying to get things straight in his head. "So, they've got you on video camera carrying the hatch out of the service station and placing it in the limousine." He waited to see if Baz made any comments, but he didn't, just as he hadn't done in the police station.

"They've charged you with theft," Mr Hughes said pointing out the obvious.

"But I posted it back to them."

"Yes, Mr Williams, but you posted it back to the wrong service station."

"What will I get?"

"If you plead guilty, first offence, some community service and most probably a fine."

"What about my work?"

"That gets a little more tricky."

"Just tell me!" Baz demanded.

"As you know, door men are no longer allowed to have a criminal record."

"So, I've had it then?"

"There is some hope."

"And what's that?" Baz asked, practically screaming at this point.

"The panel can use their discretion, and since you helped clean up the town, the council should look favourably towards you. However, you can never predict anything, and I wouldn't want to get your hopes up too much. Anyway, I would have thought you didn't need to work the doors anymore?" Mr Hughes finished.

"That's not the point," said Baz.

Heading into town in a slightly better frame of mind, Baz passed a newsagent and decided to buy the Sport for one last time. He'd bought it every day since they got back. As he glanced at the front page, he saw the usual 'up the skirt knickers' shot, which the Sport was famous for. As celebs climbed out of their cars, a photographer would crouch down low and snap away.

The headline proclaimed, 'Sex Starved Barmaids'. Baz didn't even bother to open the paper as he always guessed that they would be on the front page. He ripped the wrapper off the bar of Galaxy chocolate that he had bought – a rare event – and consumed it in fewer than four mouthfuls, hardly tasting the silky-smooth chocolate which he used to love so much before he became a gym freak.

A moment later, Baz changed direction and headed back towards his car feeling guilty about the shameless waste of calories he had just consumed. He leant against his door of his beamer and started to text Phil. 'Where are you? Fancy a work out?'

It didn't take long for Phil to reply. 'I'm at Charlotte's house, meet you at the gym.' Baz got into his car and turned the key in the ignition but nothing happened. He tried again with the same result. Baz smashed the centre of the steering wheel sending the horn into overdrive, and passers-by turned their heads to see where the noise was coming from.

Leaping out of the car, Baz slammed the door shut and yanked the bonnet up. As he looked down, he could see that there was absolutely nothing he could tinker with as the whole engine was covered in plastic and chunks of metal. He tried to slam the bonnet with no avail as it was fitted with a hydraulic cushioning device.

Next, he tried wrenching the door handle open, but nothing happened. Somehow, the central locking had locked the car and at that moment he felt like smashing his hand right through the car window. He kept pressing the remote control but the car wouldn't open. He inserted the key and still nothing.

Baz scanned his phone just in case he had the phone number for the dealership. He could feel his blood pressure rising by the second.

Speed dialling Phil's number, he got an answer after three rings. The sound was muffled, though, as Phil was on his hands free. "Alright mate?"

"No, I'm not fuckin' alright!"

"What's up?"

"The car's dead and now it's locked me out!"

"Do you want me to pick you up?"

"No just get me the dealer's number."

"I'm in the car at the moment but I'll get it for you when I get to the gym."

Baz took a deep breath and began his wait. *Why does shit always happen at the same time?* he thought to himself. His phone was quiet for about five minutes then it sprang to life and Phil gave him the number.

"Good morning, Hallows, Donna speaking, how may I help you?"

"I want to speak to the managing director."

"He's in a meeting now, may I help you?"

"Not unless you can start my fuckin' car!"

"I'll put you through to the service department."

After twelve rings, he disconnected his call and pressed redial. "Good morning, Hallows, Donna speaking, how may I help you?"

"You just put me through to the service department and no one answered. What type of Muppet outfit are you?"

"I'm sorry sir, would you like me to put you through again?"

"I'm not going around in circles all the time. I want to speak to the managing director!" Baz demanded.

"As I explained earlier, he's in a meeting."

"I don't care what meeting he's in, get him on the phone!"

"I'll just have to put you on hold, sir."

The next moment, Baz was subjected to classical music which continued for two minutes. He was just about to hang up when he heard a male voice.

"Hello sir, this is Hawkins the MD. How may I help you?"

"About fuckin' time. I haven't even had this car for two months and it's died and locked me out!"

"Ok sir, we'll send a tow truck out now. Can you give me an address?"

About an hour later, a tow truck finally arrived. "You lot don't rush, do you," Baz commented. The driver didn't answer, which just agitated Baz even more.

"What's the matter with your vehicle, sir?" the driver asked. Baz explained what had happened.

"May I have your keys?" Baz handed them over expecting his car to be carted off, but the driver simply inserted the key and turned it anti-clockwise while gently lifting the handle. He did this for several seconds until the door popped open.

Baz stood there in disbelief and watched on as the driver lifted the bonnet, pressed a button and then sat in the driver's seat and turned the key. The engine sprang into life.

"Why couldn't they tell me to do that over the phone?" Baz asked in amazement.

"Don't know. If I'd known what was wrong, I would have told you myself before having to drive all this way."

Baz pressed the switch to remove traction control and floored the accelerator, causing the car to spin out of the parking slot. He made slight adjustments to straighten the car and sped away towards the exit.

Making it to the gym in seven minutes flat, Baz slammed the door shut and marched in like a man possessed. "What a fuckin' morning I've had!" he announced this loudly as he entered, to anyone who would listen.

"They got it fixed then?" asked Phil.

"Fuckin' muppet show!" Baz replied as he tore his jacket off and marched to the changing rooms to get into his training gear.

"What are we training first?" asked Phil on Baz's return.

"Chest," Baz replied before proceeding to load up the bar with 60 kilos on each side.

"Not warming up then?" Phil asked him.

"I'm already fuckin' warm," replied Baz, as he started to punch out twelve reps without breaking a sweat.

Breaking out in a sweat would have been hard as the gym was colder than the December temperatures outside. On this particular morning, you could clearly see your own breath.

They swapped over and Phil took control of slowly lifting the bar. Taking care not to bounce the bar on his chest, he powered it to a full stretch, repeating this eight times before Baz helped him place the bar back on the stand.

Baz added another ten kilos to each side of the bar. "Are you sure about this weight?"

"I'm so fuckin' tense, I need to." Phil wasn't going to argue, so he helped Baz ease the bar from its resting point and let him take the full weight.

One of the other lads sat in the gym drinking his protein shake reading the Daily Sport. "Hey Baz, your ugly face is in this paper!" he exclaimed.

Baz momentary lost concentration and the weighted bar tilted to one side. He'd lost control. Instinctively, Phil shot his arms down managing ribs to grab the bar. He knew he had no chance of lifting the bar back up, especially when it was moving in the opposite direction with gravity against him.

Phil lifted and shoved the bar to one side and there was a huge thud as one end hit the floor with the bar bouncing on Baz's chest. Phil battled with the bar, trying to lift it as it dug further into Baz's chest. Baz tried to lift it too, but a shot of pain ripped through his chest. Fortunately, one of the other lads who had been training nearby sprinted over and lifted the bar clean and free.

Phil and the other lad took the weight of the bar and pivoted around the bench as Baz held his chest and painfully raised himself up off the bench.

"You fuckin' idiot!" Baz shouted angrily to the lad who was reading the paper. He tried to take a breath and a pain shot right across his chest.

"I think you've broken a couple of ribs," said Phil.

"That's all I need!" Baz fumed.

"Come on, I'll take you to hospital."

"Where's this picture then?" asked Phil, but the lad was looking very coy.

"I was only joking," he said in a nervous Welsh accent. Tenderly standing up, Baz slapped the lad hard across the back of the head, without trying to inflict too much pain on him.

"Get out of my fuckin' gym!" he told him.

The lad left without looking back. "Fuckin' twat!" Baz exclaimed.

Baz gave his details to the lady at the hospital reception and was passed along to the triage nurse, who assessed him quickly and efficiently and came to the same conclusion as Phil. "You'll have to wait for a doctor to give you the once over and he'll most probably want to do some X-rays," the nurse informed him.

Baz and Phil sat on some plastic seats in the waiting area reminding them both of school. Opposite, there was a poster inviting you to call a free number if you'd had an accident and promising you would receive 100% of the settlement if your claim was successful.

"There you go," Phil pointed to the poster.

"The only settlement I'll be having is with that prat!" Baz replied. A couple of minutes of silence passed as Baz and Phil watched the medical staff wander back and forth in no particular hurry.

"How are you and Charlotte getting on?" asked Baz.

"Really well, it's great to see the kids all the time."

"So, you're back for good then?"

"Bloody hope so! We had a good heart to heart on Sunday. We talked for hours and laid all our emotions on the table you know."

"I'm glad for you. You reckon it will last then?"

"I really want it to work and Charlotte keeps kissing and hugging me. I've lost count of how many times."

"I won't be working on the doors for much longer," Baz announced, changing the subject.

"Broken ribs will only put you out of action for about six weeks, mate."

"It's not just the ribs. I got arrested and charged with theft of that bloody hatch this morning."

"Shit! That's terrible, although you don't really need to work on the doors anymore, do you?"

"I wish people would stop saying that."

"It's true."

"You know that I do it more for the girls than the cash. I'd never meet any birds without it."

"Talking of birds, Charlotte's going to a hen do on Saturday night."

"Do you fancy a beer then, as I won't be working?" Baz asked him.

"The kids want to stay at my house before I get rid of it. They think it will be exciting."

"I'll come over to you then and bring my nephew. I reckon his mum and dad could do with a night off," Baz concluded.

Chapter 32

It was Thursday morning and the phone rang at the Plassey Hair Studio. "Good morning, the Plassey Hair Studio, how may I help?"

"Hi, it's Lara, can I speak to Rockin please?"

"Hold on I'll get him now," the receptionist replied.

Walking over to where Rockin was working, the receptionist whispered into his ear and Rockin made his excuses to his client as he headed over to answer the phone.

"Hi darling," he began.

"What the hell am I doing on the front page of the newspaper?" Lara shouted down the phone.

"How do you mean?" Rockin's heart raced and he felt light headed.

"There a picture of me leaving the school!"

"Shit!"

"A bloody parent handed me the Daily Sport when he was dropping his child off. Do you know how that makes me feel like?" she sounded really annoyed and panicky.

"You do realise that someone has sat in the bushes to take that picture," Lara continued. "And what other pictures have they got?"

"I don't know." Rockin's face started to drain of its colour.

"The school governors are going to go mad and I'll be lucky if I keep my job." Her voice was now raised.

"You'll be alright," Rockin said feebly.

"And what about my dad? He's going to go ape. I haven't even dared read the story!"

Lara's eyes were filled with tears and they started to spill over onto her cheeks. Her hands were shaking as she held the phone to her ear and tried to stop herself sobbing uncontrollably.

"You never think of the consequences, you're so bloody selfish," she added. Then the flood gates opened and tears streamed down her cheeks, just as the head teacher walked into the staff room.

Lara's voice never came back. All Rockin could hear was mumbled voices as the head tried to pacify Lara and find out what was the matter with her. The head mistress replaced the receiver and guided Lara over to one of the chairs, sitting down next to her.

"What's wrong Lara?" she asked. Lara didn't want to say. She was too worried about getting into trouble. As she struggled to hold back the tears, the head mistress continued to console her thinking that something dreadful must have happened.

Rockin stood by the reception desk and listened as the phone went dead. He felt like going into the coffee shop garden, digging a big hole and jumping in. Liz, the Hair Studio's receptionist, placed her hand on Rockin's shoulder and asked him, "Is everything alright?"

He didn't answer, so she took him by the hand and led him through the salon into the staff room. Sitting him down, she went off to get Marco.

Marco arrived, "What's up mate?"

"Lara's on the front cover of the Daily Sport."

"Fuckin' brilliant!"

"She doesn't think so."

"Ah, she'll be alright."

"She reckons she'll be lucky to keep her job."

"Nah, come on let's go and buy the paper."

"What about my client?"

"I'll get one of the girls to finish her off."

That's what Rockin always liked about Marco. He could always turn a bad situation into a positive one.

Back at the school, Lara passed the paper over to her boss, who unfolded it and glanced at the front page not quite knowing what she was supposed to be looking at. At first glance, she saw a bikini babe in the top right corner, but then she spotted a large picture of Lara with her long blonde hair flowing behind her as she carried her school box full of books. Worse still, the school was pictured in the background.

The headline read, 'Love rat and the Catholic school teacher'. The head looked confused. She looked at Lara, not really knowing what was going on. "Is this you?" she asked. Lara managed a nod.

Marco and Rockin raced across the car park towards the convenience store and burst through the door, nearly giving the shop keeper, Brendon, a heart attack. They headed straight for the newspaper stand.

At first glance it looked like they didn't have the Daily Sport. "Have you got the Sport today?" asked Rockin. "Yeah, it's tucked under the Daily Star," Brendon replied. Marco scrambled under the papers until he eventually found what he was looking for.

Lara had been spot-on because there, right on the front page, was a very good shot of Lara with the school sign clearly visible in the background. "Quick, turn to the centre pages!" Rockin demanded. Then a feeling of dread overwhelmed him. "What about the blow job?"

By this time, Brendon had come around to the other side of the counter to see what all the fuss was about. Marco fumbled through the pages until he saw a picture of himself and Rockin glaring happily back at them.

Another picture showed Rockin and Abigail with their arms wrapped around each other as they leant on the limo. To the left there was a picture of Abigail topless and another picture of her, that hadn't been taken recently, which the lads thought was a bit strange.

Right in the centre of the double page spread was a picture of a blonde who neither of them recognised at first, but she did look familiar. She was a blonde, like Lara, and her boobs were on full display. Rockin couldn't help but read the caption underneath the picture.

'What we think the Catholic teacher would look like topless', the caption read in barely legible small print. The bottom photo showed all the lads standing in line with the limo in the background. *Not a bad photo,* Marco thought to himself.

"Come on, let's go and show Will and Giles," Marco said pulling the paper away.

"No, I want to read the story first!" Rockin demanded.

"Love rat gets dumped at the alter after having sex with one of the bridesmaids. Then through our brilliant investigation, we find out that he is engaged to be married to an innocent Catholic primary school teacher."

Rockin wiped his brow and with a sense of relief, he said, "Thank God for that!"

"What do you mean thank God for that?" asked Marco.

"Lara's in the clear," Rockin informed him.

"Told you she'd be OK mate."

Before Rockin could read on, Marco snatched the paper and was running back across the car park to the coffee shop leaving Rockin to pay for the paper.

Rockin followed, but ambled slowly gathering his thoughts.

Lara sat and listened as the head mistress gradually read her the story. Lara felt relieved after hearing the first paragraph. Deeper into the story, came the part about 'the wicked sex with the bridesmaid' which both Lara and the head teacher knew was made up.

Next came a report of a mystery girl who had given Rockin a blow job under a table in an exclusive Italian restaurant in the Soho district of London. They both came to the conclusion that this was made up as well.

Lara was pleased that she had warned everyone around the table during their Christmas dinner. This included the governors and the priest. She had told them that Rockin had gone to London in a limo dressed up in wedding gear, because it was the only way they could hire a stretch limo.

"Hey Baz, we'll have to go out for a drink to celebrate," said Marco after telling him about the story in the papers.

"I've broken my ribs and Phil's looking after his kids this weekend," said Baz.

"He's got the kids? That's brilliant!"

"He's back with Charlotte as well, but she's on a hen do this weekend."

"Thank God for that. When we were in London, he didn't stop going on about them all bloody day."

"Why don't we all go to Phil's house for a drink and then if you lot want, you could go into town afterwards?" Baz suggested.

"Sounds good," Marco replied.

The headmistress made Lara phone Rockin, who was now back in the salon.

"Don't you ever do anything like that to me again, or I'll kill you myself," she promised.

"I won't," he promised back.

"How's the head teacher?" asked Rockin barely wanting to know.

"I'm just glad I told her what you lot were up to. I just hope everybody sees it the same way."

"They will."

A dreadful thought crossed Lara's mind. "The parents are going to love this," she informed Rockin. She paused before adding, "They love to get some dirt on a teacher!"

Rockin didn't comment, sensing that might be best. Instead, he just said, "Well I'll see you later then."

While Rockin was busy with a new client, Marco slipped out of the salon with a small piece of paper in his hand. He walked around the corner and dialled the number on the paper.

"Hello MFM, your local radio station," said a girl with a Wrexham accent.

"Hi, can I have the news desk please?"

"News desk?"

"Hi, I've got a bit of a story for you." Two minutes later, Marco made his way back to the salon.

Baz's doctor had banned him from working out for six weeks, telling him to go gently when he started again. This had pissed him off, but he had been lifted by news of the paper carrying their story.

Rockin showed his twenty-two-year-old client her blonde hair in his back mirror, and then escorted her to the desk for Liz to sort out the bill. Just then, something caught his attention. He thought he'd heard Lara's name mentioned on the radio, so he listened harder managing to block out some silly question that his client was asking.

The two DJs on the radio were discussing the newspaper article in the Daily Sport. That was all Rockin needed – not only did all the builders in the country know about Lara, but now all North Wales and Cheshire would know as well.

He heard his name mentioned next as the 'love rat' and listened on as the DJs commented on how this poor teacher must be feeling. Then, much to his horror, one of the DJs asked for the listeners' comments. "Phone us or text us with your views," she invited her listeners.

"Bloody female DJs," Rockin muttered under his breath. The salon seemed to be quiet now. All the hairdryers had been turned off as everyone listened in. The DJs played another record and Rockin stood there in total disbelief.

Meanwhile, Baz tried to climb onto his counter in excitement, but his ribs put a stop to it. Instead, he punched his arm into the air. Baz and Phil waited in the gym for the song to finish, and then the DJs were back. "We've had some interesting comments on this newspaper matter," one of the DJs began. "Joan from Rhos says he should be ashamed of himself. Paula from Acton says he used to cut her hair in the Plassey Hair Studio, and he tried to kiss her when she was out on a night at Scott's nightclub. He sounds a right one! Keep the calls coming in, and in the meantime, here's the lovable rouge Tom Jones," the DJ finished.

The children in Lara's class sat quietly reading while Lara's phone bleeped, signalling an arrival of a text message. It was Kate her best friend. 'You're on the radio,' the message told her. Lara said shit under her breath and buried her head in her hands. She just knew that this was going to grow and grow.

'What are they saying?' Lara texted back. Twenty seconds later her phone beeped again and she read the next text. 'Feel sorry for you, he's a love rat,' Kate informed Lara, which made her feel slightly better.

The DJs were on a roll. "We've got some more comments. John from Chester says his fiancée looks beautiful and how could he do it to her? An anonymous text has come in saying that the best man is a right lad and is always with a different girl. Jill from Wrexham says the fiancée looks so innocent. How could he? More after this song."

Marco's wife dragged Marco out of the staff room at the Hair Studio. "What's this about you going with different girls?"

He whispered, "I phoned MFM and told them about the story. I said they could say anything." Marco's wife shook her head in disapproval. "But why?"

"It's all free publicity and they've already mentioned the salon, so now everyone will be talking about us."

"What about poor Lara?"

"She'll be alright. She can work on reception here if she loses her job."

"I'd bet she'd love that!"

As Marco's wife walked away, she thought, *Well at least there's never a dull moment with Marco.*

The DJ was back. "We're about to break for the news but I've got a quick one here from Rob asking why all the attention is on the school teacher. What about the poor bride? And who is she anyway?"

In Liverpool, Keira laid still not moving a muscle. She listened to the silence while the radiators pumped out heat which made the conservatory seem like a sauna. Lifting herself up into more of a seating position, she reached across to take cup of tea that her mother had just brought her.

She loved it here. Her parents had bought it after she moved to London and she looked upon it as a country retreat, where she could throw herself into family life away from the hassle and bustle of city life.

Her auntie and uncle had bought the second, slightly smaller, barn conversion next door, which made her feel even more comfortable. She had a strong bond with her family and wondered whether it was due to her coming of age.

Leaving behind those adolescent years, even if she had been in her early twenties at the time, that was a different part of her life and she had been reborn. Her parents knew what she did for a living. She wasn't a prostitute, although they worried it might lead to it, but they knew not to pressurise her.

Sabir watched as Keira took a sip of her drink and gazed into the distance. He held his recently purchased binoculars steady as he lay entrenched in a small wooded area about fifty meters from the barn.

He'd bought the most powerful binoculars he could find, without going over the top on size. He made sure they had anti-reflection lenses, something he'd learnt from watching a Saturday afternoon movie. Then he'd invested in a pair of dark brown overalls to keep his clothes clean and some cereal bars and a couple of bottles of water. He didn't go over the top with the rations, as he figured and hoped that she would be going out that day.

Ten minutes later, Keira's mother entered the room with her coat on. She spoke to Keira, who eased herself off the sofa. This was what he'd been waiting for, so he packed his binoculars into his holdall, crawled deeper into the woods and joined the footpath which brought him onto the road.

On reaching the road, Sabir pressed the fob on the electronic key of his hire car, opened the boot, carefully placing the bag inside, and then unzipped the overall and stepped out of them. He just made it into the driver's seat in time to see Keira's mother pull out of their driveway in her car.

Leaning flat across the passenger seat, just in case one of them glanced into his car as they passed, he waited until they had gone around the corner and then pulled himself up and started the engine. He hoped they were going on a girlie day out shopping and maybe they'd have lunch. If he was right, he could keep his distance but watch Keira all day.

Sabir edged out of the layby at a normal speed, not wanting to draw any unwanted attention to himself, and slowly reached a speed of forty-five miles an hour. In the distance, he could see his target take a left turn at the T junction. They were going shopping; he had guessed correctly.

The previous night, after hiring a car with one of his fake driving licenses and credit cards, he had verified Keira's whereabouts and then headed into town, surveying the shopping centres and various outlets she might visit. He checked the local night life. After all, if Keira had had a few drinks, she would be easier to take. Especially if she needed a taxi home!

Sabir kept his distance as he watched Keira's mother navigate the town's traffic. She eventually came to one of the council-run car parks and turned in. He had been hoping that she would use this one. It was the largest in the town so he wouldn't be noticed so easily. He'd be fine if they didn't pass each other looking for a space.

They parked up close to the entrance and Keira dashed in front of his car sending his heart pounding. She turned her head towards him and her body language gestured 'sorry' but then she carried on towards the ticket machine. Sabir drove on and watched in his mirror as she stopped for a second, as if in thought, then delved into her pocket for some loose change.

Breathing slowly to calm himself, Sabir slowed the car and parked in a slot at the far end, towards the recycling area. He stayed in the car until he had given the ladies more than enough time to exit the car park.

He now had two options. 1. To run and catch them up and maybe get spotted, or 2. To hang back, play it cool and check out a few of the shops he had spotted the previous night. He decided on the latter.

Pulling up the collar on his coat, Sabir started heading into town. He plugged in his ear phones from his MP3 player, but kept it turned off. He'd learnt that people were less likely to try and speak to you or try and sell you something if you were listening to something, thus drawing less attention to yourself.

Sabir had soon lost his prey and after a couple of hours, he was beginning to worry that they had gone elsewhere. He was about to head back to the car park when he spotted them walking towards him. Sabir quickly jumped into the nearest shop, which happened to be more suitable for teenage boys than him. It was a video game shop selling the latest Play Stations and X Boxes.

At least it was predominately a male domain, so there wasn't much chance of Keira and her mother following him in. Picking up a copy of Grand Theft Auto he pretended to study it, but all the time watching the window. As they passed by, he carefully replaced the game in exactly the same position and walked out of the shop.

The ladies walked slowly, happily chatting away while they window shopped. Suddenly, they came to a halt and turned around as Keira had decided she wanted a pair of jeans from a shop they had just passed.

Sabir's heart pounded as they came face to face, but he had no option other than to carry on walking forward hoping she wouldn't notice him. He turned his face away as they went past, but luckily Keira's mind was elsewhere.

After several seconds, Sabir turned and watched them enter the shop opposite the one he had just left. He toyed with the idea of entering the gaming shop again but decided against it. The shop was too open and there were no mannequins to hide behind – just lots of low-level shelves which were great for spotting shop lifters but not so good for camouflage.

He leant against the wall, looking like the bored husband once again, but then, much to his delight, Keira's mother exited the shop. He watched as she entered a health food store. This was his chance, so he slipped into the clothes shop, undetected, and no one batted an eye lid.

He made his way directly to the changing room at the back, and sat down on one of the seats outside – where bored husbands tend to sit while their wives or partners tried on endless amounts of clothes.

A lady walked over to the assistant and asked for some help and the assistant dutifully followed the lady to the racks of clothing. Then his sixth sense could feel Keira moving towards him. He kept still with his head down, while Keira waited for the attendant, but there wasn't one, so she walked into the changing rooms clutching two pairs of jeans and a top.

Sabir looked around and made sure that no one was watching. He slipped through the doorway into Keira's changing room. Seconds later the attendant returned, but as far as she concerned, the changing rooms were empty.

Chapter 33

It was a Thursday when Rockin explained to Marco how he'd managed to smooth things over with Lara the previous night. To his surprise, the radio coverage had actually helped his side of the argument.

Lara dreaded going to school because she knew that all the parents would be watching and gossiping at the gates of the school. The headmistress had been kind and suggested that she take a day off sick with stress, but Lara concluded that this would only prolong the agony, so she went in extra early to avoid the prying eyes.

"Lara's going out with her mates on Saturday night," Rockin told Marco.

"Great, we can all go up and see Baz and Phil. I'll see if Will and Giles can make it, too."

"Yeah sounds good," Rockin replied, but his mind was elsewhere.

"Hey, you'll have to be careful," Marco warned him.

"Why?"

"Well Lara's going to get loads of attention when she's in town. She'll be a mini celebrity!"

"Thanks," Rockin replied sounding pissed off.

Brendon opened his shop at about five to nine. To be honest, there wasn't much call for his services this time of year, especially with the caravan site closed for the winter. He piled his Christmas trees up outside the window then went back inside and unbundled the papers that had been delivered.

A headline caught his attention and then another. Grasping the papers, he headed out of his shop, forgetting to lock the door behind him, and headed towards the salon. He walked through the salon straight into the staff room without knocking. Marco and Rockin and another stylist looked a little shocked as he walked in. "You'll never guess what, you're only in the papers again!"

He held out the newspapers for Rockin to take, but Marco beat him to it. A picture of Rockin and Marco in their wedding gear brandished the front page of the Sun and Marco's face gleamed.

The next paper – the Express – showed a picture of them all standing in a long line next to the limo with the title 'Love rats from hell'.

Marco opened the paper, turning to pages five and six, to read the full story. There was an outline drawing of them all and they each had a number. Marco soon found himself – he was number three.

'3, Best man slept with two of the bridesmaids and the bride'.

He was stunned to silence at first, but then burst into a hail of laughter and read on.

'4, Groom, Due to wed last Friday, also engaged to a Catholic primary school teacher'.

'1, William Edwards, usher. Engaged to a nurse with an unconfirmed mistress'.

'2, Giles Chambers, usher. Single but rumoured to have had filthy sex with girls of the hunt and the young farmers'.

'4, Baz Jones, usher. Long term girlfriend. Works as a doorman and is often seen taking girls back to his secret pad for sordid sex sessions'.

"Baz will love that," Marco announced.

'6, Phillip Greene, separated from wife and kids. Wife seen brandishing a black eye recently'.

"Phil won't like that," Marco continued.

"Has Baz got a secret pad?" asked Marco,

"How am I supposed to know?" Rockin replied.

"What does the Sun say?" asked Sian the other stylist.

Rockin speed read the paper. "Much of the same, expect they say that we tried unsuccessfully to get them to pay for drinks and lap dancing bars. They're taking the high ground, saying it would have been immoral."

"Here it is. The love rats spent, what was supposed to be a wedding night, cavorting with naked girls in Peter Stringfellow's," Rockin added.

One of the apprentices knocked and softly opened the door. She spoke very timidly. "You're on the radio again." They all shot through the door and into the salon, nearly knocking the poor girl over in the process.

"As the story grows, we'll bring you more later," the DJ announced. They just caught the tail end of the story. Marco turned to Liz, "Did they mention the salon?" he asked. "Yes, they did, how did you know?"

"Oh, just hopeful, a bit of free publicity."

Rockin looked at Marco and suddenly realised that Marco had tipped or pushed the radio station a little further.

"Not bad, we got into three national papers and one or maybe two locals by the end of the week. And now we've got coverage on MFM!"

"Free advertising," said Rockin.

"No think of it as fifteen minutes of fame," Marco replied.

"Not quite the fame I imagined!" Rockin exclaimed.

Keira sat perched on the edge of the cream sofa in the lounge of her parent's house cradling another cup of tea, watching the steam slowly rise as the doorbell went. She didn't move a muscle.

Her mother opened the door gently and peered out to see a man and woman in their mid-thirties with a younger WPC standing behind them. The female introduced herself as Detective Inspector Diane Hughes and turned slightly to her male colleague introducing him as Mark Edwards from the CID. The constable never got a mention.

Her mother let go of the door and they followed her into the lounge where Keira was still sitting. They introduced themselves but Keira didn't respond. She was still in her own little world trying to block everything out.

"Would you like a drink?" Keira's mother, Glenda, asked.

Diane asked for a cup of tea. The other two declined.

"My husband has just gone for a walk as he needed to get some fresh air. He'll be back in a few minutes," Glenda informed them. They all nodded except Keira, who remained motionless.

Meanwhile, Baz was getting a ribbing from the lads at the gym. His name had only been mentioned in passing in the papers with his face only showing in a small group photo. Even the radio station hadn't mentioned his name or his gym once. All the attention was on Rockin, Marco, the salon and Lara.

The story was now getting huge local media coverage and Baz wasn't getting his slice. The listeners were still ringing in or texting with their comments.

Glenda came back swiftly with the cup of tea, not wanting to leave her daughter a moment longer than she had to. They might be police but they were still strangers and would be asking unsettling questions.

"How are you feeling?" asked the DI. There was no reply.

"We just wanted to update you on our progress." Keira lifted her head ever so slightly.

"We've sent the samples from under your fingernails to the lab, and your clothes have also been sent away to see if they can give any DNA evidence, but we're not hopeful."

The sound of a key being inserted into a lock and turning made Keira jump a little, but moments later her father entered the house limply holding a newspaper. He felt guilty about not being there to protect his daughter.

After introductions, the DI continued. "We're going through the tapes from the shop and the surrounding shops in case he reveals his face, and the town's CCTV is also being looked at as we speak." The DI let this hang in the air to see if she could get a reaction, but just silence came back.

"Can you give us a description of the man?" asked Mark.

"We need some more to go on," he carried on, but silence still hung in the air.

"When will you arrest him?" her father asked.

"We think he might be a serial rapist, as he kept his face hidden when he entered the town and he was wearing gloves."

"What about witnesses?"

"We have witnesses, but no one who could give a good description. All we know is that he had dark hair and dark eyes."

A song finished and the presenter went to a call. "That man cuts my hair at the Plassey, and I'm never going there again. I think it's disgusting what he's done to those poor girls."

"OK line two."

"Hi, I agree with the previous caller. That poor teacher, and the bride must be hurting so much inside."

The phone rang in the salon and Liz answered the phone. "Hi, can I cancel my appointment?" Liz made the cancellation but then the phone rang again. "Hi Plassey Hair Studio."

"Hi, this is the Ben from the Wrexham Leader. We'd like to come and get an interview and some photos." Liz slammed down the receiver and went to tell Marco that they'd just had the seventh cancellation of the day.

Marco was beginning to feel that things were back firing. He carried on trimming his client's hair but moments later, his scissors sliced into his finger.

No blood appeared but he knew that in about thirty seconds it would be flowing. "Fuckin' new scissors," he said under his breath, as he darted into the staff room.

The phone rang again and this time it was Lara. Liz went to get Rockin. As Lara spoke to him, he could hear the tears and the anguish trembling in her voice. She wanted it all to end and end now!

Rockin didn't care what Marco thought. He had to save his relationship, and he only could think of one person who could help him and that was Baz.

"Have you ever met your attacker before?" asked the DI.

Keira burst into floods of tears and started to shake with fear. Her father dropped the newspaper letting it fall to the floor, as he placed his arm around her shoulder.

Then out of the corner of her eye Keira spotted something familiar. She diverted her eyes towards the image which leapt out of the paper. Instinctively backing away for a second, she then leant forward and picked up the paper.

Baz placed the phone back on the receiver and said to anyone within ear shot, "We're in business!" Delving under the counter, he then found what he was looking for. He flicked through the Yellow Pages until he found the advert for MFM.

He dialled the number and after a few rings a girl answered. Before she could ask how she could help, he cut in. "I'm one of the ushers from the wedding party which is plastered over the papers and the airwaves."

"Oh, how can we help?"

"I'd like to come in and speak on air about what really went on that day."

"Could I take your name and number?" She took his details and then asked, "Would you mind if I put you on hold for a few seconds?"

Keira's face drained of all its colour as she stared at the six faces in the paper. A confused swirl of memories twisted and turned in her head. She tried to speak but her mouth wouldn't work, as the images of those lads in Stringfellow's and the attack which she had bravely fought off in the changing room brought memories flooding back.

She remembered his hand slipping momentarily from her mouth, at which point she'd let out a scream for her life. Moments later, the changing room attendant rushed in and on seeing what was happening, screamed even louder. The attacker had kept his head down and pushing them both out of the way he'd made a run for it.

She had caught a glimpse of her attacker's eyes and she knew she had seen him before. And now she knew where. Dropping the paper on the floor she pointed to the wedding party, then burst into tears and curled up into the foetal position.

Baz checked himself in the mirror, flecked his muscles then opened the car door and made his way to the entrance of MFM radio. He introduced himself to the receptionist who asked him to take a seat, which he did.

After an agonising five-minute wait, a man in his late twenties, who was wearing a well-worn black suit, arrived by his side. No introductions were made. "Follow me," he ordered.

Baz was taken into an office and told to take a seat by an untidy desk with an ashtray over flowing with cigarette butts. Baz hated smoking. Moments later, he could see two men behind smoky coloured glass looking at that morning's newspaper then staring at him.

One of the men came out and sat by Baz. "So, come on then, what's the real story?"

Baz could smell his smoky breath and wanted to heave. He produced a wallet of photos of the day, proving that he'd been there.

Before he knew what was happening, he was sitting in a studio with the DJ, a girl in her early twenties with dark hair and of a slim build. *Just as I like my girls,* thought Baz. For some reason, he'd always imagined this DJ to be a bit of a minger. Her assistant told him not to lean into the microphone then handed him a pair of headphones.

"Well ladies and gentlemen, we have a guy called Baz, who was one of the ushers at the infamous wedding party that everybody is talking about. After Robbie Williams, we'll find out all the dirty details," the DJ announced.

All the lads arrived at Phil's house brandishing bottles of beer, except Marco who arrived with a bottle of vodka and a two-litre bottle of diet Coke, not wanting to consume too many calories. They were introduced to Phil's children who were being allowed to stay up late since their mum was out.

They all cracked open their drinks and sat around in the front room with the television belting out episodes of Bob the Builder. Chatting away about all the recent media coverage they had received, Rockin explained that it had been touch and go with Lara at one stage.

"Thanks for going on the radio and sorting things out Baz," Rockin said.

"No problem."

"How's family life now?" Giles asked Phil.

"Sweet mate, sweet. I've moved back in, Charlotte's all over me and the kids are brilliant," Phil explained. His daughter, Carey, who was sat on his lap, dug in deep and hugged her dad and then kissed him on the cheek.

In town, Lara and her friends necked their second bottle of WKD blue to the thumping beat of the music. She could feel eyes upon her and knew people were talking about her, but she didn't mind. In fact, she was enjoying the attention.

They moved on to Lloyds, previously a bank that had been turned into a bar. With its high ceiling and ornate plaster coving, it was a square room about 50ft by 50ft in size and packed tight with drinkers. The ladies ordered a double Red Bull and vodka each and went to mingle.

As soon as they moved away from the bar, Lara felt a hand on her shoulder. She turned to find an ex-boyfriend, who she hadn't seen for years, standing next to her.

"Are we having a game of poker then?" asked Baz.

"I don't know how to play," Marco replied.

"Even better. Hope you've got plenty of cash on you," replied Baz.

"Come on kids, bed time," Phil announced.

"Can I watch the end of this first Dad?" asked little Josh.

"OK, but then straight to bed."

"Come on Carey, it's time for bed." Carey didn't complain because she loved having her dad to herself. They went into her bedroom and she selected three books for him to read. "They'll take all night for me to read," he told her. Carey just looked at him with her big blue eyes. And that was the idea, he quickly realised, but he didn't mind in the slightest.

"You're not going to leave us again, are you Daddy?"

"No never," he assured her. Carey climbed into bed and insisted that he lay next to her to read the stories.

Lara's heart missed a beat at first. She'd met this guy at university in Manchester and they had gone out with each other for about a year and a half. But then he'd done the dirty on her one night at a party and when she found out, she went ballistic.

Her immediate reaction was to slap him, but he gave her a heart-warming smile and that thought quickly evaporated. Turning to face each other, he placed his hand on her waist and kept it there as he held her gaze.

"I saw your picture in the paper," he remarked.

"Did you?" she asked, not knowing what else to say.

"All I can say is that you've got better looking as you've got older." She blushed and said, "Less of the older, I'm not even thirty yet!" He smiled and moved around to stand next to her, slipping his arm around her back drawing them closer.

Lara went to pull away, but decided not to, instead leaving his hand where it was. She moved in closer and pushed her chest out just enough so she could have some fun.

After a few hands of poker, Baz went to see where Phil was. He tapped gently on Carey's door, but everything was silent. Baz was making his way downstairs again when he heard a thud coming from somewhere upstairs, so he turned and made his way back up.

Lara's ex-boyfriend sent one of his friends off to buy another round of drinks for himself and the girls. He was a slick lad and he made sure he complemented and gave plenty of attention to all the ladies and didn't single Lara out. He wanted to know all about Lara's boyfriend, though, the 'scoundrel', as he nicknamed him. "He certainly knows how to enjoy himself, doesn't he?" Lara just nodded.

"I bet he's one for the women," the ex-added.

The alcohol was starting to do its work on Lara. She hardly ever drank, but right at that moment she wanted to party.

Baz stood at the top of the stairs looking for any signs of where the noise had come from. He was worried in case Carey was up and about. The last thing he wanted to do was scare her, especially after what she had been through with Wayne. He listened for a couple of seconds longer and moved forward towards her bedroom, tapping first before pushing the door open when there was no answer.

Charlotte made a toast to the bride who was dressed in a pink nurse's outfit with 'L' plates on her back. Raising their shot glasses, they all downed them in one, and a few of them came up coughing from the burning sensation that the Absinthe left behind.

One of Charlotte's friends nudged her once the sensation had worn off. "Isn't that the girl who was in the papers?" Charlotte didn't grasp it at first.

"The school teacher, you know the trip your Phil went on to London."

"Oh yeah, so it is."

"You should go and say hello."

"I want to meet the guy who's groping her arse – he looks cute," Charlotte replied, and they both smiled cheekily at each other.

Baz entered Carey's bedroom which was decorated in Barbie pink with a border to match. He felt a crunch under his foot and bent down to see what he had stood on. Picking up a small doll, minus an arm which lay limply on the floor, he looked towards the bed and saw Phil lying there.

Charlotte made her way over to Lara in her NYPD outfit, complete with mini skirt and truncheon, and as they came face to face, Charlotte introduced herself. "I think we've got something in common," she said to Lara.

"What?" asked Lara.

"The limo trip to London. And maybe men?" Charlotte explained, winking at Lara's ex, who was called Lee.

"I'm Phil's partner. Phil went to London with your boyfriend."

"Oh, my God!" Lara exclaimed and proceeded to hug her.

"You've been through the mill this week, haven't you?"

Baz leaned over to where Phil and Carey lay sound asleep. Placing his hand on Phil's shoulder, he nudged him, being careful not to wake Carey. Once Phil opened his sleepy eyes, Baz said, "Come on you lightweight, you're supposed to be playing poker."

"I'll be there in a minute," said Phil before laying his head back down on the pillow.

The hen party left the pub first and Lara and her friends followed as they all headed to a nightclub called Liquid and Envy. One thing that Charlotte had said was bugging Lara, "Do you get a sense that someone's watching you?" she'd asked Lara, and Lara had no idea why she had said it.

The lads carried on playing cards and Marco was having his usual luck taking a good share of Baz's money.

Once in the night club, the girls sorted themselves out with drinks and went for a wander. It wasn't long before a few lads came over to speak to Lara, after recognising her, but she kept looking over her shoulder still thinking about what Charlotte had said. Soon her friends dragged her on to the dance floor, where a few more men fancied their chances with her. Needing the toilet, Lara quietly slipped away. She'd never understood why girls had to go to the loo together to be honest.

At five to one in the morning, the doorbell rang in Phil's house. All the lads looked at each other. "Who the fuck is that?" Will asked, as if anyone should know.

"It'll be Charlotte," Baz guessed, as he stood up and made his way over to the front door. He was only half way here when the bell rang again.

"I'm coming!" he yelled.

Baz opened the door and saw two policemen in full uniform standing in front of him. "Phil Evans?" the officer asked.

Chapter 34

The officers pushed past Baz, forcing him against the wall, and Baz struggled to resist the urge to grab them and teach them some manners. After the sixth officer had passed, Baz followed them into the front room. "Where's Phillip Evans?" One of the officers demanded at the top of his voice. Another two officers forced their way into the kitchen.

The shouting woke Phil from his deep sleep. At first, he assumed he'd been dreaming, until the shouting continued and he heard his name echoing into the bedroom. Easing himself out of the bed as quietly as he could so as not to wake Carey, he placed both his feet on the floor and started to lift his body up. At that moment, the door burst open and a cosh powered down on to the back of his neck sending his body limply to the floor.

DI Diane Hughes and Mark Edwards CID watched Phil being dragged down the stairs. His hands were cuffed tightly behind his back. "Let's have a look at the bastard," said the DI, while Edwards lifted his head by the scruff of his neck.

Phil's eyes had rolled back into his head and were barely open. "Lift his head higher," the DI demanded. As Phil's head was raised, she slapped him hard. His eyes rolled again as he tried hard to focus, but the images were blurred.

Two middle-aged women with hard faces entered the house and looked at Phil with disgust. An officer guided them upstairs. The first woman marched into Josh's room and swept him up into her arms. At first Josh thought it was his mum, and he placed his arms around her.

The second woman lifted little Carey into her arms and her head fell softly forward onto her shoulder. Both children carried on sleeping, as the social workers made their way downstairs.

Baz was at the doorway of the lounge watching the DI recoiling her arm for another blow. He lurched forward grabbing her hand and twisting her body around so that her hand was pinned against the wall. She let out a scream as Josh and Carey reached the bottom of the stairs, instantly waking them.

Josh looked around dazed and confused and seeing his father bent over in agony with blood dripping from his mouth, he let out a terrifying scream. He proceeded to kick and punch the social worker as hard as he could. She held one hand under his bottom and one hand tightly around his wrist as she struggled to keep hold of him, but then Josh had an idea.

His dad had once taught him how to escape if a 'bad man' tried to take him away. Sharply flipping his wrist to free his hand, he used the other hand to gauge at the woman's eyes, sending even more screams into the tiny hall way. The trick worked, and he immediately found his two feet firmly planted on the floor.

He ran forwards screaming for his dad and pounced on the heavily armoured policeman who was holding Phil by his handcuffs. Circling round, and without thinking, Josh kicked him in the balls and floored him instantly.

By this time, Carey was fully awake and in total confusion about what was happening. The last thing she could remember was her dad reading her a story while she held his hand tightly, never wanting him to go again.

She began following her brother by frantically scratching at this stranger's face with all the strength that she could muster. As Carey began to dig her fingernails in deep, an officer grabbed her from behind and pulled her away. Carey let out a terrifying scream that only a four-year-old girl could do, and the whole house fell silent except for Carey.

Baz instantly smacked the DI's head against the wall as hard as he could. He didn't give a shit now. They'd gone too far and whatever Phil was supposed to have done, the kids didn't deserve this!

He lunged at Edwards, who took the full force of Baz's fist, sending him crumpling to the floor and releasing Phil's head. Baz took a swing at the officer holding Phil, who was in mid recovery, but he ducked and Baz missed.

Baz pushed on forward towards Carey and wrenching his hand back, he powered it into the back of the officer's head. Before the officer fell to the floor, Baz had swiped Carey from his grasp and instantly clung on to her for dear life as he watched the tears streaming down her face.

Phil was outside the front door, being propelled towards the awaiting squad car, and another officer grabbed Josh and made his way towards the exit. With immaculate timing, Marco brought his fist up and slammed it into the officer's face making contact with his nose. Josh was free again and ran for his life – out of the door and into the dark cold night.

Two more officers entered the chaotic house with taser guns at the ready. They jabbed Baz in the back sending ten thousand volts through his body and into Carey's tiny body. Instantly, this sent Carey's muscles into spasm as her body relaxed. Then the jolting spasms started again, her innocent eyes bulging out of their sockets as they expanded. Her mouth opened but no noises came.

Baz held her blonde head in his own. "Carey, Carey!" No reaction came and at that moment the officer behind him kicked the back of his legs and sent him into free fall. Baz lost hold of Carey as the officer punched him in the back.

The policeman raised his cosh for another blow, but then he caught sight of Carey's limp, lifeless body impact on the laminate flooring, her head bouncing like a cricket ball.

As sirens pierced through the night air, Phil started to come around. He eyed up his surroundings and felt the pain of the handcuffs cutting into his skin. "Why have I been arrested?" he asked one of the officers.

"Don't give me that shit," the officer replied.

"No, please, tell me!"

"Didn't they read you your rights?"

"No," said Phil, "they didn't."

"You've been arrested for the brutal rape of two women – and that's just so far."

"That's bullshit," Phil said, having no idea what they were talking about.

Baz pulled Carey's body towards him and laid her flat on her back. Leaning forward, he breathed into her mouth, filling her lungs. He checked her chest was rising and then started compressions – one, two, three, four, five.

He started again, watching her tiny chest rise before continuing with compressions. By this time, Rockin had moved to her side. "Carey, come on Carey, can you hear me Carey?" Phil lifted her eyelid, but he wasn't sure what he was looking for.

"They've got DNA evidence," the officer continued.

"What DNA evidence?"

"From the girl, you brutally raped five years ago – a perfect match."

"That's crap!"

"You thought you were clever wearing a condom, didn't you?" Phil remained quiet.

"You're going away for a long stretch in prison, and I doubt you'll ever see your kids again."

Chapter 35

Ten days later, on a bitterly cold morning shrouded in mist, Carey's body was lowered six feet to her final resting place. Her pure white coffin scratched against the cold dark clay.

Phil fell to his knees, hands cuffed behind his back, and his body trembled uncontrollably as the voice of the priest echoed around his head. Two minutes after the funeral had finished, Phil was led back to the awaiting police car.

Exactly one year to the day that Carey was laid to rest, Sabir was arrested on suspicion of murder. When his apartment was searched, he was charged with a further six murders and eight rapes. Phil was released from jail two days later with all the charges dropped.

Phil went straight to Carey's grave and spent the night propped up against her head stone as his body trembled with anguish and the freezing temperature. At first light, he kissed the ground on Carey's grave, shedding yet more tears. He stumbled along the path and made his way to an all-night café and ordered a mug of hot chocolate with squirty cream (Carey's favourite), he started to write his last will and testament on a napkin.

Forty-two minutes later, he stepped in front of a freight train killing himself instantly.